FOR LOVE OF THE LAND

The Legacy of Mildred Kanipe

FOR LOVE OF THE LAND

The Legacy of Mildred Kanipe

By
Lois Christiansen Eagleton

iUniverse, Inc.
New York   Bloomington

FOR LOVE OF THE LAND
The Legacy of Mildred Kanipe

iUniverse books may be ordered through booksellers or by contacting:

iUniverse
1663 Liberty Drive
Bloomington, IN 47403
www.iuniverse.com
1-800-Authors (1-800-288-4677)

ISBN: 978-0-595-50688-0 (pbk)
ISBN: 978-0-595-61612-1 (ebk)

Printed in the United States of America

DEDICATION

To Mildred Kanipe, who provided a wonderful story that begged to be told. I feel that I have made a good friend. Perhaps we shall meet one day in the afterworld.

And, to my husband Mark, who put up with my lengthy absences, both physical and mental.

I think it a great honor, a great privilege to be able to live on, to own, and to operate the same ranch as my forefathers did.

I feel that the land is a sacred trust and we should hold it dear. That we should take care of it; should protect and preserve it; should enhance its productivity and its beauty as much as we can; and above all we should love the land, which I surely do.

Mildred Kanipe, August 24, 1974

Mildred Kanipe with her sheep and favorite dog. (1940s)

Contents

ACKNOWLEDGMENTS

This book would never have found print without the generous help of so many. To the following, thank you from the bottom of my heart.

Nancy Nowak, whose kind encouragement and effective editing made the completion of the book possible.

John Robertson, for his kind comments in the foreword for this book. He has been a solid supporter in so many ways.

The Douglas County Museum of History and Natural History, and especially Karen Bratton, museum Research Librarian. I was given free access to the boxes and boxes of related documents and photos in possession of the Museum, and Karen brought things to my attention that she thought might be of interest.

John Howard and Kathryn Howard Weathers, Mildred Kanipe's sister Leah's children, who both provided valuable information during personal interviews, and Kathryn especially, who generously loaned the Kanipe family album so that I could scan photos that add immeasurably to the stories told here. Kathryn also provided copies of the original stories that her mother, Leah, and Mildred wrote, which provide a unique window into who those people were and the life they lived.

Maxine Baimbridge, a distant relative of Mildred Kanipe through her mother, who knew Mildred well and cared for her when she was no longer able to take care of herself, until it was necessary to place her in a nursing home where she passed away.

Bill James "Wild Bill" Cantrell, who knew Mildred Kanipe and contributed the story of his memories.

The staff of the Douglas County Courthouse and the Oakland Library for their patience and assistance.

Ticor Title, Roseburg, which provided a copy of an important land document that the Douglas County Courthouse, for some reason, did not have.

Former Douglas County Park Director, Jeff Powers, and current Park Director Jim Dowd, for their overall support, for allowing me to poke around inside the historic buildings and for providing access to park records and the taped interview made by Mildred's good friend Ed Boehrs before he died.

Mildred Kanipe Memorial Park caretakers Paulette and Chuck Jones for their friendship and support of this huge endeavor.

The staff of the Oregon State Parks Department of Historic Preservation and Liz Carter, Historic Preservation Consultant, for their valuable assistance in preparing and processing the applications for inclusion on the National Register for the English Settlement School and the Baimbridge-Kanipe Farmstead.

Don Dole, Mildred Kanipe's attorney, for his valuable interview and interpretation of Mildred's will; Bill Talburt, who knew Mildred well; and Audie Campbell, who was a local law enforcement officer. Also, the many people who shall remain nameless, because I spoke with so many, whom I met in passing in places like the supermarket checkout line or waiting for my car repairs to be completed, whom I have no names for.

Everyone who knew Mildred Kanipe has a story to tell. I am sorry I was unable to use them all.

If I have inadvertently left anyone out, please forgive me.

And yes, I am forever grateful to Mildred Kanipe herself, who many refer to as a pack rat because she had a reputation of never throwing anything away. She would not have known that one day I would be digging through the boxes of papers that she saved, recovering bits and pieces of history that made it possible to tie this story together.

ILLUSTRATIONS

FOREWORD

I have had the great pleasure of working with Lois Eagleton as vice chair of Friends of Mildred Kanipe Memorial Park Association for nearly four years.

Our organization was formed to preserve the ranch with all its buildings for this and all future generations to enjoy.

This most informative book will set the record straight, by eliminating suppositions and hearsay of the park's history. It is informative and entertaining for all who read it, and is a part of Douglas County history that needed to be written.

John Robertson, President, Douglas County Historical Society

PREFACE

I fell in love with Mildred Kanipe Memorial Park while exploring its beautiful trails on horseback. When I learned that a management plan for the park completed in 2001 mentioned, *"Compile an up-to-date historical record of the Mildred Kanipe Ranch and Park and utilize it in educational and publicity endeavors for the Park,"* I decided that researching and writing the story would be a way I could thank Mildred for her precious gift—the almost 1,100 acre ranch that she left to Douglas County for a park when she passed away in 1983.

I could not foresee the adventures this decision would lead to. When I decided to pursue the project I thought that my long-term interest in history, mediocre computer skills, experience writing my own family histories, writing for several small local newspapers and anthologies published by An Association of Writers of Roseburg, would provide me with the tools I needed.

It turned out that I was absolutely unprepared for what I had gotten myself into! I am seventy-four years old, and if learning new things does keep one young, I think I must be getting younger every day.

Reading reference materials and interviewing people were a snap, but, among a lot of other things, I had to learn how to find and read historic land records, often finding that what other "experts" had previously written was incorrect. On those, I have endeavored to set the record straight.

When the suggestion was made by then County Commissioner, Dan VanSlyke, that the County should return the park to the Mildred Kanipe Trust, a meeting of people who love the park convinced the commissioner that the park should be kept and formed the Friends of Mildred Kanipe Memorial Park Association, which later became a corporation in the State of Oregon and a 501 (c) (3) tax exempt charitable organization. These required new skills in writing for me, as I, as the person who knew the most about the history of the park, was the one best equipped to do the necessary. That was only the beginning.

As Chair of the new Friends of Mildred Kanipe Memorial Park Association, I have now prepared successful applications for the National Register of Historic Places—no small task—and most recently have been introduced to the art of grant writing.

This is my first book. I hope readers will enjoy reading it as much as I have enjoyed the process of getting it into their hands.

INTRODUCTION

In 1983 the people of Douglas County, Oregon received a precious gift. Mildred Kanipe, a colorful local personality, passed away and left her ranch to the public for a park— almost 1,100 acres of rolling hills, forests, meadows, creeks and historic buildings.

She respected history and wished the buildings be maintained and a ranch museum be developed. Two sites on the Ranch, the English Settlement School with one acre of land, and the Baimbridge-Kanipe Farmstead with more than eighteen acres, which includes the ranch house, barns, related ranch buildings, and what remains of an old heritage orchard, have, in 2007 and 2008, been included on the National Register of Historic Places, confirming their importance to local, state, and national history.

Mildred loved the land and wished it to be enjoyed and cared for. She loved horses and requested that equestrian trails be established. She asked that the trees in the park be preserved and not cut—unless "necessary".

Mildred Kanipe Memorial Park* is located about eight miles northeast of Oakland, Oregon, on Elkhead Road in what is still called the English Settlement because of the origin of the pioneers who settled there. The town of Oakland, once an important agricultural center and railroad shipping point, is today a popular destination for antique hunters.

The goal, in writing this story, is to bring to life the history of the land and the people who made it what it is today, especially Mildred, who loved it the most and entrusted it to us.

Stories written by others were provided by those who wrote them or their heirs. They add greatly to the story. No attempt has been made to edit them as they speak better for the writers left in their own words.

Additional information such as trail and historical maps of the park, a few revealing recipes from Mary Baimbridge, Mildred Kanipe's aunt who raised her and her sister, historic orchard tree information, and copies of the applications for inclusion on the National Register for the English Settlement School and the Baimbridge-Kanipe Farmstead have been included.

This book has been produced at no cost to the Douglas County Park Department. All royalties earned will go to Friends of Mildred Kanipe Memorial Park Association, Inc. for the sole purpose of helping to care for the historic buildings at Mildred Kanipe Memorial Park.

*Not to be confused with another park of the same name that was left to the City of Oakland by Mildred Kanipe and is inside the Oakland city limits.

IN THE BEGINNING

Land and Climate

Millions of years ago the land that would one day be called Oregon was under water— except for two groups of islands that today are known as the Blue and Wallowa Mountains in the northeast and the Klamath Mountains in the southwest corners of the state. It is there that rocks up to 400 million years old, the oldest in the state, can be found.

The land mass of the Western Hemisphere has been drifting westward since it broke free from Europe some 200 million years ago. It has traveled about 1,500 miles at a rate of one to two inches per year, and continues to do so.

Pressures from the westward movement caused the crust of the ocean floor to dip and slide under the continent's western edge, gathering in ups and downs to form the hills and valleys that became Oregon's Coast Range. As it moved, the lower basalt layer dipped and moved closer to the core of the earth, and heat caused the basalt to melt. This molten rock was then pushed back to the surface, creating volcanoes which formed a string of new islands. As the continent continued to move, it collided with them, making them its own. The roads of Western Oregon cut through that ancient rock, and from them can be seen the layers, thick and thin, straight and folded, of the buckled ocean floor.

The newest volcanoes can be seen in the Cascade Range, those awe-inspiring snowcapped mountains, some still active and others merely dormant.

Oregon's weather went through a long tropical period when tree ferns grew trunks as large as ten inches thick. Then, about 70,000 years ago, the climate changed. Ice sheets up to more than six miles

1

thick in places, extended south to 45 degrees latitude—to the present sites of Keizer and Baker City, Oregon.

When the Ice Age ended around 11,000 to 10,000 years ago, the earth began another warming period. When the huge glacial covering melted, North America experienced the greatest floods in its history. The rushing water carved out many of today's rivers and lakes.

As the ice melted, the water carried tons of silt from the eastern part of Washington State to the future Willamette Valley in Oregon, making it a rich agricultural area.

Oregon weather, which had at one time had been hot and humid, with plants abounding that we now see only in tropical climates, had experienced its coldest period. Over time, it settled into the climate that we enjoy today.

The area between Sutherlin and Elkhead, Oregon, is made of marine basalt and marine mudstone, in other words, old ocean floor. Here, mercury deposits occurred. The Bonanza Mine, located seven miles east of the small town of Sutherlin, was the largest and the longest running mercury mine in the country, operating until 1961. There were smaller mercury mines in the Elkhead area. Today's Mildred Kanipe Memorial Park is in a direct line between those two areas.

Though the weather of Western Oregon is famous for being wet, the whole of Douglas County is notorious for being very difficult to find a good source of water for a well. When sufficient water is found, it may have salt in it, making it unusable.

Native people and the early settlers established their homes near creeks and rivers, which were not only a source of needed water, but teemed with fish and attracted wildlife, making them an important source of food as well.

Now with global warming, the vegetation of Oregon is expected to undergo more dramatic changes. Some experts predict that the very nature of Oregon's great forests will change, with traditional varieties of trees unable to survive. Already, many creeks that used to run year-round dry up every summer.

The First Settlers

There is evidence that human beings arrived at North America around 14,000 years ago. The common theory is they came across the land bridge at the Bering Strait that joined Asia and North America between 70,000 and 11,000 years ago. The "bridge" occurred when vast amounts of ocean water became tied up in the enormous glaciers of the ice age, lowering the level of the ocean and exposing the land which connected the two continents. It is believed man first settled along the coast because of the food sources the ocean offered, but possible early village sites are not accessible since the ocean level rose again with the melting of the ice from the ice age, making it impossible to authenticate.

The Yoncalla Indians were the southernmost tribe of the Kalapuyas (Kalipooyas, Calapooias), a group of Indians whose home area stretched as far north as the falls on the Willamette River at Oregon City. Today's Mildred Kanipe Memorial Park is located in the area where they lived. Historical records suggest that the Yoncalla associated with their neighbors, the North Umpqua tribes to the south and the Molallas to the east.

These first people were peaceful, living with the land, hunting, fishing, and harvesting a bounty of local plant foods such as berries, camas root, and oak acorns. The tall native grasses were burned by the natives each fall to fertilize the soil, keep the brush down, and kill insects. Toasted grasshopper was a favorite treat that resulted from this custom.

The Newcomers

The Spanish poked around a bit off the west coast of today's United States in the 1500's, but there is no record of their landing on the Oregon Coast.

As exploration of the "New World" expanded, British and American ships discovered the mouth of the Umpqua River. The year 1791 brought the American Brig, Jenny, from Bristol, Rhode Island, and a year later, in 1792, the Englishman Captain Robert Gray visited the river. The Umpqua became the principal way of accessing the valleys inland. Ships traveled up the river as far as present day Scottsburg, and mule trains carried on from there with ferries at river crossings.

In 1804 President Thomas Jefferson sent Meriwether Lewis and William Clark to explore the western part of the continent and find a route to access it from the United States. When they reached the mouth of the Columbia River and built Fort Clatsop to spend the winter, the only people living on the land were Indians. Lewis and Clark were not the first white men the Indians had seen, however, as ships had frequented the Mouth of the Columbia for some time, trading for furs.

However, the Lewis and Clark expedition was the first to bring the white man overland from the eastern part of the continent. It proved that it was possible to reach the west coast by land and disproved the commonly held theory that an inland passage waterway connected the Atlantic with the Pacific Ocean. The flame of interest was lit. The vast lands with rich soils and what seemed at the time limitless resources became much desired.

In 1826, the British botanist David Douglas explored the Umpqua valleys. His notes indicate that he had been in the area of today's town of Oakland and the future English Settlement where Mildred Kanipe's grandparents settled. Douglas was particularly keen on finding the pine trees that had produced some very large pine nuts he had seen while in Portland and was told had came from the Umpqua area. He asked the local Indians if they knew where these could be found, and some of them agreed to take him up the South Umpqua River to where the huge Sugar Pines grew. His notes mentioned observing the Indians spearing salmon as much as six feet long from the river on that trip.

The first established post in the North Umpqua area was a small fur trading post built in 1832 by the Englishman Thomas McKay and his men where Calapooia Creek enters the Umpqua River. It was staffed by two French Canadians, which may account for the "French Settlement" that developed in the area.

When the Hudson's Bay Company built a substantial fort and trading post at Elkton in 1836, Fort McKay disappeared into history. The new fort was the first settlement that planted fruit trees and vegetable gardens and raised livestock to feed the fur trappers that it served. The few local Indians who remained after the devastating kill of the "fever" of 1830-1833 were happy to bring furs to trade for the amazing items the foreigners had to offer, such as knives, beads, colorful cloth, and metal kettles for cooking. Later they traded for guns as well.

The British Hudson's Bay Company, headquartered in Canada, had thus preceded the Americans with the first permanent settlement of non-Indian people in the Umpqua area.

Not only the British and the Americans but the Russians were also interested in the new lands. The people on site, however, felt a sense of kinship. Most helped each other, without regard to nationality, while their governments tried to figure out how they could get the upper hand and acquire control over what they considered to be "new" lands, there for the taking.

The first white men came to the Land of the Umpqua to extract resources, mainly pelts for the fur trade. Originally they didn't come with the idea of staying and making it their home. Some did, however, marrying native women and settling down to raise families.

Around 1842 the British and the Americans agreed to share colonization.

In 1843 thousands began coming overland by wagon train. Others came around the Horn by ship to Scottsburg or Portland, and then to the Umpqua Valley by wagon, or came by wagon via the Applegate Trail, the southern route, which brought them through the area. Some decided to stay. Others went on to other places.

The reasons people left where they had been living were many. Some were excited about the opportunity for adventure. Many were looking for a better future for their families. A few were running away from the law or overwhelming debts. The economy in the Eastern United States was having problems, and the situation was also tough in Europe. When stories of free or cheap land and opportunity reached receptive ears, many Americans sold out and lined up to join wagon trains. In Europe, men from country after country packed up their families and, with whatever they could scrape together, found a way to pay for passage across the seas to the United States, often crowded together with no comforts—like so many cattle. From this came the term, "steerage."

On June 15, 1846, Great Britain and the United States signed a treaty establishing the boundary between Canada and the United States at the 49th parallel. This set the stage for the Americans to take over the land that lay south. The Russians, who had never acquired a competitive toehold, dropped out of the picture.

The natives, who were not recognized by the "white men" as having any claim to the lands they had lived on for generations, were peaceful and helpful to the strangers who were invading their homeland.

Land Ownership

The Donation Land Claim Act

In 1850 the US government passed the Donation Land Claim Act, which was intended to encourage Americans to settle the West. In Section 4 it *"granted to every white settler or occupancy of the public lands, American half-breed Indians included, above the age of eighteen years, being a citizen of the United States, or having made a declaration according to law, of his intention to become a citizen, or who shall make such declaration on or before the first day of December, eighteen hundred and fifty, and who*

5

shall have resided upon and cultivated the same for four consecutive years, and shall otherwise conform to the provisions of this act, the quantity of one half section, or three hundred and twenty acres of land, if a single man, and if a married man, or if he shall become married within one year from the first day of December, eighteen hundred and fifty, the quantity of one section, or six hundred and forty acres, one half to himself and the other half to his wife - - - - - - ". Section 5 went on to say that, *"all white male citizens of the United States or persons who shall have made a declaration of intention to become such, above the age of twenty-one years, emigrating to and settling in said Territory, and settling there between the times last aforesaid,* (those who arrived between December 1, 1850 and December 1, 1853), *who shall in other respects comply with the foregoing section the provisions of this law, there shall be, and hereby is, granted the quantity of one quarter section, or one hundred and sixty acres of land, if a single man; or if married, or if he shall become married within one year after becoming twenty-one years of age as aforesaid, the quantity of one half section, or three hundred and twenty acres - - - - - ".*

The United States was clearly rewarding the early settlers and encouraging additional citizens to hurry up and get out there to claim free land. It also provided a monetary incentive for single male settlers to get married!

Between 1854 and the passage of the Homestead Act in 1862, settlers had to pay for their land at a price of $1.25 an acre. They were limited to 320 acres. As time went on, the price went up and the amount of land allowed went down.

By this time the newcomers had taken over much of the land, decimating the food resources that the native people relied on for their very existence, and many were facing starvation.

Resentment grew, and feeling the need to defend their homes and families, many Indians in the region participated in a general uprising in 1855-56.

Outnumbered, in 1856 most tribes reluctantly agreed to a truce. It stipulated that the Indians would be taken to the 6,000 acre Grande Ronde Reservation in Yamhill County, Washington. Each adult male was to be given as much land as he had occupied in the Umpqua Valley, with a house as good or better than the one he had left, and he would receive pay for the property he had abandoned. Clothing was to be supplied for himself and his family until they were settled in their new homes. How these promises were not carried out is another story.

With the Indians removed, the white man took over unimpeded.

The Homestead Act

In 1862, President Abraham Lincoln signed the Homestead Act into law. Ten percent of the area of the United States was claimed under this act, some 270 million acres. The Homestead Act differed from the Donation Land Claim Act in some very important ways. While the Donation Land Claim Act singled out "white male citizens" (with the exception of "half-breeds"), the Homestead Act made 160 acres of free land available to any head of household over the age of 21, regardless of sex or race. "Former Slaves" are specifically listed as qualifying. A Homesteader was required to live on the land, build a home, make improvements, and farm for 5 years before they were eligible to "prove up." A filing fee of $18 was required. After that the land was theirs. (William and Mary Baimbridge, brother and sister of Mildred Kanipe's mother Sarah Alice, each acquired 160 acres of land under the Homestead Act.)

Later arrivals had to buy their land. They could purchase it from someone who acquired it via the Donation Land Claim or Homestead Acts or bought it earlier, or they could buy up to 160 acres of Oregon & California Railroad land for $2.50 an acre, land that the government had given to the railroads to sell to settlers as a reward for building the railroads. This was to encourage development, but too much of the land ended up being sold to logging companies instead of settlers, which was not the intent, so the government took the remaining land back and operates it today under the Bureau of Land Management— referred to as the O. & C. (Oregon and California) lands, managing it as a timber resource.

The first transcontinental railroad was completed on May 10, 1869, making it possible to travel from the East Coast to San Francisco in six days, rather than the four to six months required before. Settlers on their way to Oregon traveled north by land on the Oregon-California Trail or took a ship up the coast to the Umpqua River to Scottsburg or up the Columbia River to Portland.

OAKLAND AND VICINITY

The Neighborhood

The first wagon train to travel across the new southern route into the Oregon Territory, later called The Applegate Trail, came through the Oakland area in late 1846. Exhausted by the trip, the Rev. Joseph A. Cornwall and his family, and another family by the name of Campbell, built a cabin and endured the winter, moving on north in the spring. It is said that they avoided starvation due to the kindness of the local Indians. The creek by which the family stayed the winter became known as Cabin Creek.

In 1851, Dr. Dorsey S. Baker established the region's first grist mill and town across the creek from the site of Cornwall's cabin. He called the town Oakland for the many oak trees in the area. Oakland became the convenient County Seat of what was called Umpqua County. Dr. Baker's home was the voting place for the newly formed voting precinct of Green Valley. Baker served on the first election board, receiving two dollars per day for his services. After the county business had increased to a volume where a central location was needed, County and United States District Court were held in his house. Calapooia Creek, which in 1832 had been described as being "navigable" and provided power for grist and saw mills, formed the boundary between the Umpqua and Douglas counties. Umpqua County was absorbed by Douglas County in 1862.

The Oregon & California Railroad was built from Portland as far south as Oakland, Oregon, in 1872. When it arrived, it bypassed the town. Citizen Alonzo F. Brown's answer to the problem was to move the town the three miles to a new location by the railroad. He bought land from early settler Reason Reed, divided it into lots, and donated a site for a railway station. Many of the buildings of the original town were put on skids and moved. A few of those are still standing in 2007. Dr. Baker's home stayed where it was and can be seen in its original location today.

The railroad ended in Oakland for a period of six months, giving a boost to the local economy. Then in October, tracks had been completed to Roseburg, eighteen miles to the south. The first railroad car arrived there on October 20, 1872. The railroad was to dead-end in Roseburg for the next ten years because the company that was building it had run out of money. Construction was resumed in 1882 under new management. It took only a year for the new company to become bankrupt as well and the railroad reverted to its old owners. Finally, on December 17, 1887, the last section connected to tracks in California. By that time Southern Pacific Company had acquired the line.

The major industry in the area became farming, but resource extraction continued to contribute heavily to the economy. As the fur trapping industry fizzled out, salmon from the Umpqua River became an important resource. Fishing became a major industry when preservation by salting and canning made it possible to ship to east coast markets. (According to an item in the Roseburg News Review on November 23, 1914, 1,000 to 1,200 pounds of salmon were being brought daily from Elkton to Oakland by stage to be shipped out by rail.) Deer were harvested in large numbers. Some settlers made hunting their livelihood, shipping venison to Portland markets.

As fish numbers declined, fish hatcheries came into being and species were introduced where they had never been before. Commercial salmon fishing on the Umpqua became a thing of the past. Rivers and streams that at one time were teeming with fish now had relatively few. Both game and fish became regulated in order to protect remaining numbers.

Mercury mines closed. The largest and the last to close was the Bonanza Mine east of Sutherlin, which operated until 1961.

With the arrival of the railroad, it was practical to transport wood products to other parts of the country. That, and the need for building materials for a fast developing nation, fueled the development of logging and lumbering, which became a major economic force in the whole of the Pacific Northwest.

Harold A. Minter in his book, *Umpqua Valley Oregon and Its Pioneers*, said, "*Oakland was never a large town in population, but its economic influence was felt throughout western Douglas County. More wool, grain, prunes, and turkeys, have passed through its warehouses than through those of any other town of its size in Douglas County. Thousands of hogs, sheep, and cattle have been shipped from its stock pens.*" He went on to say that, *"its wood-processing plants now play a prominent role in the economy of the town."* Minter's book was written in 1967. In 2007 the wood-processing plants he referred to have long been gone, along with much of the timber that supplied them.

Oakland was the first town to have agricultural fairs, and it was here that the broad- breasted bronze turkey, the bird that today graces tables across the country on holidays, was developed. It was referred to as the "Turkey Capital" of the world.

In 2007, with a population just over 1,000, Oakland is a small town that honors its history with its many antique shops and old style downtown. Descendants of pioneer families still populate the surrounding farms, and Stearns Hardware, which opened in 1887, is still in business on Main Street.

Oakland, Oregon (2007)

FROM ENGLAND TO OREGON

Thomas and Emily Baimbridge

In the year 1870, Mildred Kanipe's maternal grandparents, Thomas and Emily Baimbridge, left Derbyshire, England, with six young children, headed for the English Settlement near Oakland, Oregon, where friends and relatives had already settled. It took them three weeks to cross the ocean from Liverpool to New York. From there they traveled by train to San Francisco. The Transcontinental railroad had only been completed the year before. They sailed by boat to Astoria, Oregon, and continued up the Columbia River to the Willamette River, which they followed to Marysville, which today is called Corvallis. From Marysville they continued their journey by land, with horses and a freight wagon.

A daughter, Avis, became ill from Diphtheria while on the boat. She died on November 7, less than two months before her third birthday. They buried her in Portland before continuing on their journey.

Thomas Baimbridge's original diary of this trip is at the Douglas County Museum. It provides a valuable insight into the details of their trip and the type of hardships that immigrants experienced coming to America in the 1800s. The original document was written on paper embossed, "Pacific O.C. & W. Mills," by hand, with very little punctuation and numerous spelling errors, common in documents of the era. Paragraph breaks have been inserted by the author to facilitate readability.

THE THOMAS BAIMBRIDGE DIARY

Mr & Mrs Thomas Baimbridge & family of six children leave home (Derbyshire England) on the 3 day of October 1870 came across the Ocean in the vessel Italy a very fine vessel accommodation for 800 steerage and 250 cabin they is about 900 passengers now altogether and 600 tons cargo besides all the luggage and she seems like a feather on the water a 600 horse engine she is 433 ft long set sail from Liverpool at five oclock Queenstown three on

Thursday all well

Friday morning a heavy sea wind ahead so we cannot get along so fast about 330 steerage passengers in the same room as we are in and not more than 10 this morning but what was sick wife and all the children sick had to carry them on deck cannot taste food

Saturday the came a most awfull sea it was just like the hills on land and when the vessel struck the waves it upset her and down we came on our backs I had to carry the children on deck and take any rugs to keep them warm but the mighty sea came dashing over us and almost drownded us

I got wet through and had to sleep in my clothes I now begin to think of chance made me think of swimming in the sea. But thought of Abraham taking his son. Cant have the windows open and this place is enough to suffocate one having so many asleep in it. Wife not well we are traveling at the rate of 13 miles the hour

Tuesday all better came on deck by 7 oclock and took the victuals to them I have not been sick if I had don't know what would have become of us.

Wednesday fine but cold wind ahead, crossing the banks of the New Foundland saw a whale 40 feet long and some fishing boats

Thursday fine but cold wind all well.

Friday morning a heavy sea water rushing on deck and she rides 15 to 18 feet out of water many people sick. Wife and children sick had to stop in the room all day they was a child died to day and buried at 12 o lock to night and one born the same day

I do repent coming out steerage the victuals was good but being packed so close together all the room we had was 6 ft 9 wide 2 ft d 16 so we had to crawl in and cant sit as our boxes was packed away and we could not get any clean clothes.

Sunday fine morning wet afternoon

Monday favorable and children better

Saturday morning fine and a beautifull sea all well

Sunday fine and warm a sea of glass most beautiful expecting a Pilot to watch us to day.

Monday 9 oclock land in about 2 hours but it was about 7 oclock at night before we got it Castle Garden was bustling about the luggage all day and nothing to eat since breakfast we got treated well in Castle Garden got our tickets started at five oclock the 18 cars are very comfortable stoves at each end Coaches 75 ft long seats for 150 passengers had to check my Baggage at Buffalo and at Omaha on Sunday the 23. New York State a fine place Oiho and Illinois to Chicago a fine level country you may travel 100 or 200 miles and not a tree or a bush to be seen plenty of coal and cheap

Land is double the value it was a year ago. From $5.00 to $16.00 per acre on easy terms no houses to be seen except a station and so level you cant tell if you are going up or down hill. I never saw an acre of Land Cultivated all through Nebraska not as much as a garden spot and none worth it not worth having if they would give you a 1000 acres Antilopes to be seen by the score and Buffaloes by the hundred and some gray wolves when we got into Wyoming. The hills all covered with snow for 60 or 70 miles. Twice as large as any I ever saw I ever saw in England.

Stoping at Ogden to day the 27th 40 miles North of salt Lake City plenty of Indians they brought 120 mules and shipped them for the east. When we got into Nevada it was cold hills from 7000 to 11000 feet high we went through a wood tunnel 60 miles long on the Nevada mountain that is to keep the snow of the track when we got of the mountains into California it got warmer and a fine Country all mining in the hills good farming land in the valleys fields of Corn from 10000 to 15000 acres belonging to different farmers. Plenty of game

The oldest part of Sanfrancisco is wood houses the new part is fine stone buildings stopped (?) days some of the children sick took my boots of and cant get them on again my feet are so swelled from having them on so long.

Start for Portland Nov 5 little Avis sick on the 6 died on the 7 of Dephtheria buried her on the 8 at Portland went up the Willamette river to Marysville. Then four days in a wagon to Oakland arrived on the 17 of November being 42 days on the way from home went to George Halls and found a good home with them for a week.

Cost $350 for our fare from England

March 1871
   Flour 100 lb $3.00 Wheat 1 bushel .73

In 1870, when the Baimbridge family arrived, the State of Oregon was only eleven years old, having obtained statehood on Valentine's Day 1859.

When Thomas and Emily and the five remaining children arrived in Oakland, they headed for the English Settlement east of town where they were reunited with old friends and relatives. They moved into a cabin owned by George Hall, a relative who owned a ranch. Then they leased a ranch owned by Dick Thomas in nearby Driver Valley. Mr. Thomas owned the Thomas Hotel in Oakland, and his wife was a Hall, so they too were related to the Baimbridge family.

Interestingly, stories vary as to how and when the Baimbridge family obtained the ranch that would remain in the family for over 100 years.

One version is the story as Mildred Kanipe related it to a relative, Maxine Baimbridge, who told it to the author as she remembered it.

Buying The Ranch From Winslow Powers

'Thomas Baimbridge came to the Oakland area from England in 1870 with his wife and five children. After renting a farm for two years he found one that he wanted to buy. When he approached the owner, Winslow Powers, Powers told him that he had no intention of selling. It would seem that that would have been the end of it, but it wasn't.

The story relates that Winslow Powers had purchased another ranch in Eastern Oregon and wanted to raise sheep on it but there were no sheep there. So, Powers gathered together a nice flock from the Oakland area to take to his new ranch. Because there was no other means of transportation in those days, Powers had to drive the sheep all the way to their destination. He left Oakland with his son, a hired hand and a Baimbridge boy. The Baimbridge boy was the only one mounted on a horse. The other three were walking.

(Maxine thought the Baimbridge boy was about 15 years old at the time, but if he was William Baimbridge, Thomas Baimbridge's only son, he would have been only 11— in this version of the story at least!)

When the group reached Eugene they were told there had been some Indian trouble in the pass. The Baimbridge boy grew nervous. He wasn't comfortable with the idea of "Indian trouble".

The group headed up the trail which followed the McKenzie River toward the old pass over the lava beds. Along the way they found a schoolhouse that had been burned down by the Indians. That was enough for the boy. He took advantage of the fact he was riding a horse, turned tail, and rode by himself all the way back to Oakland!

The remainder of the group continued on their way. When they got to the lava beds they were attacked by the Indians. The sheep were scattered every which direction while the three men hid among the rocks. The Indians tried to find the men, but were unable to do so.

After waiting for what seemed an eternity, Winslow Powers, his son, and the hired hand, came out from their hiding place. The story goes on to say that the hired hand was so scared that he ran all the way back to the Willamette Valley and was going so fast he ran right past Eugene before he realized where he was! Powers and his son tried to find their sheep, to no avail. They finally returned to Oakland, dejected, and now in financial trouble. Powers had overextended himself buying the Eastern Oregon ranch and the flock of sheep. He found himself without money and still needing sheep so he remembered Thomas Baimbridge's offer to buy his Oakland ranch and decided to sell it to him."

The very different story below is a sample of how history gets fouled up—the accuracy depending on who writes it down. We have a tendency to believe that once something is in print, it IS the TRUTH!

The Powers and the Deardorffs

The other version of the story came from the Winslow Powers family. Powers' son James wrote a book about his father, *Frontier Days, the Life of Winslow Powers and the Early Settlement of Eastern Oregon*, published in 1940. According to James, his story about the sale of the ranch and the trip with the sheep was a first hand account, saying that he accompanied his father on the described trip.

James Powers claimed that his father obtained a Donation Land Claim of 640 acres near Oakland. That was not possible, as Powers was not married at the time and therefore didn't qualify under the law for 640 acres. A study of the land records revealed that Powers did have a Donation Land Claim, #796, of 320 acres, having qualified for it by arriving in Oregon on December 14, 1847. His DLC was secured November 18, 1853 and he received the patent for the land on May 24, 1867.

He acquired an additional 327.66 acres on April 12, 1859 when he purchased Joseph and Elizabeth Deardorff's Donation Land Claim, which was contiguous to his on the west. The terms of the Donation Land Claim Act had changed after 1850. Single men qualified for only 160 acres, and married, 320 acres. Since Deardorff was married when he arrived in Oregon on August 25, 1853, he qualified for 320 acres. The Deardorffs secured their Donation Land Claim # 802 on "June/Sept 1854." Interestingly, the original document said they had qualified for 320 acres, but later in the same document it said they had received 327.66 acres! This could explain why there are some discrepancies in future land records. When Deardorff sold the land to Powers, it was listed as "320 acres more or less," but when Powers sold it to Baimbridge, it was again 327.66!

The house, which was long thought to have been built in 1851 by Winslow Powers "on his Donation Land Claim," turned out to actually be on Joseph Deardorff's Land Claim. James Powers said his father first built a log cabin, and then, *"after he married Harriet Tower in 1855, he built a good barn and several years later, a larger house."* Who actually built the house that Mildred Kanipe's grandfather and family moved into in 1872, Deardorff or Powers? Where was the cabin Powers was supposed to have built? He was required to live on his own land claim and farm the land in order to receive the patent for it from the government, so it would seem reasonable to assume that there was a cabin on his Land Claim. Also, he didn't buy the Deardorff property until 1859, four years after he got married.

The purchase price recorded for the Deardorff property was $1,000, and records show that Powers sold his place in Linn County, Oregon, where he had first settled, for $1,000 on October 18, 1853. Perhaps that is how he got the money to buy the Deardorff place six years later?

The Douglas County Calapooia Precinct 1870 Census listed Winslow Powers (49), his wife Harriet (37), and five children, Sarah (14), William (13), Mary (10), Anna (8), Francis (6), and James (1).

Powers was involved with the English Settlement School, apparently the first one, that was on Oldham Creek about a mile and a half south of were the current school is located. In April, 1863, he was elected clerk. (Apparently he was interested in education for his children as he is credited with being one of two persons who built the first school in Wallowa after moving there—he and the other person "having the most children.")

James Powers said his father left Oakland because the wet climate of Western Oregon did not agree with him. According to James, he rented his ranch to Baimbridge (a page from Thomas Baimbridge's diary substantiates this and placed the date at June 10, 1872), packed up his family, household goods, and farm animals and headed east to Wallowa, where the weather was drier, to find a parcel of land to his liking. In 1878, after getting settled in their new home, he took James with him and made the trip back to Oakland, a distance of over 400 miles, to negotiate the transfer of the farm to the Baimbridge family.

(Winslow P. Powers was issued a patent, document #702, for 160 acres under the Homestead Act of 1862 at the LaGrande, Oregon Land Office dated December 30, 1882.)

James's book said the agreed upon price for the Oakland property was $3,000 and 1,100 young ewe sheep. His story also had the sheep being driven on the journey. This time all but 200 were lost, not due to pesky Indians as in Mildred's story, but to a dishonest (white) hired hand. The sale was recorded on March 13, 1880, with Winslow and Harriet Powers signing the papers in Grant County, not Douglas County, so either it took Baimbridge a couple of years to pay off the cash part of the purchase, or, the trip back to Oakland occurred two years later, which may make more sense as that would have made James eleven years old rather than nine. Also, Harriet did not go to Oakland. The actual transfer included the 647.66 acres made up of the original Deardorff and Powers Donation Land Claims, plus 91.28 acres in section 6. The official sales price for the total 738.94 acres was listed as $6,000, which would average around $8.12 per acre. (Perhaps the sheep were considered to be worth $3,000.)

When Thomas and Emily Baimbridge rented the Powers ranch in 1872, they received what might be called a "ranch starter kit." The receipt listed the following: rent - $150, one bees - $5, Three jars - $3, churn - $2, vinegar & crock - $7, barley - $11.25, geese - $9.75, barrel - $1, hay - $28, oats - $11.80, flour - $3, meal - $3, sundries - $4. Total = $239.00. It was dated June 10, 1872.

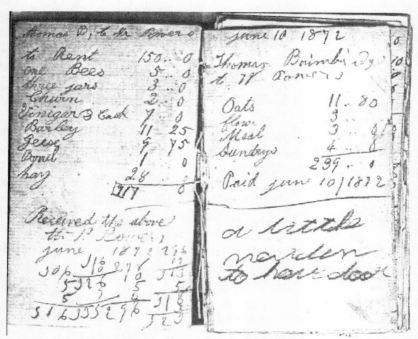

Thomas Baimbridge rental notes (1872)

The oldest known picture of the house—no horse barn.

On July 21, 1876, a daughter, Sarah Alice, was born in the house that was to be in the family for over one hundred years. Thomas and Emily Baimbridge again had six children.

The Baimbridge Children. (1890)

BACK, L to R: Sarah Alice (Baimbridge) Kanipe, (Mildred and Leah Kanipe's mother), July 21, 1876 – December 18, 1907 , William Baimbridge, December 7, 1861-April 12, 1947, Emily (Baimbridge) Young, July 20, 1863-December 23, 1947

FRONT, L to R: Hannah (Baimbridge) Green, January 4, 1870-November 30, 1950, Mary Ann Baimbridge, September 2, 1865-October 6, 1955, Elizabeth (Baimbridge) Dearmin, March 10, 1860-February 22, 1924.

(Written by Mildred Kanipe)

"After my grandparents death (Thomas 1891, Emily 1896) my mother, Sarah A. Baimbridge, inherited this part of the ranch. She lived here and operated it, raising sheep, until her marriage.

My fraternal grandfather, John A. Kanipe, came with his wife and small son, from North Carolina to Oakland, Oregon in the 1880s. They lived on different ranches in the vicinity until my father, John H. Kanipe, was grown and then they moved on the Dr. Langley Hall ranch which is about three miles from here. They lived there for a number of years and my father raised grain and Percheron horses and hay for stock feed.

After my mother and father married they lived here and he continued raising grain and horses for years. Later he raised mostly sheep and a few horses and cows and hay for stock feed.

After the death of my father I inherited this part of the ranch. I have lived here and operated it since that time. I raise sheep and cattle and hay for stock feed. I was born on the ranch. I have lived all my life here. I intend to always stay here.

The house where I live was built in 1851 by Winslow Powers on his homestead. (**1**) *It was built of hand hewed wood timbers mortared together with wooden pegs and whip sawed lumber nailed with square steel nails. The original roof was made of hand shaved cedar shingles nailed with little square steel shingle nails. It lasted some 75 years. This is the oldest house in the country still in practically its original state.*

Mr. Powers bought the Deardorff homestead which joined his on the south. (**2**) *When my grandfather bought Mr. Powers ranch he got that land too. My Aunt, Mary Baimbridge, inherited that part of the land, and my father bought it from her. I inherited eighty acres of it. Of the land I now own, some 1,100 acres, 240 acres* (**3**) *are of the original ranch bought by my grandfather Thomas Baimbridge.*

Notes by author:
1. (1) Winslow Powers did not own the land where the house is in 1851.
2. (2) The Deardorff property joined the Powers property on the west, not the south.
3. (3) According to the survey made at the time of her father's death, Mildred inherited 290.77 acres of the original ranch.

Apparently some details were passed down from generation to generation incorrectly.

MILDRED KANIPE

Who Was She?

Mildred Kanipe was born September 30, 1907. She joined her father, John H. Kanipe, her mother, Sarah Alice (Baimbridge) Kanipe, whom everyone called "Sally," and Leah Kathryn, a 2 ½ year old sister who was born February 12, 1905.

Mildred was born in the house her maternal grandparents, Thomas and Emily Baimbridge, had rented from Winslow Phelps Powers in 1872 and later purchased. Her mother, the only one of the children to be born in America, was born in the same house on July 27, 1876. Her father came with his parents, John Anderson and Nancy Jane Kanipe, from Tennessee in 1883, when John was nine years old.

Mildred's mother, Sarah, passed away on December 28, 1907. There was a rumor at the time that Mildred was delivered by a country doctor who delivered two other babies on the same day and all three mothers died, suggesting there could have been a problem with sanitation. However, Sarah passed away about three months after Mildred was born, and the cause of death on her death certificate was listed as "Le Grippe." (French for influenza.)

Sarah Baimbridge Kanipe, Leah and Mildred's mother

Mildred's full name was Mary Mildred Kanipe, but she never used her first name, perhaps because her mother's sister Mary moved in with the family after Sarah died to take care of the household and raise the two girls. Mary lived in the house with Mildred until she had to be placed in a nursing home toward the end of her life. Two Mary's under the same roof could have been confusing.

Aunt Mary on her 90th birthday— with Mildred, September 2, 1955
(Mary passed away on October 6, 1955, one month and four days after her
birthday.)

Aunt Mary had a reputation of being an excellent hostess and a very good cook. (A few of her recipes are included in the back of this book.) Mary raised her two nieces as her own. She never married. This was her family. Why she and John Kanipe, Mildred's father, never married, though they lived for thirty three years under the same roof, (until John passed away in 1940), was their business. Perhaps the arrangement suited them. Mary slept in the spacious attic room with the children and John used the only bedroom, which was downstairs.

Mildred and Leah Kanipe (1915)

Mildred and her sister Leah attended the first eight grades of school at the nearby one room English Settlement School, which was built on the family ranch just a short walk from their home. When the girls reached high school age, they traveled the eight miles to the town of Oakland by horseback. After their father purchased a buggy and hooked it up to their beloved pony Pete for the purpose of taking them to school, Mildred sometimes walked behind the buggy, "so that Pete wouldn't have to work so hard."

Three girls on Pete the pony at the English Settlement School. Leah is in the middle and Mildred is on the right--in back.

Mildred and Leah graduated from high school together in the spring of 1924. Mildred was sixteen years old. The teacher of the English Settlement School graduated the two girls together from the eighth grade even though there was two and a half years difference in their ages.

When the author asked Mildred's niece, Kathryn, what her mother and Mildred's childhood was like, she said simply, "It was all about horses." Many of the pictures of those early years show the two girls with their pony. Later, when they got older and Leah had left home, Mildred is shown on her favorite horse, Blue, or with a favorite buckskin colt.

Mildred on Blue.

Mildred with her buckskin colt. (1926)

While her sister Leah became a teacher, married, and had two children, John and Kathryn, Mildred remained single. After graduating from high school, Leah taught for two years at the English Settlement School, which she and Mildred had attended.

There are a number of stories that hint at reasons why Mildred never married. They include a mysterious rodeo cowboy who was tragically killed riding a bull, which allegedly broke her heart. She did correspond with a man who worked as a cow hand for ranchers in Eastern Oregon. In one of his letters he asked for a picture of her on her horse Blue. No one really knows, but Mildred claimed she just never had the time, and given all that she did, that could very well have been the case.

Reports are that Mildred was a very beautiful young woman and was even at one time referred to as "The Belle of Oakland." After she settled into the life of a rancher, she seldom wore a dress. Her usual costume was jeans, or as she called them, "overalls," a blue work shirt, and rubber boots. In cold weather she added a jacket and hat, and for a time wore an aviator's cap with ear flaps.

In the days when Mildred was young, people got together for community picnics and barn dances. It was at one such picnic that she showed up wearing an organdy dress. One of the women I interviewed grew up next door to the Kanipe ranch. She remembered being surprised and impressed with how beautiful Mildred looked that day.

Mildred enjoyed attending the annual rodeo at nearby Yoncalla and always rode in the rodeo parade. She bought a new blue shirt and pair of "overalls" for the occasion.

She loved land. Perhaps this is one of the things she learned from her father and grandfather. After coming from England and buying the Winslow Phelps Powers ranch, Thomas Baimbridge accumulated enough additional land that he was able to leave about 160 acres to each of his six children. Mildred's mother inherited the quarter section (160 acres), where the house and ranch buildings are, possibly because she was the one born in the house. The other five children had come from England with their parents in 1870.

After John Kanipe married Sarah Baimbridge, he proceeded to buy back the portions of the original ranch that his wife's father had purchased from Winslow Powers in the 1870s, restoring the integrity of the original 647.66 acre ranch, the combined Joseph Deardorff and Winslow Powers Donation Land Claims.

Mildred's Uncle William bought and sold a lot of land, and both he and her Aunt Mary obtained land through the Homestead Act. As soon as Mary got the patent (title) on hers, she sold it to her brother William.

Mildred often said that she was her father's only son. She learned ranching by his side. Working together for thirty three years before he died must have made them very close indeed.

Mildred with her father—having fun.

Mildred loved horses. She learned how to train them from her father, who bred Percheron horses, selling them as trained teams ready to work. He also shod horses and kept a stallion at stud for extra income.

As a teen Mildred trained horses and helped with miscellaneous ranch chores for neighboring ranchers. Instead of spending the money she earned on nice things to wear or fun things to do like the other girls her age would have done, she purchased 167 acres of precious land from G. R. Underwood for $2,500. Even though she eventually ended up owning almost 1,100 acres, she always referred to that first 167 acres as "my place." Maxine Baimbridge, a distant relative on her mother's side, who knew Mildred for many years and cared for her before she died, said that whenever Mildred was feeling depressed, she would go there to sit under the trees she loved.

It was here that Mildred first experienced farming on her own. Others told her she should cut the trees to clear the land, but she loved the trees, so she instead she cleaned out the brush by the creek and in the meadow and raised grain on that. After her sister married, Mildred hired her brother-in-law, Romie Howard, to build a barn on the property. His son, John, remembered going with his father when he was building it. It was later called the Drill Barn because for many years a horse-drawn seed drill was parked in it.

When John Kanipe died in 1940, the Powers Ranch was again split up. According to the survey done at the time, Mildred inherited 290.77 acres, mostly on the west side of Elkhead Road. It included the English Settlement School and the house where she was born and related barns and outbuildings. Her sister Leah inherited 353.32 acres on the east side of the road. This adds up to 644.09 acres, which is more than the 640 acre section two ordinary Donation Land Claims would have been but less than the recorded 647.66. The difference could be a reflection of different survey methods or may be accounted for by Elkhead Road.

Mildred now owned two disconnected pieces of land. She solved the problem by buying the 633 acre Underwood ranch which connected the two. The popular story is that in order to pay for this, she ran a Grade A dairy for eight years and saved every penny she could set aside to apply to the land purchase. Cows need to be milked twice a day, 365 days a year, regardless of the weather, whether you feel like it or not. She hauled the milk to Cottage Grove every day to be sold, and, since it was a "Grade A" dairy, she was required to keep the barn, cows, and milking equipment at a high standard of cleanliness, which was no small chore in itself. She told of once being so ill with the flu that she could hardly drag herself out of bed, but she had to feed the cows, do the milking, and drive the milk to sale. Another time she drove with an injured foot, one that would have incapacitated almost anyone else.

In March, 1954, the Eugene Farmers Creamery sent her a "*Notice of Patronage Equity*" which reported "*Pounds of Butterfat you delivered in 1953 in Milk or Cream...3,393.55.*"

The dairy represented additional work over and above what Mildred normally did running her ranch. She raised and sold beef cattle, rabbits, chickens, sheep and goats, sometimes on the hoof and other times butchered and sold as meat. This required not only managing the stock but also the pastures, repairing fences, harvesting grain, putting up hay, shearing the sheep and selling the wool, and collecting and selling eggs. She maintained an orchard of over 80 trees, with apple, pear, plum, peach, and walnut trees. In fall, she stored apples under the hay in the barn and ate them all winter.

Mildred standing on a truckload of wool.

It took her ten years to pay off the Underwood land. She paid $2,500 down in 1949 and $1,000 a year until the $12,500 purchase price was paid in full.

Now Mildred had a good piece of land, a total of 1,090.77 acres, or what is commonly referred to as, "almost 1,100 acres."

In 1963 Mildred considered buying more land. Neighbors, Alberta and Leslie C. Perrin, owned three quarters of section 14, 480 acres, and all of section 23, 640 acres. In April of that year, Perrin offered to sell all 1,120 acres, or "if she preferred," just the 480 acres in section 14, for $65 an acre. He offered to throw in "up to one mile of line fence". The price for the two parcels would have totaled $72,800. If Mildred had decided to take him up on the offer, she would have more than doubled the size of her ranch. Mildred must have thought his offer was unreasonable, however, as she had just, only four years before, finished paying off 633 acres for which she had paid less than $20 an acre and that property included a large house and fine barn.

Mildred kept meticulous records. Each animal was named. This was her way of tracking them. Today we do it with numbers and computers. She did it in her head and with short notes in small booklets. Her records of calf purchases had a short description of each and on one was an additional comment, "pretty." She kept a running record of her rabbits in a separate little book. They had names like "Diamond," "Floppy Ears," and all sorts of girls' names. When she butchered one, she recorded the date with its name and weight. She noted when she bred a female.

With the Underwood land under contract, Mildred obtained permission to do some logging on it. Between the years of 1955 and 1966 she had several contracts with lumber companies. Letters on record at the Douglas County Museum suggest that she was not always happy with how the contracts were carried out. She complained that one logging contractor had logged outside of the boundaries of the contract and requested "triple stumpage," or three times the contract price for those logs. She also felt that they had not cleaned up after logging in the manner that had been agreed upon. One contract allowed her $3 more (per what - it didn't say) if she cut and hauled the logs herself rather than have the company do it. Receipts at the museum show sales to what was commonly called a "stud mill," one that specialized in turning out eight foot lengths of boards for construction. She sold logs 12-18 inches in diameter, and all were 8 feet long. This made sense, especially when she was cutting and hauling them herself, as she was transporting them on a "one axel log trailer."

Edmund Boehrs and his wife Avis were good friends of Mildred. At one time they lived in the English Settlement schoolhouse, which was on her property. In 1954 she sold them a piece of land in the area but not part of her ranch. Ed worked for Mildred and was a partner in some of her activities. After Mildred passed away, and while he was still alive, Boehrs taped an interview for the Douglas County Park Department about his memories of Mildred. That interview has provided much valuable information for this story.

Mildred and Ed jointly purchased a chain saw and an old caterpillar tractor." They paid $4,000 for the "cat." The trailer was hers, but Boehrs was allowed to use it. They did some logging on a nearby place called "The Chicken Ranch," paying $2,000 for the timber they harvested there. This would account for at least some of the receipts for logs sold.

Mildred on her "cat".

One day (in 1972 or 1973) while she was taking the cat across a bridge over Batchelor Creek, the bridge collapsed and Mildred found herself pinned under the cat in the creek. Apparently her maker was not ready to take her as the only injury she received was to her leg. The cat was winched out of the creek by a man by the name of Robinson. Sadly, she accidentally backed the cat over her favorite dog, the one seen in several of her pictures, killing it. The dog is buried behind the house underneath the bedroom window.

For a time Mildred milled logs she harvested from the Underwood land. She had a large saw and cut the logs into rough lumber. The site can be found today by a stream of bark that flows down the hill from where the saw was. This can be seen on the slope next to the old road on the west side of Batchelor Creek. Ed Boehrs said that she didn't cut standing timber—only harvested "downed" trees. However, the few old moss covered stumps that are visible from a couple of today's trails, are testimony to the fact that some trees were cut.

Mildred was either loved and respected, or disliked intensely. She stubbornly remained her own person, a woman of extremely strong will, with her own ideas as to how things should be done.

She didn't trust many people, perhaps for good reason. She was not like everyone else, and that invited criticism and even harassment at times. She used metal ear tags on her sheep to identify them. One time some teenage boys took to shooting at the shiny tags. When they began shooting at her house, she became frightened and left to spend the night with friends.

Running a huge ranch was a lot of work, and many a young boy was referred by the Oakland High School to work for her. Her carefully recorded notes as to the hours worked and the type of work done showed that much of the help needed was with haying and cutting wood. One who worked for her said he thought he saw some things that could have been done—in his mind—a better way, so he suggested them to Mildred. She said politely, "That is interesting, but we'll do it my way." Several who had worked for her described her as "good to work for." One described her as "a little gruff, eccentric, and very private." He said she never talked about herself nor invited him into her house. She paid in cash every day. He continued, almost as an afterthought, "She was pretty nice—and fair." Then he related how she shot skunks and skinned them, intending to sell the beautiful pelts, but the demand for skunk pelts had declined so much she couldn't sell them, so she just tacked them up around the property lending a distinctive perfume to the air.

Mildred also had a number of hired hands who at times lived on the place in a small trailer. They were paid partly in groceries and other purchases. Mildred didn't smoke, but her records show many purchases for cigarettes, apparently for the hired hands. One former employee wrote her a couple of long letters from the Oregon State Penitentiary. He complained about the difficulties of life there and how hard it was to get letters out. He wrote as though he was very lonely and Mildred was someone he felt comfortable with. He called her "Honeypot" several times in his letters, which could suggest that there was more than an employer employee relationship between them—at least in his mind—or, he was just one of those men who speak to all women that way. Mildred apparently checked into his background because her papers include a report on him from the penitentiary that detailed a history of mental illness and criminal activity. It mentioned that he was married and it was unknown where his wife was. He was in the penitentiary for theft.

One person who remembered Mildred said, "She drove around in her truck looking for loose livestock wandering by the road. If she saw one she loaded it into her truck and took it home." Everyone knew Mildred's pickup when they saw it. It had stock rails on the sides to which she tied baling twine that she got from her hay, and it streamed in the wind as she drove.

Mildred had disagreements with neighbors over fences and livestock not staying where they were supposed to. The neighbors felt certain that she was cutting the fence to get free feed. Her position was that they were not maintaining the fences that were their responsibility.

There were also arguments about who pumped more than their share of water out of Batchelor Creek in late summer when the water was low. Ed Boehrs said that every fall everyone had to quit watering and "that was too bad" because it was the time of year when the crops needed the water the most. The creek that once ran two feet deep in the summer and had lots of cut throat trout and salmon in it had become so low that there wasn't enough water to go around.

A couple of people I interviewed referred to Mildred as a "thief," but Audie Campbell, who worked for many years as a policeman in the area and knew Mildred, said that he never had any reason to believe that she was anything other than completely honest.

In Mildred's mind, it was a sin to waste anything. She rarely spent money when she could avoid it. She lived her whole life in the house where she was born nearly the way it had been lived in for over 100 years. A bathroom was never put in. Only in later years electricity was run to a single bare light bulb on the dining room ceiling, which replaced the beautiful gas candelabra that her nephew John remembered hanging there when he was a boy. The only other electric light evident in the house today is a screw-in light bulb socket at waist height on a corner in the kitchen. There is also an electric outlet by a built-in ironing board in the kitchen. At the same time electricity was brought into the house, water was brought to a double stainless steel sink that was put in the kitchen, mounted in a minimal section of rough, hand-made kitchen cabinets. Her friend Ed Boehrs made these improvements. He also built an addition on the back of the house that was said to be for a bathroom, but it was never finished.

Cooking was always done on an old fashioned wood range, and the house was never heated with anything other than wood. In 2007, the house, neglected since Mildred moved out of it when her health failed before she died in 1983, has remnants of the ancient wallpaper hanging from the ceiling and the walls in the old living room and bedroom, showing the cheesecloth under it that was first applied to the bare wood. The exposed single construction walls show planks of rough clear grain wood, some as wide as twenty inches.

Ed Boehrs said he often stopped by on a Saturday and found Mildred butchering a few rabbits. These she would take to the market in Oakland to sell and then go straight to the auction and buy a suckling calf or two with the money. She brought the calves home and fed them milk from her goats. She had one nanny that would stand on a box while Mildred put a calf on each side to nurse. When they had enough, she pulled them off and stuck another two on. She did this until the goat ran dry. This was a twice a day procedure until the calves were old enough to be weaned.

It was Ed who went with Mildred one of the two times she traveled outside of Oregon. Mildred, who had been selling Christmas trees locally, decided to haul some to Los Angeles. They loaded up two trucks and trailers with about a thousand trees and headed south, Ed in the lead because he was the one who had experience driving in cities.

When they stopped in the first town Mildred wanted to know what the sign meant that said, "X-Crossing." She had never seen one.

They stopped for breakfast at one of those coffee shops you see by the side of the highway. Ed was hungry so he ordered the works, pancakes, bacon and eggs, hash brown potatoes, and coffee. Mildred, not in the habit of eating breakfast, ordered a glass of water. The waitress looked at the thin, scraggly looking woman with pity. Ed was sure she was thinking that the poor woman couldn't afford to buy anything to eat. He said, "Little did that woman know that Mildred could have bought her many times over."

When they reached Los Angeles, they got lost a few times before they finally got the trees sold and could return home. Mildred decided that the big city wasn't her kind of place.

On the way home, Ed was again in the lead. He glanced at the rear view mirror and saw no sign of Mildred's truck, so he turned around and went back to look for her, thinking that she may have had mechanical trouble. A few miles back he saw her truck parked by the side of the road. Mildred was walking around picking up pieces of cotton that had apparently spilled from a cotton truck. When he asked her what she was doing, she said, "It was just going to waste!"

The other time she went out of state she also went to Los Angeles. The National Rodeo was being held there and Mildred loved rodeos.

There are many stories about Mildred's penny-pinching, but she had her generous side as well. Her attorney, Don Dole, said she loaned money to many people the banks and others turned down, drawing up the contracts herself and fully expecting to be paid back. He knew about this because on occasion he had to represent her in court to get her money.

But, Mildred would not be messed with. She carried a pistol, and around the ranch a .30-30 rifle. She was most probably an excellent shot, as everything she did she did well, even though not everyone agreed with how she did them.

Hunting in a dress.

A retired nurse I met while downtown one day remembered checking Mildred into the hospital one of the times she had to go there. She could still see Mildred removing her clothes—and her gun.

Mildred was strong and is said to have been able to keep up with any man when it came to working. "She would pick up a bale of hay and throw it into the barn like it was nothing."

Being a rancher, Mildred had no problem butchering livestock when needed. She would kill a sheep and take it into the kitchen to skin and cut it up. As previously mentioned, she also raised and sold beef, chicken and rabbit meat for income. Boehrs reported that when the County went out to the ranch after Mildred passed away, they found two chest freezers on the porch full of meat. Apparently the electricity had been turned off for some time because when the freezers were opened the meat was pretty ripe.

Mildred also loved her animals and had a special relationship with them. Maxine Baimbridge related an experience she had one time she visited. Mildred said she needed to go bring her cattle in and asked Maxine if she would like to come along. Maxine said she would, and the two hiked to the top of a hill and sat down on a log. Then Mildred began calling— "and Mildred had quite the voice." First one cow poked its head out of the bushes, and then another. This went on until Mildred said, "I guess they are all here." Then she stood up and walked back to the barn, the cattle following her like she was the Pied Piper.

Mildred sitting on her shorthorn bull.

One gentleman remembered Mildred and a "doctor" riding their horses into town drunk. She would fall off her horse, and he would laugh and shout that she didn't know how to ride. Then he would fall off and she would do the same to him. Apparently, Mildred did drink on occasion. She kept diaries in small notebooks, usually entering only one line per day, such as "Butchered calf.", "Put hay in barn.", or "Went to rodeo." On one day she entered, "Got drunk." The next day the entry said, "Took it easy." (She must have had a hangover.)

In later years Mildred had a reputation for being unkempt. Given the fact that she lived alone, had no way to take a proper bath or do her laundry, and was working many hours a day with farm animals and other ranch chores, it is perhaps understandable that what we refer to as personal hygiene was not high on her list of priorities. She did clean up, though, if the occasion warranted it. Her attorney of forty years, Don Dole, reported that whenever she came to his office, she was always clean and neat, and her clothes were ironed.

While Mildred was taking care of everything else she was not taking care of herself, and her health suffered because of it. One of the times she was in the hospital, the Farmer's Co-op decided to send her flowers because she had been a substantial customer for many years. Instead of sending them a thank you note, Mildred sent a note admonishing them for "wasting money in such a manner." Perhaps she was secretly pleased.

Mildred loved her land and was very possessive of it. When she purchased the Underwood ranch, there was a small pioneer cemetery on a knoll across the creek north of the Underwood barn. Mildred rented out the Underwood house, and a daughter of the family who lived there, whose married name was Helen Ortiz, remembered picking flowers as a child where five graves were surrounded by a picket fence. When Mildred bulldozed the evidence of the graves away, she told Helen, "I don't want strangers poking around on my property." Apparently at some time someone had come looking for family graves. Today, the exact location of the graves is unknown, as are the identities of those buried there. Helen thought it was a Charlie Hall's first wife and two children and a neighbor's wife and child who had all died at the same time, perhaps in a fire, but extensive research has not shed any light whatsoever on this mystery.

On October 8, 1996, Helen Ortiz went with local historian Pat Gausnell and park caretakers, Chuck and Paulette Jones, to try to locate the gravesites. She was only able to identify the general area on the knoll, saying it had been so many years and the trees had grown so much that it all looked different. They had a metal detector with them and were only able to find a couple of rusty nails, one of a type that it may have been in the picket fence, and the other—a horse-shoe nail. Helen said that Mildred had asked her to see that the site be restored after her death. That was not to be.

When Mildred's health failed and she was no longer able to live alone in her beloved home where she had spent her whole life, she moved into the house in the town of Oakland that she had inherited from her paternal grandparents. When she was no longer able to live there, she moved in with her relative, Maxine Baimbridge, who cared for her at her home until it became evident that she needed professional care. On July 13, 1983, at 75 years of age, Mildred passed away in a nursing home. She was unable to stay in her house until she died, as she wished.

Mildred Kanipe left an estate valued at $1,077,865.50.

In January 1981, she had summoned her trusted attorney, Don Dole, to document her wishes in a will. She, who had been a penny-pincher in life, was generous in death. No one really knows why she decided to leave her beloved ranch to the people of Douglas County for a park. Only Mildred could have answered the question, but in addition she left:

A total of $32,000 to various friends and relatives.

"the approximately five acre tract which I own on Northeast Locust Street within the City of Oakland to be used by it only as a city park to the City of Oakland."

Two separate trusts were set up. The first was to handle the $70,000 fund mentioned below. In 2007 the bank closed this trust and distributed the funds in the percentages outlined. They claim that the size of the trust was not worth their time.

"My trustee shall set aside the sum of $70,000 and pay the net income therefrom in perpetuity as follows:

1) To the City of Oakland for use in maintaining the "Kanipe Memorial Park", (the five acre one inside the city limits), - - - - - - - - seven and one-half percent (7 ½ %) of annual net income.

2) To Cedar Hills Cemetery of Oakland, Oregon, for upkeep and maintenance of the Kanipe Lot and adjoining land, particularly the northeast corner thereof, seven and one-half percent (7 ½%) of the annual net income.

3) To the Oakland Community Church situated on Eighth and Locust Street for the use of said church for local church purposes, fifteen percent (15%) of the annual net income.

4) To the First Church of Christ, located at Second and Pine Street in Oakland, Oregon, for local church purposes, fifteen (15%) of the annual net income.

5) The balance of the net income thereof (55%) shall be paid to or for the benefit of first year's tuition and incidental fees for a

*deserving student of Oakland High School, or its successor, of high
scholastic and moral standards, which student shall be selected by
the School Board and which student shall be a native of Douglas
County, preferably farm raised, who is entering a college or
university intending to study for a degree in Agriculture, Forestry
or other subjects."* (The will detailed how any excess of this
should be apportioned to the same or other students for
college or university)

The second trust was to take care of the ranch as outlined below.

*My trustee shall in perpetuity pay the net income of the remainder of the
trust to Douglas County, Oregon for the use of its Park Department in the
maintenance and upkeep of the "Mildred Kanipe Memorial Park" or of
the "Mildred Kanipe Ranch Museum" established pursuant to paragraph
FIFTH of this Will.*

*FIFTH: I hereby give and bequeath unto DOUGLAS COUNTY,
OREGON, my ranch, together with the contents of my home and
any farm tools and implements for use in the "Mildred Kanipe Ranch
Museum", consisting of approximately 1,100 acres situated in Section
18 and 19, Township 24 South, Range 4 West, Willamette Meridian
and in Section 12 and 13, Township South, Range 5 West, Willamette
Meridian, to be used by it only for park purposes and only upon the
following conditions;*

a) *This park shall be named and known as the "Mildred Kanipe
Memorial Park".*

b) *So far as practicable, my home and its contents, together with the
barns and other out buildings and the trees and area immediately
surrounding these structures shall be restored and maintained for
public use as the "Mildred Kanipe Ranch Museum.*

c) *No portion of the property is to be transferred, sold or traded.*

d) *No hunting or trapping is to be allowed.*

e) *All animals, birds and fish are to be protected as in a refuge,
provided, however, that the County, for park purposes, may plant
and permit fishing in the ranch ponds.*

f) *Trapping and hunting of predatory animals should they become a
nuisance and harmful to domestic and wild animals both within
the park and on adjoining lands may be carried on by the County.*

g) *The County may establish a limited picnic ground and in
conjunction therewith facilities but no motorized vehicles are to*

be permitted within the park except may be required for park construction and maintenance.

h) *Pasture lands are to be cared for and continued in grass and equestrian trails shall be permitted.*

i) *No timber shall be cut or harvested except as may be necessary and cutting then only upon a sustained yield basis with all revenue from timber cutting used by the County in capital improvements upon the park.*

DOUGLAS COUNTY, OREGON may disclaim this bequest in whole or in part and should DOUGLAS COUNTY so disclaim this gift, or fail to establish this park pursuant to the foregoing conditions within three (3) years of the date of my death, or after the establishment of said park violate or permit to be violated to any degree any of the conditions of this gift as outlined above, then this gift shall lapse and the interest of DOUGLAS COUNTY, its successors and assigns, is said property shall automatically terminate and title to all of said property shall vest in my Trustee hereafter named, to become a part of the trust established under paragraph SEVENTH of this Will.

Another mystery is the way Mildred requested that she be buried. Her will stated, *"I hereby direct that I be buried on the ranch in the little open space south of the yard fence in the center between the big cedar and the big oaks and that I be dressed in a shirt and overalls lying on my right side, with my feet towards the east or county road - - - "*

No one knows why Mildred instructed that she be buried lying on her right side, but we know that she was buried that way, because after her casket had been lowered into the ground, Chris Dukehart, Trustee for her trust, requested that it be brought back up and opened. After he verified that she was lying as instructed, it was lowered again and the burial was completed.

People have different ideas as to why Mildred requested to be buried that way. Some say she wished to be positioned so that she could watch the sun rise in the morning. Others think perhaps she wished to be facing a favorite part of the ranch. One neighbor joked that she wanted to be able keep an eye on him after she died.

This mystery remains unsolved, but a photo at the Douglas County Museum shows Mildred's mother Sarah lying in state in her casket on her right side. Mildred was only 3 months old when her mother died, so she certainly didn't remember the occasion. Had she seen the picture?

Family members interviewed had no idea, but Derbyshire, England, where Mildred's mother's family emigrated from over a hundred years before has a strong Druid history and many Druid historical sites! Was the request connected to a Druid custom?

(See STORIES BY OTHERS for more about Mildred and her family.

MILDRED KANIPE MEMORIAL PARK

A Beautiful Gift

The house with park land beyond (2005)

The equipment shed with park land beyond (2005)

When Mildred Kanipe passed away on July 13, 1983, Douglas County officials were thrown into a state of shock upon learning that they had suddenly acquired a new park of almost 1,100 acres. It was left subject to restrictions outlined in the will that would result in title reverting to Mildred's trust if they are not followed, severely restricting management of the park, which has been a source of frustration ever since. (County officials are still trying to figure out how they can log for income—something that Mildred clearly did not want, and they have passed a resolution that will prevent accepting future donations that would restrict use.)

Nevertheless, the property was accepted for a park by the Douglas County Commissioners, Bill Vian, Doug Robertson, and Bruce Long, on June 4, 1986. Park Director, Tom Keel, signed the acknowledgement of the receipt on June 20, 1986.

Description of the property was listed as;

The northwest quarter less Medley-Elkhead County Road No. 50; that portion of the southwest quarter lying westerly of County Road No. 50 in Section 18 T24S R4W.; That portion of the northwest quarter of the northwest quarter lying westerly of County Road No. 50 in Section 19 T24S R4W.; The southwest quarter of Section 12, T24S R5W.; All of Section 13, T24S R5W.; All in Douglas County and containing 1,088.56 acres, more or less. (Original land records of individual parcels added together result in a total of 1,090.77 acres.)

Now the County was faced with a problem—what to do with it?

The land and buildings had been vacant since Mildred was forced to move out because failing health prevented her from managing the place. The site of the house and farm buildings was overgrown with grass and weeds, the barns full of old deteriorating hay, and the house was a legacy to a woman who never threw anything away, stuffed with piles of every document she had ever had, down to the most insignificant receipts for the purchase of groceries, Louis L'amour and Zane Gray paperback books that she loved to read, boxes of items she had apparently purchased when they were on sale and never gotten around to using (such as the box of brand new never-worn jeans), piles of egg shells in the kitchen, and much more. Among all of that were precious family antiques, including the steamer trunk her grandmother Emily Baimbridge brought with her on the ship from England over a hundred years before. To move about the house, you had to make your way through the narrow pathways between the piles of stuff! Apparently Mildred had suffered from a condition that has recently been dubbed, "Compulsive Hoarding Disorder." When the Douglas County Museum staff attacked the monumental task of inventorying the house contents, records show that they found more than one "large live brown bat" among her things, one described as being under the mattress of the bed. Mildred's house was not unoccupied.

Mildred, as the colorful character that she was, inspired many stories. At times it is impossible to know which ones are just stories and which ones are based on fact. There are two such stories related to the cleaning out of Mildred's house. They are both about valuables. One alleges that she had hidden large sums of money and "gold" in the walls of the house. Was someone looking for treasure when they removed the boards on the kitchen side of the dining room wall? Why did they stop there? Did they find something? The other story relates how several adults and children were going through the things in the house and someone began looking through one of the paperback books—and found money inserted between the pages! The story goes, "The children were immediately sent away, and nobody knows how much money was found or what happened to it." Probate records show "Cash in residence, $11.00." After the museum staff had inventoried what was in the house, they carted off many of the antiques, family heirlooms, and boxes and boxes of records. These are at the museum today and have been a valuable resource while researching for this book.

Park Department staff cleaned out the barns and burned "250 tons" of old hay.

The County had a huge sale and in the frenzy to "clean up the place," items were sold that many thought should have been kept for the Douglas County Museum or for the Ranch Museum that Mildred had hoped would be developed at the site. Mildred's pickup with the stock rails and the hay string would have been nice to display at the Ranch Museum. So would many of the other things listed on the auction sale advertisement.

ESTATE AUCTION SALE
SATURDAY FEBRUARY 18TH 11:00 A.M.
NEAR OAKLAND, OREGON
FARM EQUIPMENT, CAT 2 TRACTORS, 2 PICKUPS, FURNITURE, MISC.

Mrs. Kanipe left her 1100 acre ranch to Douglas County to be used as a Park and made many other requests in her Will. One stipulation was that she was to be buried on the property in a certain spot in a certain way in certain clothes. This should be a real interesting sale.

SAMPLE OF WHAT WILL BE SOLD

A lot of this equipment is a step back in time. Most of it is old but appears to be in serviceable condition. International TD-6 with angle blade and winch (1950's), I.H. Farmall Cub with mower attached - good rubber, Ford tractor - 8N with 3 point - good rubber, Ford mower, 1960 Chev. Apache ½ ton pickup with metal stock rack, 1954 Willys pickup, old "New Racine" threshing machine on iron wheels, New Holland hay baler, Case side delivery rake on rubber, manure spreader on rubber, Easy Flo and Lilly fertilizer spreaders, rubber tired and iron wheeled hay wagons, 8' offset tandem disc with 24" blades, springtooth seeder, fanning mill, M.M. old gang plow with 3-14" plows, horse drawn cultivator, hay rake, 3 walking plows and Fresno, iron wheels, work harness, double trees, Harpoon hay fork.

MISC. - 250 gallon gas tank, 12 50 gallon drums - some with diesel, stack of wood, various water troughs, field feeders for sheep and cattle, pump and tank and motor, large irrigation pump with 30 hp electric motor (needs work), rabbit hutches, 7½'x14' portable bunk house or storage building on skids, 11 peacocks and hens.

FURNITURE AND MISC. - You'll have to see it to believe it. The home is old and it's filled with things from tall old cupboards that were really nice once, two iron beds, feather ticks, wicker chairs, antique kitchen work tables with flour type bins below and just about anything else old that you can think of. We may sell the whole contents of the place at one time and let you remove it.

Lunch wagon will be there.

Location - 5 miles from downtown Oakland. Follow auction signs East on County Road 50 3 miles, turn on Elkhead Road 3 more miles.

Estate of Mildred Kanipe
C.A. MORRISON, AUCTIONEER
Phone: 479-9761

Estate sale advertisement (1984)

Bill Talburt, who knew Mildred well and worked for her at times, said he bought all the horse drawn farm equipment that could still be used. He offered to bring it back and demonstrate it for the public to enjoy, with his own horses, should a historic function be held at the park.

Some unusable items of old farm equipment were left at the park. They are now on display in the equipment shed.

In 1994, Mildred's beloved ranch was formerly dedicated as a county park and a bronze plaque was placed near her grave. The County put in a paved drive and parking area in the ranch buildings area, (which became known as the "Day Use Area," and since January 29, 2008, is on the National Register of Historic Places under the name, "Baimbridge-Kanipe Farmstead Historic District.") Public restrooms with flush toilets were built, picnic tables and iron grills were brought in and placed near the historic house, and a single-wide manufactured home was moved in to house a caretaker.

Park improvements (1994)

Local equestrian groups zeroed in on the condition of Mildred's will that "Equestrian trails shall be permitted." and, with the County Park Department's blessing, began to build trails throughout the park.

The Roseburg chapter of OET, (Oregon Equestrian Trails), a statewide trail riding organization, put in a fenced enclosure for a picnic site and in 2006 built a 24' X 24" shelter inside the picnic enclosure. (The fence is necessary to keep the cattle out which roam the park and bring in grazing fees to help pay the cost of park operation.) OET has a work party every year when the park opens in March to equestrian use. They clear and repair the trails that have been damaged over the winter.

County officials looked at the land and saw timber. According to probate documents on file at the Douglas County Courthouse, the timber had an estimated value of $416,875 at the time of Mildred's death. Twelve years later in September, 1995, the County commissioned the "Kanipe Ranch Timber Sale Proposal." It estimated that the volume of marketable Douglas Fir at the time was 3.0 million board feet with an estimated value of $1,350,000. At this writing, the trees have been growing for another thirteen years. It would seem reasonable to assume that that factor, combined with inflation, should result in a significant increase in value.

The 1995 timber sale proposal indicated that two thirds of the income from selling timber from the park would be required to put in the necessary roads to take it out. It did not mention how this would affect the trails or the value of the land as a park.

The county did build the bridge over Batchelor Creek that was recommended in the Timber Sale Proposal. Equestrians who enjoy park trails joke about the "10,000 pound horses" that the bridge was engineered for!

The logging study proposed that the forest growing on Mildred's first land, the 167 acres for which she did farm chores and trained horses to earn the money to buy, should be the first to harvest. It is the easiest to access, just a short distance up the hill after you cross the bridge.

When the word got out that Douglas County was planning to log in the park, the public was outraged, and the plan was dropped—for then.

In 2001 a steering committee was formed to develop a management plan for the park. It was made up of six individuals: Mike Black, Oregon Department of Fish and Wildlife; Francis Eatherington, Umpqua Watersheds; Jill Talburt, Oregon Equestrian Trails; Bill Talburt, Oregon Equestrian Trails; Mel Thornton, Douglas Forest Protective Association; and Jeff Powers, Director, Douglas County Parks. The resulting plan was completed in August, 2001. It was approved by the Douglas County Commissioners but not by the Trustee for Mildred's trust because it included plans to cut trees that may not be in agreement with the terms of Mildred Kanipe's will.

In 2004, the County Park Department approved a public survey of users, which at that time were mainly equestrians enjoying the trails. The results showed a strong interest in preserving the natural assets of the park. The vast majority objected to logging of any kind. They saw the trees as a source of pleasure. The County considered them a source of revenue.

At the end of 2004, County Commissioner Dan Van Slyke announced that the County was seriously considering "giving the park back" to Mildred's Trust, due to the burden it posed to the county. Mildred's will forbade the county to sell any part of the land but allows it to be returned to the trust.

Don Dole, attorney who prepared Mildred's will, said that if the property was returned to the Mildred Kanipe Trust, it would be sold to the highest bidder and the proceeds obtained thereof be used to set up another trust to be administered similar to the one established by C. GILES HUNT. The county would lose its largest park. The new trust would provide a source of grant funds for other interests.

A New Direction

On February 18, 2005, a public meeting was held at the Umpqua Regency Inn in the nearby town of Sutherlin to protest the potential loss of the park. An e-mail network and posters put up around Roseburg, Sutherlin and Oakland, brought in a standing-room only crowd. People were packed in the room so tight that many who came to the door had to turn around and leave. There was "no room left at the inn." Fortunately, the fire marshal didn't show up.

The group sponsoring the event had invited Jeff Powers, Douglas County Park Director, to address the crowd, and invited all three Douglas County Commissioners to attend. When Commissioner Dan Van Slyke arrived, Park Director Jeff Powers declined to speak and turned the meeting over to him. He was the commissioner in charge of the Douglas County Park Department at the time and the only one of the three commissioners to show up. Van Slyke had arrived a bit late and had a difficult time maneuvering through the tight crowd of bodies to get to the podium. The numbers in the room apparently sent a strong message as he changed his mind and promised to keep the park. In return, members of the public made a commitment to "help the County in every way possible" in order to lighten the burden of managing the huge park. The "Friends of Mildred Kanipe Memorial Park Association" was formed. Eight months later it became a nonprofit corporation and successfully petitioned for federal nonprofit charitable tax exempt 501 (c) (3) status. Then it went one step further and joined the qualified list of the Oregon Cultural Trust, which adds another dimension to contribution benefits. Donations to the Friends group are tax deductible, a matching donation to the Oregon Cultural Trust is an Oregon tax credit, and, the Oregon Cultural Trust makes grant monies available to members on the list.

When County officials looked at the buildings when they acquired the park, they decided the restoration and continuing maintenance that would be required to save them was impractical and perhaps financially impossible, so they adopted a "do nothing" policy, or what has been quoted many times over the years, "Let them melt into the ground."

The County's decision to do nothing to preserve the buildings resulted in the loss of four buildings and the further severe deterioration of the others

The rabbit hutch, that had stood between the horse barn and the dairy barn, was not savable. It was gone soon after Mildred passed away. The Salt Barn, which was about in the center of the Underwood ranch land and had been repaired by Oregon Equestrian Trails volunteers in the 1990s in an attempt to save it, collapsed and was burned by the county in 2004. The Underwood House, the only building at the park, other than the English Settlement School, to be included in the Douglas County Historic Buildings Inventory, collapsed, and was burned by the County in January of 2005. The beautiful Underwood barn is still there.

The Underwood House (1990)

In 2006, the Drill Barn, which was on the first land Mildred Kanipe owned and her brother-in-law Romie Howard built, was falling down. The County tore it down, salvaged what lumber they could and used it to repair the equipment shed. (The thinking had begun to change.)

The English Settlement School had stood in water every winter for almost 100 years. Foundation timbers had suffered significant rot. The roof of the school had also been leaking for years. The building had been used as a barn, and the floor was covered with sheep manure. By 2005, the balloon frame building was twisting and starting to pop apart at the corners, threatening eminent collapse.

The house, where Mildred Kanipe and her mother were both born, had been leaking for years. This had caused major rot through the roof, the attic floor, down the wall and through the kitchen floor. A neglected minor repair had resulted in major damage. Bats had taken up residence, and, rather than one or two as was the case when Mildred died, there was now a large bat nursery. Broken windows provided easy access. The floors downstairs and up were covered with bat guano and dust. The building was sagging here and there as well.

The barns needed attention.

The land was suffering from serious invasion of noxious weeds.

Mildred Kanipe Memorial Park is almost exactly in the center of the English Settlement, named for pioneers who had emigrated from England and settled there. Like many immigrants, the English brought plants that made them feel at home. Where they came from, hawthorn was commonly used for hedgerows. It makes very effective living fences. Unfortunately, birds eat the berries and have spread hawthorn everywhere. It is fast-growing and very difficult to eradicate. Most of the meadows which once grew hay and provided pasture became overrun with ten-foot tall hawthorn.

Another nuisance foreign plant is the Himalaya Blackberry. These plants were brought to Oregon many years ago by a well meaning farmer who intended to grow them and sell the berries. Birds have spread them all over western Oregon and Washington states.

Various varieties of "Scotch" Broom have also made their way into the park. These have perfected the art of survival. One plant can produce 100,000 seeds in a single year, and those can lie on the ground for 85 years, sprouting a few at a time.

The new Friends of Mildred Kanipe Memorial Park Association, wrestling with how they could best take some of the load off of the Park Department and the County and at the same time help fulfill Mildred's wishes as expressed in her will, came up with the following mission statement.

"The mission of this organization shall be to provide volunteer services for the purpose of restoring, improving, maintaining, and protecting the natural resources of the park such as land, plants and animals, the historic structures in the park, and the other park improvements such as fences, restrooms, picnic areas, etc., for the purpose of providing recreational, educational and cultural experiences for the public, in accordance with the conditions of Mildred Kanipe's Will, and to raise funds to cover as much as possible of related costs."

The group had their first work party on July 16, 2005—purely cleanup. They then worked up a priority list of critical needs and presented it to the County. The County came through with flying colors and helped complete every major item on the list except fixing the house leak, which they did the following year. It was a start.

In the first two years of existence, the Friends group accomplished the following:

- Cleaned up the Underwood house site. They salvaged the historic bricks that had been in the chimney and were made in the old kiln in Oakland, cut blackberry vines, and hauled loads of trash to the dump.
- Cleaned the inside of the English Settlement School, removing sheep manure that had resulted from using the

structure as a barn, and cut blackberry vines and English Hawthorne and other weeds in the area surrounding it.

- Removed old rusty barbed wire that was on and near trails around the park.
- At their request, former Commissioner Van Slyke authorized necessary repairs that saved the English Settlement School from imminent collapse, thus buying time.
- Repaired and replaced where necessary the perimeter fence of the park, which had been in a sad state of repair with some sections lying on the ground. Cattle were getting out onto neighboring property.
- Washed the windows in the historic house so that the inside can be viewed by the public and replaced several panes of glass that were broken.
- Cleaned out, with help from county crews, several buildings and set up the beginnings of museum displays in keeping with Mildred Kanipe's request that her house and farm buildings should be developed as a "Ranch Museum".
- Researched and purchased two Century Farm signs of the style that Mildred Kanipe would have received had she ordered them in 1974 when she received the Century Farm Certificate from Governor Tom McCall. (See the note for her speech below.)

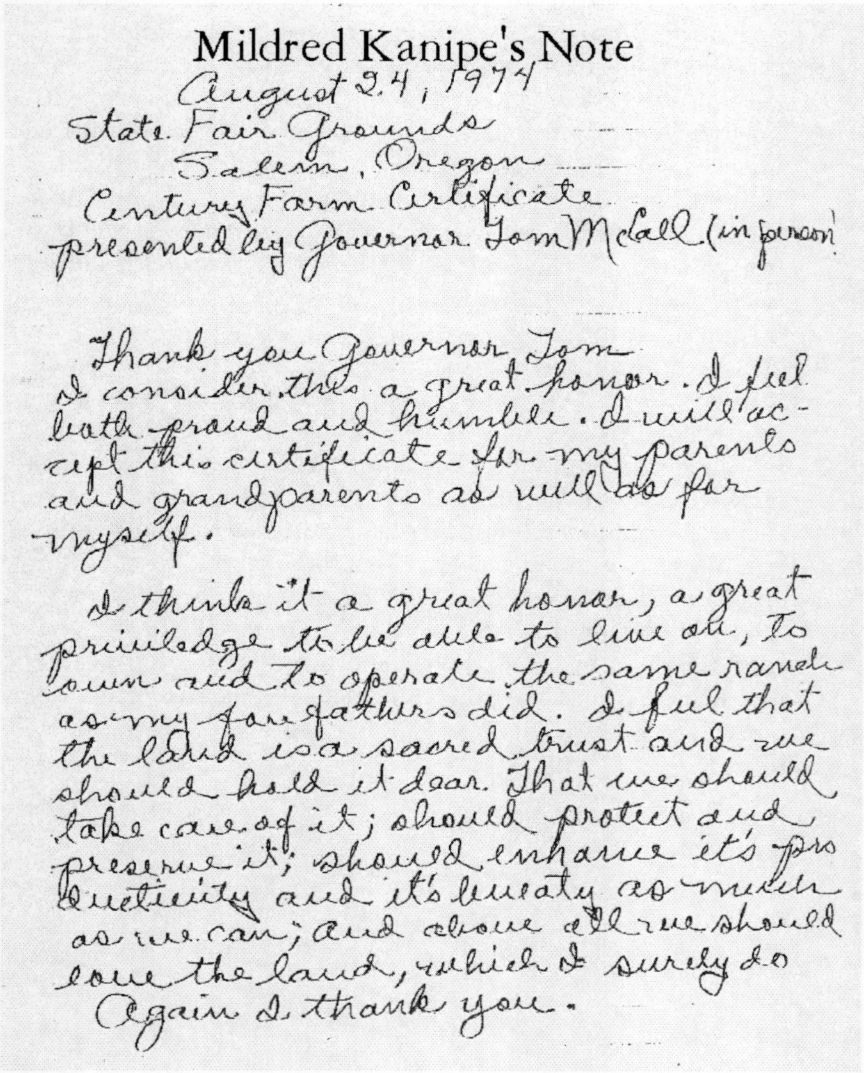

Mildred Kanipe's Note

Handwritten note:

August 24, 1974
State Fair Grounds
Salem, Oregon
Century Farm Certificate
presented by Governor Tom McCall (in person)

Thank you Governor Tom
I consider this a great honor. I feel
both proud and humble. I will ac-
cept this certificate for my parents
and grandparents as well as for
myself.

I think it a great honor, a great
priviledge to be able to live on, to
own and to operate the same ranch
as my forefathers did. I feel that
the land is a sacred trust and we
should hold it dear. That we should
take care of it; should protect and
preserve it; should enhance it's pro
ductivity and it's beauty as much
as we can; and above all we should
love the land, which I surely do
Again I thank you.

Mildred Kanipe's note (1974)

The group, noting that many terms of Mildred's will had been put into effect but her wish that the buildings be taken care of and a "Ranch Museum" developed had been ignored, decided to find out if it was too late.

On Sunday, April 3rd, 2005, the Friends invited Kingston Heath, Director of the Historic Preservation Program at the University of Oregon School of Architecture and Allied Arts in Eugene, Oregon and

George Kramer, a Historic Preservation Consultant with Kramer & Company, Ashland, Oregon, to come and tour the park buildings to evaluate whether they are of historic importance and if so whether it is possible to save them. The answer was that indeed the buildings are important historically, and that anything "that has not fallen down is restorable." They recommended that, at the very least, the buildings should be stabilized. They also recommended that they be nominated for the National Register of Historic Places, as listing would verify the historic importance of the buildings and make it possible to obtain grant monies to help with the cost of taking care of them.

Working with SHPO, (State Historic Preservation Office), it was decided, since the Underwood house was gone, not to apply for the Underwood Barn. It was further decided to submit two separate applications, one for The English Settlement School and one for the cluster of buildings including the house, two large barns, a sheep shed, an equipment shed, the buggy shed, and an old heritage orchard.

On February 5, 2007, applications for the English Settlement School, with one acre of land, and the "Baimbridge-Kanipe Farmstead," which includes the house, farm buildings, and the orchard, along with over eighteen acres of land, were mailed to SHPO.

The English Settlement School was placed on the National Register of Historic Places on September 4, 2007. The Baimbridge-Kanipe Farmstead Historic District followed on January 29, 2008. (You may review the final applications in the appendix.)

At the September, 2006 annual meeting of the Friends, it was suggested that better signage on the trails would help people who don't know the park well find their way around. A committee was formed, and a trail naming and marking proposal was developed and submitted to the Park Director and the Park Advisory Board. Once it was approved, a new map was developed showing the six color-coded major trail loops (see Trail Map in Map section). In October, 2007, trailhead signs for the newly named Oak Savannah Trail (red), Fern Woods Trail (purple), Underwood Hill Trail (blue), Mildred's Forest Trail (green), and the Schoolhouse Trail (orange), were placed in the park. Colored diamonds will mark the trails as weather permits and volunteers can get them done.

Fern Woods Trail sign (2007)

Many are enjoying the extensive network of park trails which are open for horses from March 16 through October 31 each year, and all year for hiking. Equestrian groups hold Poker Rides and other functions. Individuals, including the author, enjoy their horses on the trails regularly.

Fern Woods Trail (2005)

In January, 2008, the "Friends" completed a solar-powered electric fence around the English Settlement School. Cattle were rubbing against the historic building, damaging the exterior.

Weddings, family reunions, and individual picnics are held at the "Day Use Area," which is now on the National Register of Historic Places as the "Baimbridge-Kanipe Farmstead Historic District."

Park grounds are used by teachers as an outdoor classroom to teach science, ecology, native plants, and stream bed restoration.

Peacocks still populate the park. They represent a tradition, as Mildred had them for years, referring to them as her "watch dogs." If you go there for a picnic, be prepared to have one or more peacock try to join you. If not shooed away, they will jump right up on the table and eagerly partake of your lunch. Sometimes they will wait by your car door when you park, hoping you will have a hand-out for them. Remember to take some bread along to toss to them. They will be happy and you will be able to enjoy the beautiful birds.

Douglas Soil and Water Conservation District, via grants, has been eradicating noxious weeds such as English Hawthorne and Himalaya Blackberries, and thinning the oak trees to restore the oak savannas, which are threatened ecosystems in the State of Oregon. They have cleared several meadows of invasive shrubs and are putting in fish friendly culverts, trees, stumps, and rocks in the creek beds to improve the severely eroded creek beds. Salmon have been recorded making their way up the stream again in the fall.

Delivering a fish-friendly culvert. (2006)

According to local people who grew up next to it, Batchelor Creek used to run two to four feet deep all year around, and, "There were so many huge cutthroat trout that all you had to do if you wanted fish for dinner was to take a pitchfork to the creek and spear as many fish as you needed."

"We kids used to get a mason jar from our mom, put some Ovaltine and milk in it, take it to the creek and put it in the water to keep it cold, then build a fire and spear a couple of fish. After the fish were roasted over the fire we retrieved our cold drink from the creek and enjoyed a wonderful picnic!"

Mildred Kanipe's nephew, John Howard, related that the unnamed tributary to Batchelor Creek that runs behind the house, Dairy Barn, and Sheep Shed, always had water and fish in it when, as a boy, he visited his grandfather there. He said, "Grandpa loved to fish, so he took me out to the creek behind the house, and there was always plenty of water and fish there." Now that creek is dry every year in the summer. John said, "That started when they clear-cut the headwaters."

The creeks will probably never be what they once were, but hopefully they can be restored to much better health than they have today.

The park is a game preserve, per Mildred's wishes, and it is credited with having played an important part in the Columbia White-tail Deer being taken off of the Endangered Species List.

Whitetail deer (2006)

The Friends dream for the English Settlement School is to restore it to the point where it can be used to bring school children to experience a day in school like their great-grandparents did.

The Farmstead is being developed as an open-air museum where students and the public can learn about and enjoy history on site. The Friends are now working with local schools to develop programs which will allow students to learn history where it was made. Annual "Living History" functions are envisioned.

The Historic Preservation Department of the University of Oregon School of Architecture and Allied Arts is currently exploring the idea of developing credit classes for University students to get involved with using the Kanipe sites and buildings to learn how to plan and conduct restoration.

Douglas County's financial situation has continued to deteriorate with the decline of the local economic mainstay, the wood products industry, and cannot be relied on to provide financial help for projects. Therefore, funds for restoration and maintenance of the historic buildings will need to come mainly from grants, in-kind donations of materials and labor, and cash donations from the public.

The Douglas County Park Department will continue to manage the park. The Friends of Mildred Kanipe Memorial Park Association, Inc. will do what they can, and other groups will continue to do their part to support various uses in the park.

History does not stand still. Changes continue. Only time will tell what happens to the historic buildings and the land that Mildred Kanipe loved so.

STORIES BY OTHERS

These treasures have been left as they were written. Editing would have changed them, and the intent is to let these special people speak for themselves. The "creative" spelling and grammar add to rather than detract from the flavor.

MY MEMORIES OF MILDRED KANIPE

by Bill James (Wild Bill) Cantrell
January, 2005

I remember Mildred Kanipe as a tall, slender, big boned woman. The first time I saw her was in 1960 at Stricker's Auction Yard in Sutherlin. She was selling sheep. I knew who she was. She came over to me and introduced herself and said she wanted to buy one of my sheep dogs. My dogs had a reputation because they did so well at the dog training trials. I didn't have any dogs to sell at the time …..just pups. Later she came to my house in Drain to see if I had a trained sheep dog to sell, but I had already sold everything but my own working dogs.

Later I became foreman at the Fisher Ranch, which was also known as the Less Pellet Place, as they manufactured alfalfa pellets. It was right next door to Mildred's place.

Sometimes her cattle or sheep, or ours, would wander. We worked together on returning them to where they belonged as we each knew the other's stock.

Mildred like rodeos and never missed the one in Yoncalla. Every year she would show up in a new set of clothes. They were always the same, a cowboy hat, a blue shirt, Levis, and cowboy boots.

I remember seeing Mildred so many times in Oakland in her old Jeep with hay strings hanging on the racks blowing in the wind. She never threw away the strings from hay bales, but tied them on the wood sheep racks on the back of her truck. Mildred would be in town buying feed, groceries, and whatever else she needed. She always shopped locally.

One time I was out looking for the Fisher bull and saw smoke coming from Mildred's place. I went to investigate, thinking there was a fire. I found Mildred, sitting on her old International caterpillar tractor, smoke billowing up all around her. My eyes were burning just standing there talking to her, but she just sat there as if it didn't bother her at all.

Another time when I was hunting for some lost sheep I came across an old saw mill site. All that was there was bark shavings and pieces of wood. It looked very old and I thought perhaps it had been her father's saw mill, but it turned out that it was on the Underwood property that Mildred bought after her father died.

My boss didn't get along with Mildred, so I had to do all of the dealing with her. Mildred always packed a .30-30 rifle and didn't trust anyone but me. She and I were neighbors and friends.

The Fisher Ranch, where I worked, had a registered Polled Hereford bull that we called Ferdinand. One day he got out and decided to go visiting. When he got to Mildred Kanipe's place, he tore down the fence and picked a fight with Mildred's long horned scrub bull. Mildred's bull was much smaller than Ferdinand, so, of course Ferdinand came out the winner. As victor, he seemed to think that he had won the right to stay awhile and enjoy the company of Mildred's cows.

About a month later, on a cold rainy day, Mildred headed out all by herself, walking, as she herded the 2,000 pound bull back to where he belonged. She had nothing but a stick to control him with. It was a two mile walk and Mildred had become frail with age. Bulls can be very dangerous animals and should never be trusted. Most farmers, at a minimum, kept a pitchfork in their hand when working around or with them, but that was not Mildred's style. After I put Ferdinand in the barn and fed and watered him, I gave Mildred a ride home. When we got there she invited me in. The house was dark. I don't believe she had electricity, just the wood burning stoves, a fireplace, and perhaps a kerosene lantern or two. The furniture looked like it was very old. She offered me a cup of coffee, probably still warm on the cook stove from morning - nothing fancy to go with it.

We talked about farm things. Mildred's house was not especially tidy, as this lady had little time for housework. She always had too many chores to do. It kind of looked like a bachelor lived there. There was a chair by the fireplace that suggested she liked to sit there in the evening enjoying the peace and quiet and the warmth of the fire.

Mildred's rubber boots stood by the fireplace and her raincoats hung nearby. She had a pile of sticks of wood to put on the fire when she needed them.

Attached to the house was a woodshed where she stacked dry wood. She cut her own – probably mostly from oak trees that blew down on her place.

Mildred's farm equipment included the old green army Jeep with sheep rack on it, the International cat, a wench and a tractor. Perhaps in her father's time there were work horses, but in the many years I knew her I never saw any. (Mildred's father, in fact, raised registered Percheron horses.)

Mildred had irrigation sprinklers that she changed every day. She watered the pasture to keep it green and raised hay for the cattle and sheep. In the fall, when the water in the creek got low, everyone had to shut off their irrigation. What a pain! It was lots of work stacking all the irrigation pipes in a pile. Bachelor Creek runs into the Calapooya, and it supplied water for the City of Oakland.

Peacocks and chickens ran around Mildred's yard pretty much everywhere. There were grouse, raccoons and many deer. Her goats ate the poison oak and berry vines on the place. They were for work. Stray cats took care of the mice.

Mildred had a herd of mixed breed milk cows for the Grade A dairy that she ran for eight years during the 1940s after her father died. She drove the milk to Cottage Grove every day to sell. Having a Grade A dairy meant she had to keep sanitation of the animals, her barn and all the milking equipment up to standards, in addition to having to milk all of the cows twice a day and feed and care for them on a daily basis. That was a lot of work, and Mildred did it all herself. One time she was sick with the flu. It took all the will power she could muster to drag herself out of bed and take care of her chores.

Before I quit the Fisher Ranch I stopped by to see Mildred, as I hadn't seen her for a while. I found her once blondish brown hair had turned grey........shoulder length – poking out of her straw cowboy hat, blowing in the wind. She had lost most of her front teeth. They were just snags, broken off at the gums. I'm sure she had toothaches and probably couldn't eat properly. What a sad state of affairs for such a proud hard working woman.

Mildred was a survivor. She lived a life I doubt very few of us, especially a lone woman, could handle, much less master.

As the story goes, Mildred was buried on her ranch, on her right side so in spirit she could see the sun come up. As she lived and worked, she was buried in her work clothes.

MY LIFE

By Leah Kanipe Howard (Mildred Kanipe's sister)

(This story was provided by Kathryn Howard Weathers, Leah's daughter. The original was written by her mother in pencil on a "Little Chief" pencil tablet. At the bottom of the cover where there was a place to enter "school", Leah wrote, "of Hard Knocks".

No attempt has been made to edit the document or rearrange it in chronological order. It was obviously written as Leah remembered things. The abbreviations are hers.

This important document provides a window into many aspects of Leah and Mildred Kanipe's life and clears up a few historical questions as well. Thank you, Leah.

Many of the photos are added from scans of pictures in the family album. Thank you Kathryn.)

I was born February 12, 1905 as Leah Kathryn Kanipe, the first child of John Henry Kanipe and Sarah Alice Baimbridge. My sister, Mary Mildred Kanipe, was born September 30, 1907. My mother was sick after her birth and gradually grew worse until she died December 28, 1907. My Aunt Mary Baimbridge, my mother's sister, took over the job of raising us to adulthood. She had promised my mother that she would be a mother to us, so she was.

My father, John Henry Kanipe, was born in McDowell County in N. Carolina on October 12, 1871, the only son of John Anderson Kanipe and Nancy Self Kanipe. His family moved to Tennessee when he was a small boy and later they moved to Oregon. He attended school and as he grew older he taught his mother how to read a little and how to write. His father never learned. Johnny became a farmer and a very good one too. He was also a good horseman, he rented my

Uncle Will's property which was the side of the mountain until it was sold to J. D. Jones. He bought the 160 A. that was Aunt Emily's and the 160 A. that was Aunt Hannah's.

He owned a Percheron stallion and raised that breed of horses.

He owned a threshing machine in partnership with the Cockeram brothers, Ward and Albert. The first one was a horse power driven one. Albert withdrew from the partnership. They bought a large steam engine to run the new thresher and went in all the neighborhoods near Oakland threshing the grain that was grown. My father used his team on the water wagon to haul the water for the steam engine. I can remember him being gone from home for 6 weeks in late summer while the threshing season was on. He usually got home on Sundays to take a bath and get clean clothes, and see how things were going at home. Later after the separator had been smashed up badly by being turned upside down they traded it on a new Case tractor and separator and just threshed in the immediate vicinity of home. Farmers had cut down considerably on the amount of grain they raised.

Piling grain for threshing.

Bringing water to the steam threshing machine.

Threshing with a tractor.

The Case threshing machine.

My father liked to fish and hunt. In early spring he always caught trout in all the small creeks and streams in the English Settlement. He could catch fish where no one else could, just a knack I suppose.

Fishing

He hunted pheasant, grouse, pigeons, etc. and sometimes wild ducks. The beautiful blue grey squirrels with the bushy tails were plentiful in the oak hills around home, so he killed them for meat. Then he hunted deer too for meat. When we needed some fresh meat he would ride up on "Ben Moore" Mt. and come home with a deer slung across the saddle. Those days there was no deer hunting season. Later when there was, he went on campout trips with friends to get their deer.

Deer hunting

On one of those trips my cousin Edwin Young and Ike Flannery of Oakland were along. That evening as they were prying bark off an old snag, it let loose and came crashing down upon them. My father had his skull fractured and they had to spend the nite in camp not knowing what would happen. That was a very, very long nite for Edwin and Ike. As soon as there was some light one of the men walked out of the woods for the Dr. and help to pack out my dad. He was very sick for weeks but finally recovered. He had another bad accident where he got his skull fractured again.. This time he was riding a horse and while going thru an iron gate they became squeezed and he was thrown.

In later years several times he went mule deer hunting in Central Oregon with my husband, Romie, and I. He was very proud of my son Johnny and always called him Mike. Of course he never knew my daughter, Kathryn, because he died the day after she was born.

My dad had a black mare named "Black Butte" that he rode or drove. She was a good trotting horse. When he lived on the old Hall (Medley) place he could drive her to a 2 wheeled cart into Oakland in 15 minutes. When the road was smooth we could drive from home to Oakland in 1 hr. Black Butte and Babe (a bay mare) were our saddle horses and driving team. Butte trotted so fast that Babe had to gallop to keep up. Babe and Butte each lived to be 32 years old.

Soon after my grandfather moved his family to Oregon, a boyhood friend of my father's, Henry Clay, came from Tennessee and made his home with them. They lived on Red Hill on the place that is now Bob Allen's. They moved from there to a place called Tibbet's place about one mile out of Oakland on the English Settlement road. Later my father rented the Hall place which became the Jeff Medley farm. It was while living here that he met my mother and married her in 1903. Then he bought Aunt Mary's property when was joined to my mother's and moved there.

My grandfather, John Anderson Kanipe, was born in 1834 and died in 1920, at age 86. My grandmother, Nancy Jane Kanipe, was born in 1837 and died in 1914, at age 77.

Grandfather was one of 22 children. His father had two wives, so some of them were half brothers or sisters. I remember one of his half sisters, Mrs. Hogan, coming to visit one time when grandpa was living with us. She told us how grandpa had a negro nanny as a wet nurse when he was a baby. This was sure a jolt to him, because he hated the negroes so much. He blamed them for the Civil War. He served in the civil War, in the Confederate Army, was in the battle of Gettysburg and wounded 5 times there. He was left on the battlefield for dead but the Red Cross nurses came along, found him, and saved his life. He had nothing but praise for the Red Cross. He said the little stream running thru the meadow where he fell was running red with blood. That was a terrible battle. Both of his hands were crippled. He had some fingers missing and some drawn down so he couldn't straighten them, and he carried a bullet in his neck just under the skin as long as he lived. However, he could hold an ax handle or saw when he cut wood. He wasn't happy unless he was cutting wood for someone. He received pay for his work. He cut mostly oak wood, both for cook stove and for fireplace. The cook stove wood he split and tiered up. He always kept us in plentiful supply, in fact he was cutting wood right up to the time of his death.

Grandpa and grandma Kanipe bought a house on 5 acres in Oakland and lived there until grandma died in 1914. She became completely paralyzed and was bedfast for 8 months. I remember my Aunt Lizzie doing the house work for them. They had to have a nurse too.

When they were living on the farm Grandpa would drive the cow up from the pasture and tie her but Grandma had to milk her. He wouldn't milk or maybe he couldn't due to his crippled hands. I remember while he lived with us if my father was away Aunt Mary always had to go to the barn and do the milking. He would put the cows in and feed them. He loved to talk about the war so when I was a kid I knew quite a lot about the Civil War.

Henry Clay married Annie Cockram who lived on Red Hill. Her mother was a niece of my grandmother Baimbridge.

My grandfather Baimbridge was Thomas, born September 15, 1834, in England. My grandmother, Emily Baimbridge, was born June 29, 1832 in England. They had born to them 5 girls and 1 boy in Derbyshire, England and then a girl in the English Settlement 7 ½ miles out of Oakland. While their family was very young they sailed from England for America. In those days 1870-71 it took a long time to cross the ocean. One little girl about 3 years old named Avis, became sick and died and was buried at sea. The mother was in such a worn out condition from caring for the ill child that she didn't have enough milk to nurse her baby. There happened to be another woman on board who was nursing a baby and she had plenty of milk so she nursed the Baimbridge baby too who was named Hannah.

They landed in America, came by train across to San Francisco, took a boat from there to Portland, Ore., then by boat up the Willamette to Corvallis, then by team and wagon on to Oakland. They went to the Thomas ranch which is about 8 miles out from Oakland on the Driver Valley road. They were friends of the Thomases, so lived there until they could find a place.

Grandfather Baimbridge bought a large ranch from W. P. Powers. This Mr. Powers had property in Eastern Oregon, which he was moving his sheep to. He started with a large flock of over a thousand sheep. Uncle Will helped with the drive for a ways down in the Willamette Valley. Going up the Columbia River the Indians attacked them. They killed and stole many of the sheep. Because he lost so many sheep he sold the ranch to my grandfather. Before this he was just leasing it. Here they lived and reared their family and died. Thomas died April 20, 1891 and Emily died November 15, 1896.

Elizabeth Baimbridge Dearmin was born in May 10 1860 in Derbyshire, England. After she was married she lived in Baker. She had 3 children, a son, Willy, a daughter, Lillian, and a daughter, Edna.

She and her husband separated. She came back to Oakland area to live after her family was grown. She died in 1924 at Aunt Emily's and was buried in the I.O.O.F Cemetery, in my father's lot. She had asked him permission and he granted it. Aunt Lizzie was a large woman and jolly. At one time she kept house for Mrs. J. T. Bridges in Oakland. Mrs. Bridges worked in their grocery and dry goods store.

William Baimbridge was born December 7, 1861 in Derbyshire, England. He grew up to be a stockman. When a young man he took up a homestead on the side of Ben Moore Mt. Then he inherited 160 acres of land from his father. He married Elma Crow. At one time they rented and lived at Elkhead on Jazak's place. They had 2 children, the first died at birth and was buried in Shoestring Cemetery, the second, Heston, grew up. He is buried in Fir Grove Cenetery in Cottage Grove. Uncle Will owned a home in Cottage Grove with an acreage with a barn and corral. He kept a horse for many years, had a Hambletonian stallion which he drove to a buggy. He and his horse were in a Buster Keaton motion picture made up Row River and his horse was ridden by the army general in the movie.

Aunt Elma was born September 3, 1880. She grew beautiful flowers and had a lovely yard. Uncle Will grew a good garden every year. He owned a flock of sheep as long as he lived, had them leased out on the shares.

I remember visiting Uncle Wills when I was small. That was a long trip and we stayed several days. Aunt Emily, Aunt Mary, Mildred and I went downtown one day to visit a friend. Uncle Will had started us out on the right street, so we had no trouble going down but coming back we were confused and ran into dead end streets. Finally Aunt Mary said, "Well, let me get out where I can see the big oak tree that stands by the barn. Then I can find it.", and so we did.

Uncle Will died April 13, 1947

Aunt Elma died January 16, 1953.

Heston was born July 22, 1901. He died September 2, 1955.

Aunt Hannah was born January 4, 1870 in Derbyshire, England. She was just a baby when the family sailed to America and may have starved to death if it hadn't been for the good woman on board the ship who nursed her along with her own baby. Aunt Hannah married Ed Green who was a neighborhood boy and they lived at The Dalles for several years, then they moved to Alberta, Canada and lived there and became Canadian citizens. They reared a family of 6 children, Roy, Afton, Itha, Albert (deceased), Ruth and Harry (died). They were farmers raising much grain. Aunt Hannah came back several times for visits with her relatives. I remember her. She died November 30, 1950.

In 1927 Ruth Green came to visit her grandmother Green and her aunts and cousins. I got to know her while she was here that summer. One day she and I and 3 other girls, Juanita Pinkston, Fontelle and Isobelle Harvey, took a horseback ride over to London Springs.

Roy Green Steinhoff came to visit several times when he was a young man.

Itha Green Steinhoff came twice to visit Aunt Mary and I got acquainted. She has been to visit me several times.

In 1965 I met Afton Green for the first time. He and his wife and Itha were here. He and his wife were here again for a visit a year or so later.

Aunt Emily was born July (?), 1863 in Derbyshire, England. She married James Young, son of Ed Young, and they lived in Oakland. Jim Young had a brother Gary who was a banker. Jim attended to the ranches and livestock in the E. G. Young & Co. He died May 11, 1911. Aunt Emily reared 4 children, Hazel Young Clarke, Gertrude Young Garrison, Edwin G. Young, and Martha Young.

Aunt Emily had a barn where my father would stable his horses when he went to town. When we all went we always stopped with her for dinner. My cousin, Martha, was a little older than I and we had such good times playing with her. When Mildred and I went to high school in Oakland the first year 1920-21, we drove our Shetland pony to the buggy every day from home 7 ½ miles each way. One of us rode Pinkston's pony because we were too much load for the buggy.

Ready to go to high school.

We stabled our ponies and buggy in Aunt Emily's barn. She used to have a black mare named Bird that she drove to a buggy. Many a time she drove Bird out to our place to visit. During the summer vacation Martha would stay a week at a time with us. When deer season came Edwin would come out and go deer hunting with my Dad. I remember when he shot his first deer. He was so proud. We had to take pictures of it for him. He never cared to hunt after the trip when my father was injured so badly. Edwin was a banker until he retired. The E. G. Young & Co. Bank in Oakland started by his grandfather, E. G. Young, was where he worked for years and lived in Oakland. Then after Douglas Co. State Bank, a branch of E. G. Young bank, was started in Roseburg he moved to Roseburg and worked in it until his retirement. Edwin married Cecile Goss of Walla Walla and they had 2 children, Gerald and Barbara. He died in January, 1967.

Aunt Emily died December 23, 1947.

Hazel married Rush Clarke of Millwood and they lived there a short while. Then they bought what was called the old Shuey place 3 miles out of Oakland on English Settlement road. When the Young estate was settled Hazel inherited the Wheeler place on Batchelor Creek about 2 miles farther up. They run sheep on this property. Rush also had his property at Millwood. Hazel sold her property to Perrin and later they sold the big ranch and moved to Roseburg.

Gertrude was a soprano singer but she didn't perform. She worked in the E. G. Young bank for years. She married T. B. Garrison who was a banker. They lived in Oakland awhile, then moved to Roseburg. She died (blank)

Martha became a high school teacher and taught until she was old enough to retire. She lived and taught in Seattle, Wash. for many years but moved back to Roseburg recently.

Martha and Gertrude inherited a big ranch known as the Quant place on Hall Creek and they sold it to Davidson. They took a trip to England and visited the place where Baimbridges had lived and some relatives also.

I remember getting Martha's dresses she had outgrown. I thought more of her dresses than new ones.

The old house where I was born is still occupied by my sister, Mildred Kanipe, It was built in 1852.

My mother, Sarah Alice Baimbridge, was born July 21, 1876 on the Baimbridge place in English Settlement where she lived all her life and died December 28, 1907. She and Aunt Mary lived here after the death of their parents and operated the ranch. The land she inherited had the old home on it and Aunt Mary's was joined to it. They operated it for about six years until Sarah married John Kanipe, then he took over and he bought Aunt Mary's 160 A. but she lived with them much of the time. My mother was a very good horsewoman. She and Aunt Mary had good riding horses and they rode sideways. My mother's nickname was Babe, her whole family called her Babe and some of her friends did too.

Edna Harvey, who lived over the hills west and a little north of our place was a very dear friend to my mother. The Harvey family was English too. Aaron Harvey was the father. There were several other girls, and Bob and Tom were the boys.

Mary Ann Baimbridge was born Sept. 2, 1865 in Derbyshire, England. She was only 5 years old when her family set sail for America but she always remembered the crossing of how sea sick she was and others too. She never had any use for bodies of water. I remember when we were going to the coast we had to ferry across the Umpqua. My dad drove the team and hack onto the ferry boat. Aunt Mary said, "Wait a minute and let me get out and walk." She meant that she wanted to stand on the ferry instead of sitting in the hack. She never married. She was always very small, about 5' 2" and weighed about 100 to 110 lbs. She always walked with a limp due to a bad knee she had sprained several times when a girl, but she was very active anyway. At one time she worked in the Thomas Hotel in Oakland. She lived with my mother and father much of the time. She was there when I was born and also when Mildred was born. She became a mother to us after our mother died. Nearly everyone in the neighborhood called her Aunt Mary.

When I was six years old Aunt Mary bought a Shetland pony for Mildred and me. He was a large sized Shetland, sorrel with a white face and flaxen mane and tail named Pete. She bought a pony buggy and harness too so we could either ride him or drive him. He was just young so we had to train him and it was several years before he was trustworthy. Then we rode him everywhere.

Mildred, Leah, and Aunt Mary, with Pete.

Giving the dog a ride.

Aunt Mary said if Pete could climb the stairs that we would ride him to bed. She would take us and go horseback to visit a neighbor or cousin. She rode the saddle horse "Black Butte" with Mildred on behind her and I riding Pete. We rode up to the Cockerams on Red Hill and up to Ward Cockerams in Driver Valley as well as all over the English Settlement.

The first year we were in high school we went from home each day. One of us in the pony buggy, the other on the Pinkston pony. The other 3 years Aunt Mary moved with us into Oakland in the house that had been my grandparent's, that my father inherited. My dad came after us on Fridays and took us out to the ranch. We cleaned the house and cooked food for him for the following week. Then on Sunday afternoon he took us back to town. After Christmas vacation we had to stay in town for 3 months because the days were so short and the roads so muddy we couldn't make it Friday evening after school.

The road was finally graveled as far as our place and my dad bought a car, an Oakland car. Then during the school year we could go home every weekend.

John Kanipe's car

Mildred and I were always riding somewhere and Aunt Mary worried about us so much. One of us rode the horse, Black Butte, and the other Pete.

Aunt Mary always washed on Monday. While Grandpa lived with us on wash day he turned the washing machine and also helped pack the water. After he was gone when it wasn't school time I helped with the washing. Aunt Mary liked to go wild strawberry picking also blackberry picking too. When she was a young woman she took out her naturalization papers to become a U. S. citizen and then she took up a homestead up on Ben Moor Mt. by the Boon place which had been homesteaded earlier. She had quite a time proving up on her land, living way off up there on the mountain by herself. She didn't stay any more days than was legal. After my dad died Aunt Mary continued to live with Mildred. She did all the housework and cooking and tended a garden until the last four years of her life.

When she reached her 80th birthday, Ida Pinkston gave her a big birthday party at the Pinkston's home. Aunt Mary always wanted to reach her 90th birthday and she did. She became quite ill in the spring of 1955. My cousin Itha Green Stienhoff of Alberta, Canada, came to visit her. She was in the hospital awhile with an attack of pneumonia and then she moved to a nursing home down Garden Valley way. She was here when her 90th birthday came and they had a nice party for her.

Aunt Mary's birthday (1955)

Mildred moved her to a private home for invalids in Roseburg where she died October 6, 1955. She is buried in the I.O.O.F. (now Cedar Hills) cemetery in Oakland in my father's lot beside Aunt Lizzie Dearmin, her sister.

She was like a grandmother to Johnny.

Mary Mildred Kanipe, my sister, was born September 30, 1907 in the old house on the old Baimbridge place where she still lives today. After our father died she inherited the old home place and the rest of the Kanipe place on the west side of the county road. She bought the old Underwood place which lies just west of this and runs cattle and sheep. She never married and lives alone since Aunt Mary's passing.

Samual Baimbridge 1866-1891 was a cousin of Aunt Mary's who came to this country. He and his wife Hattie had two sons, Harry Baimbridge, (another son, William, deceased), who married and reared a large family. Samual died when only 25 so his widow married again. She became Mrs. Whitney and reared a family of 5 girls, Edna, Nellie, Doreen, Pansy, and Nettie Dellia. I can remember going to her house to visit. She had the most extensive flower garden I had ever seen.

Elizabeth Whittaker was a sister to Emily Baimbridge. She died January 27, 1903 and was buried beside her sister in Old Town cemetery. She had a son Harry and a daughter Sally (and another son, Samuel and another daughter, older). Sally became Mrs. Harvey Cockeram and her children were Ware, Albert, Ann Ada, Ralph, Harvey Agnes, Veta, and Leo. Mrs. Whittaker's husband died before she left England and her oldest daughter remained there. When she first came they lived on a ranch 2 or 3 miles N.W. of Oakland out where the Metz Hill Road takes off from 99. Later she had a house in Oakland.

I was born February 12, 1905 in the old house on the old Baimbridge place, the same house in which my mother was born. This old house was built in 1852 and is still lived in by Mildred. Grandfather Baimbridge added the kitchen part onto it after buying the ranch.

The House in 2005.

I was not yet 3 years old when my mother died so I couldn't remember her but I do have a dim recollection of the horse running away with the buggy. She ran down the hill from the county road, past the barn, and into the yard gate. To get into the yard we had to go around to the other gate until my father came home and removed the buggy.

Aunt Mary was the same as a mother to Mildred and me. The fall after I was 6 years old I started to school. Those days the school term was 6 months and all 8 grades were taught in one room. There were large boys in school too. I remember the oldest Medley boy, James, was so good to help the little children get their rubbers on when it was time to go home.

Roy Medley had been in school several years when I began and I caught up with him in the fourth grade, we passed into the fifth together. Then Roy had a fight with the teacher, who was a man that year, and he quit school and never did go anymore.

Mildred started to school my second year because she was so lonesome at home without me. She was only 5. By the time I reached the 8th grade there were only 4 students in our district, and later two of them moved away, so there were only Mildred and me left. We had a very good teacher and finished our work early so then I reviewed getting ready for the 8th grade exam and Mildred studied with me. When it came time for the county 8th grade exams, both of us took them and both passed. The teacher had made us promise to not tell the folks what she was doing until after the exams. So we were both ready to start high school together, but Mildred was too young for the work. In her second year she almost had a nervous breakdown. As I have stated before, our first year we went from home. Then the other 3 years we lived in Oakland in my dad's house that was his parents place. Aunt Mary lived with us of course. When we couldn't go home to the ranch in the winter my dad would come in every so often and bring the cream for Aunt Mary to churn. In the spring he would bring us blue grey squirrels all dressed out ready to cook or sometimes a grouse. He would also bring vegetables out of the garden (carrots, parsnips, etc.).

The English Settlement School—old photo.

When I was a senior I took teachers training. Part of the course we did training teaching down stairs in the grade school under supervision of the regular teacher. One day I had a group of primary kids who were behind the rest of the class. The regular teacher went home for her lunch and turned the class over to me until noon. The little kids were excused at 11:30 every morning. I had been standing up at the blackboard for ½ hour with a pointer pointing to words on the board when I became faint. I dismissed the children and sat down for awhile. Then I started up the stairs to get my coat to go home for dinner. I felt faint again and just as I reached the top I fainted away and fell backward down the first flight of stairs. Naomi Pinkston was the first girl to come along and found me all crumpled up. She ran back and got the teacher who was on duty during the noon hour. She was Miss Alta Spalding who later married the minister and became Mrs. J. K. Howard. I revived by drinking some of her hot tea, then she got a boy who drove his car to school to take us home and she told Aunt Mary to keep me home that afternoon. I wasn't hurt very much, one shoulder bruised and my nose skinned.

My class was the class of 1924 and it was the largest class up to that time to graduate from Oakland High School. There were 16 graduates, 4 boys and 12 girls, and I was the valedictorian.

I taught school in English Settlement for 2 years, then went to Southern Oregon Normal School in Ashland for one year. I also had 2 summer terms. I needed about 1 more term to graduate. I taught one year at Elkhead. When I went to Ashland I took my saddle horse, Cheyenne, with me. I boarded with Mr. and Mrs. George Jones and daughter Agnes. They had a small barn where I kept my horse. I had much enjoyment riding about the countryside. I would ride with a group of girls when they rented horses to ride. Sure was funny sometimes as they were such greenhorns. One day I rode to the top of Grizzley Mt. with my girl friend Agnes and a boy. I also rode with her out to her sister's ranch at Dead Indian, 22 miles from Ashland. One summer while I was attending school I drove a team of horses hitched to the running gears of a wagon over to Dead Indian for these same ranchers.

The school year of 1927-28 I taught the Elkhead school, I rode my horse, Cheyenne, from home every day. I stabled her in Collie Pringle's barn and walked on down to the school house. After it got bad weather and the days short I boarded with Howards, Romie and his mother.

On September 22, 1928, I was married to Romie Howard in Roseburg in a little church near the courthouse. All the neighborhood here came to chivaree us the evening of the 24th. Romie and I hid in the hay mow and they couldn't find us. We finally came up to the house when they gave up hunting. We didn't have any honeymoon trip until the next July 1 to 4th when we went to the coast at Bandon, Coos Bay, and Winchester Bay. We lived with Romie's mother and took care of her until she died in 1930. We bought the Howard estate which was this place of 120 A. and the homestead they took up in Central Oregon near Lapine. We rented the Lapine ranch out for many years, then finally sold it.

Here in 1935 we bought from Bertha Moore her property and the old Coates place. We sold the Bertha Moore part to Harley and Mildred Bowman in 1946. After my father died in 1940 we had the property I inherited in English Settlement about 350 A. to operate too. I sold this property to Dale Roberson in 1963.

My first child, John Noel, was born January 6, 1930 in the Sacred Heart Hospital in Eugene. I went to Eugene about 2 weeks before his arrival and boarded with a lady. It was a very bad winter, much snow and ice. My second child, Kathryn Marie, was born June 26, 1940 in the same hospital.

In the fall of 1936 I had an attack of rheumatism, the Dr. called it but they didn't really know. I was in the hospital for weeks in terrible pain, a very high fever, and paralyzed. They thought this condition was caused from my diseased tonsils so the Dr. removed them before I came home. I was in bed and had to be turned in bed. After 3 months I was up again some but used a wheel chair for awhile. It was a long time before I was able to do very much and I never was able to do some of the things that I had used to do. While I was laid up we had Lucille Cramer do the housework and when Romie was out she waited on me too. She later became Mrs. Percy Langdon.

Romie worked as road patrolman for Douglas County in this area. I helped him with all the ranch work as he worked 6 days a week on the road most of the time. I have done everything but plow. We did our farming with a team of horses. When Romie sowed the grain I rode my saddle horse behind the harrow and drove the team instead of walking. When we hauled hay I did the loading and Romie said it was packed down so solid because I was always heavy. I was fat all my life. I remember when I was 12 years old I weighed 144 lb. and I never weighed any less than that although when I lived in Ashland I lost weight and that spring at the end of school I was down to 150 lb.

During World War II I was the chief observer for our observation post. The post was located in a tent between our house and barn from Pearl Harbor Day until spring of 1943 when we built a little house over in our pasture for the post. We operated there until it was closed in fall of 1943. I spent 2500 hours in the service of my country and received a lovely pin from the government for it. I had quite a job organizing and getting someone to take each shift. Many a shift I took myself because no one came.

When Kathryn was a little girl a Sunday School was started in the neighborhood. It was held at the old school house or "Hall" as they call it now. When it fisseled out I started taking Kathryn to Sunday School at the Methodist Church in Yoncalla. Johnny had been going with Opheims to their church. I joined the Methodist Church and later became a teacher of the class for 1st and 2nd graders. I sure did enjoy this. I taught for over 10 years until I was so disabled I couldn't make it. After the Sunday School began giving pins for perfect attendance and Kathryn had one for 12 years, then they stopped the practice of giving pins. I was real proud of my pin as I felt it showed what I had done for my Lord.

I did lots of horseback riding, I rode Cheyenne until she was 28 years old.

Then I bought a nice 8 yr old grey horse named "Shorty". Cheyenne lived until she was 30.

I rode Shorty until I got so crippled with arthritis that I couldn't get on him anymore. He was so good for my grandchildren to ride when they visited. He got sick and died when he was 23.

My knees began hurting with arthritis first, then it was in my feet and gradually went into my hips. I went to the uranium mines at Boulder, Montana, and was helped greatly. I went back several times but the last time 1960 didn't seem to help me much, was in my back then too. I took to using a wheel chair in 1960.

One year in the 40s I had sores on my fingers like my pet lambs had on their lips and noses, called canker mouth. Went to a Dr. in Eugene, he didn't know what it was, sent me to the hospital. They gave me shots of penicillin and terramyacin but the sores were worse. Dr. was very worried I was going to loose my thumb. He called in other Drs. One day I had 7 doctors to see me and they didn't know what it was except one who was a veterinarian. He agreed with me that it was the sheep disease. Then they began giving me sulfa drug and that killed the disease. I said that I had handled sheep so much guessed I was part sheep so that was why I got the disease from my pet lambs. People are not supposed to have the disease.

In the fall when deer season came Romie and I would go to Central Oregon mule deer hunting. Most of the times someone else went with us, like Frank Bradford once, Ed Hawkins, Howard Brink, Emma Record, my dad, etc.

Johnny would stay with his Uncle Al and Aunt Valerie Trobee and attend school and they would do the chores for us. Before he was old enough to go to school Johnny staid with Aunt Mary and his grandfather and Uncle Mildred. A hired man put him up to calling her Uncle because Mildred always dressed like a man. So he always called her Uncle Mildred. He liked to stop off there while we went to Roseburg too. He was like a grandson to Aunt Mary.

For the holidays we traded, one year Aunt Mary would cook the Thanksgiving dinner and we would have the Christmas dinner then the next year we would have Thanksgiving and they have Christmas.

Aunt Mary with turkeys.

One year Romie and I went in the truck to Montana and camped beside Boulder Creek while there and drove up to the mine twice a day. We went into the uranium mine you walked back into. A later year we went in the Enterprise mine which has an elevator to take you down a long ways into the ground. I was in my wheelchair then and could not manage the walk in one. When we started home we visited Virginia City, Mont. Which was real interesting. We went to see what the earthquake did in the area near West Yellowstone and on into the Park. We saw the falls and canyon of the Yellowstone, the famous fishing bridge and "Old Faithful" geyser. We saw it erupt and saw many, many other phenonomens. Yellowstone Park is an awe inspiring place. This trip we were in the car and stopped in motels at nite.

I had a very happy childhood. Mildred and I rode our horses all around the country with the dogs, chasing squirrels and jack rabbits. There was one big old jack we named Jed Thumper from a story who lived in the big briar patch down in the cow pasture that we would chase regularly, but we never caught him. In winter time we hitched our horses to little sleds when there was snow and had so much fun driving around. That was much more fun than riding a sled down hill. We would also spend hours playing in the hay mow in the barns. When it rained too much outside we also rode the horses in the barn. The big horse barn had a stable at each end with a lard shed down one side. So we would ride from one end to the other when there were no other horses stabled.

Bringing in the hay.

We had one shepherd dog that learned to climb the ladder up to the hay mow, we carried the little terrier dog up and they would hunt mice in the hay. We also enjoyed riding our horses thru ponds of water. One time on a cold day while riding thru a small pond a mile or more from home Pete stumbled and throwed Mildred. She was soaked & about frozen by the time we reached the house.

The Howard family came from Texas to Corvallis, Ore, in 1886 where they lived a year. A brother Dave Howard settled there, but my husband, Romie Howard, was born April 3, 1893 on this place where we live. He was named William Jerome and because his father was William they nicknamed him Romie and he has always gone by that name. when he was 12 years old his family rented out this place and moved to Central

Ore., near Lapine and took up a homestead. They lived there 7 years and then moved back here and spent the rest of their lives here. Romie lived here on this place all of his life except those 7 years.

Romie's father was William Henry Howard born 1852 in Pen. Died 1922. His mother was Sarah Jane Lewis Howard born 1855 in Ken. Died 1930. They are buried in the cemetery up here on the hill called Shoestring cemetery.

Romie had one brother and four sisters.

Fannie was born January 29, 1876 died 1958. She married Geo. Gilkison and he died before their child Ethel Gilkison Skidmore Hunt, was born. Then she married John Watkins who had been married before and had 2 sons. She and John had 3 children, Albert Louis, and Virgie.

Lula was born Sep 22 1885 in Texas and lives on a ranch near Lorane. She married Bill Witt and they lived on Coast Fork above London. They had 3 children, Ivan, Alta Witt Jack, Herman (deceased). Her husband died and she married Bob Wills and they reared two daughters, Velma Wills Mitchell and Mabel Wills Kingsley.

Velerie was born March 12, 1888 and died July 19, 1968 in Riverview Terrace Apts. in Cottage Grove. She married Al Trobee and they lived many, many places. They had no children. After Al's death in 1953 she married Olaf Olsen and they lived in Cottage Grove a few years until he died. 1964.

Mary was born 1890 and died 1952. She married Don Caldwell and they lived in Portland many years. She worked in a place where they made coffins. They had no children. They moved to Bend where he had a job with an irrigation ditch Co. They were both buried in the Veterans Cemetery in Portland.

When Velerie was born she had a twin sister but it died and is buried in the family plot in Shoestring Cemetery. The grandparents Mr. & Mrs. Enoch Lewis, are also buried there as well as Fannies firs hisband Geo. Gilkison. The grandfather Lewis was a soldier in the Northern forces in the Civil War.

Romie was in the army during World War 1 stationed at Fort Lewis, Wash. And then at Los Angeles, Cal. Where he was when the Armistice was signed. He lived at home and helped his parents as long as they needed him. He worked on the county roads, being a road patrolman for 30 years. He finally retired with a public employee's pension. The last few years the county combined our area with Drain and Romie worked under Roy Spalding, driving a gravel truck mostly.

He was bothered with an ulcer in his stomach for years. In Dec. 1951 he had an operation for the ulcer. In April 1962 he had an operation for prostate glands. After he was 65 he began drawing his social security and a few years prior he was granted a veterans pension. He was admitted to the Veterans Hospital in Portland for his operations and went every 6 mo. for check-up.

He dearly loved to go deer hunting in Central Ore. and went every fall. He built a camper to put on the flat bed truck to camp in so he would be warm and comfortable. Had a little light plant he took for lights too.

He had a welding outfit and was always making something. He built a hay elevator to put the bales into the barn, a winch on the tractor, a buzz saw on the tractor, etc.

He died Oct. 7, 1970 after a few days illness of a heart attack. He went on his deer hunt but became very sick so Johnny brought him back to the hospital in Cottage Grove. In four days he was gone. I am thankful that he did not have to suffer a long illness. It is very difficult to live without him, he was so kind and gentile. I miss him so much.

Note added by Kathryn, "Leah K. Howard died June 25, 1971 at home in her afternoon nap."

ODE TO AN OAK

By Mildred Kanipe (1974)

When I was a kid growing up, about sixty feet from our kitchen door there stood a mighty black oak tree. It was six feet thru on the stump, one hundred feet tall and a limb spread of well over one hundred feet. It was a majestic monarch. The massive trunk rose some twenty five or thirty feet to the first limbs and many of the bigger limbs were large enough to make big individual trees. It was thickly branched and made deep cool shade thru the summer and protection from the summer rains. It was a very friendly, inviting tree and yet carried such a strong, watchful, protective bearing. A large iron ring was fastened in the trunk on one side, about four feet from the ground. That was our hitching post — the place to tie a team or saddle horse. Many a time my pony stood hitched there in the shade of the old oak tree.

Every spring, usually about May, the buds on the end of all the little branches would begin to swell and then almost overnight there would appear from each bud a little cluster of catkins hanging daintily. They are a dark red and gold color and gave the tree, especially when the sun shown on it, a sort of golden halo. In about a couple of weeks the little leaves began to come and the blooms dropped off. The leaves, when they first start coming are a dark red. The tree from a distance has a sort of purple hue. As the leaves grow they soon change to a light green color and keep getting darker as they get older until when full grown they are a dark glossy green. Then the old tree was ready to shelter us from the hot sun and showers for another summer.

Along in October, when the nites began to get "nippy" the leaves would turn gold and brown and then start falling. By winter the tree was bare and ready to stand the riggers of winter storms.

Many are the happy hours I spent playing under the spreading branches of the old oak tree. What can't be done by the vivid imagination of a healthy active youngster if left to his own devices. The old oak tree had one fault. I could not climb it. I climbed all the other trees close around that I could get up in and I always managed to climb back down again. Despite my Aunt's dire predictions, I never did get hurt climbing trees. Oh, I got scratched and skinned and my clothes torn badly, but I never really got hurt. My favorite trees for climbing were some little slender oak saplings. I would climb slowly and carefully up until the slender swaying top would no longer hold my lite weight. Then I would grasp the tree tightly with both hands, kick my feet loose and out and come swinging down thru space to light on the ground. I'd let go and the tree would spring upright again. O' what fun – what a thrill it was. What if the tree had of broke? Well, they never did. Oak trees are made of mighty tough material. Some of those trees grew on a steep hillside and swinging on the downhill side made a much longer distance to go. One was close to the creek bank and it took pretty close calculating to lite on the bank and not go over into the creek. Some would not bend far enough to let me reach the ground. Then I would have to let go and drop. A few years ago I read where Robert Frost, the poet, wrote about swinging in the birches on his father's farm. He too had learned the secret of climbing carefully to the slender top, then the thrill of swinging down thru space.

The old oak tree had a sort of sunk in place on the trunk where maybe a limb had been years before. It was about twenty feet from the ground and looked sort of funny and I was curious as to what was there. Finally one day I found a long board, dragged it to the tree and after much effort got it set up against the tree. Then I "cooned" up the board and managed to reach to the place and it was just sort of punky stuff. That was my nearest attempt at climbing the old oak.

In the summertime we often parked our wagons or harvesting machinery under the old oak tree in the shade if we were not going to use them for a few days. One particular fall we had finished threshing and parked our threshing machine under the tree waiting a more convenient time to take it to the machine shed and put it away for the winter. It was a hot fall day, not a bit of wind, and my aunt was home alone. She heard a loud cracking and popping noise and went outside the kitchen door to listen and see what it was. Pretty soon she heard it again and knew it was the old oak tree. She became frightened and ran out away from the house to the foot of the hill to be in the clear. At short intervals the cracking and popping continued, getting louder and more persistent each time until finally, with a mighty cracking and groaning and rending of fibers down came the old oak, all in a heap, like the "Wonderful One Hoss Shay". The limbs and branches were a huge jumbled mass, completely surrounding the massive trunk. The broken, jagged top was about twenty five feet from the ground. The short side of the spread of the tree was next to the house. The end of some of the branches fell on the fence and some small limbs were pressed against the buildings but they did very little damage. The old tree gave ample warning. If there had been someone there with a means of pulling the threshing machine out in the clear there was plenty of time. However, none of the big limbs fell across it and while it was mashed and broken quite a lot, we cut it out and repaired it and used it the next summer.

We spent all of our spare time that winter cutting wood and piling and burning brush. The great big limbs that were too big to work up into wood, were terrific to split, so we cut them into logs and rolled them into piles to burn. I helped my Dad pull the cross cut saw to cut them - no power saws in those days. We cut the trunk off leaving a stump about four feet high. We burned the trunk and tried to burn the stump. It was sort of cloty in the center and that part burned, but the rest of it was too tough and we could not burn it.

Mildred standing on the stump of the oak tree holding a golden eagle she had shot. This was legal at the time and a common practice among sheep farmers.

We missed the old tree so much I got the idea of planting a little tree there. I got a small maple, oaks have such big tap roots I couldn't dig one up, and planted it in the burned out place of the old stump. I thought if it grew the roots would go down the burned out part into the ground and the stump would protect the tree from the stock while it was little. It was sort of half heartedly growing when some little kid goats discovered the old stump and decided it was a wonderful place to play., They ate all the leaves off the tree and killed it. The next year I planted another, a bigger and better tree, and it was growing real good until some kind of black bugs ate the leaves. I couldn't find anything to the keep the bugs off and they killed it. The next year I planted another with the same result so I gave up.

As time passed by the old stump rotted some and we burned more of it. Finally a few years ago we cut off what was left and I hauled dirt and filled the hole and planted grass on it so that now there is not a trace left of the old oak tree. It will always remain etched deep in my memory.

This country where I live has much oak timber on many of the foot hills and along the streams, both black oak and white oak. They range from scrub oak bushes thru saplings, small grubb oak, on up to big grubb oak and then the big old oaks. The limbs on many of the old oak are bent and twisted and gnarled from their battles with the elements. Occasionally one whole big limb will be ripped off but seldom does an oak tree blow down. They are very deeply rooted to the soil. They are very tough and will bend but are extremely hard to break or split.

While oak trees are exceedingly tough the little new twigs and leaves can freeze. They are pretty good judges of the weather. When the oak tree leaves are as big as squirrel ears it is time to plant beans and corn for there will be no more killing frost. I have seen them nipped a little a few times but only once have I seen them badly mistaken and that year we had a freak frost in June. The oak leaves were half grown and it sure "cooked" all of the new growth. They were a black sick looking bunch of trees. I worried if it might kill them. In a few days all the black stuff dropped off and soon new buds appeared and dauntlessly they put out new leaves. They didn't bother with any blooms this time. It was much later in the season the weather warmer and the days longer so the leaves came on much faster. They got all leafed out and you would never have known that anything had gone wrong.

The bark on the black oak is fairly smooth and a sort of steel grey in color with occasionally white spots scattered over it. The bark on the white oak is rough, seamed, and ridged on the trunks of the big trees and a white grey color. The main limbs and trunks of the trees are more or less covered with a sort of greenish brown moss. All the small limbs and branches are hung with a fringelike light grey colored moss (lichen) so the trees are not bare even in winter.

I think that the early pioneers who settled here acquired much of the same characteristics of the oak trees among which they lived. They had to in order to stay and survive.

At the present time oak timber has no value, at least not here in this vicinity, but the time will come when it will be valuable. I hope it is in the far distant future for then the oaks like the firs will be doomed. I am afraid there won't be any protective U.S. Forest Service to save any of the oaks.

SCHOOL ASSIGNMENTS

By Mildred Kanipe (Age 14)

English II
English II, Story
A+
No date

FAITH RESTORED

Jack Keats was a rancher by name and a man by nature. Nevertheless he was a thief by his own making. He was a good upright fellow until, when attending college he was thrown over by a fickle girl. He, like many others, lost faith in mankind and went wrong. He thought that there was nothing more worth living for.

Jack quit college and went back to his father's ranch. That winter, at the death of his father, he was sole owner of the ranch. He practically left it to run itself while he done anything he pleased.

One day Jack learned that one of his neighbors, Old Sawyers, had six months wages in his safe to pay off the men at the end of the week. Jack decided that it would be easy earned money so he planned to go and take possession of it.

Along in the middle of the afternoon Jack saddled his horse and rode away to the east. As he topped a small raise he saw a horse and rider coming, from the south, toward his ranch. He turned his horse and rode behind a small clump of trees where he could watch, unseen. As the rider came steadily onward Jack distinguished it as Old Sawyers' daughter. He surmised that she was riding over to his ranch to visit the housekeeper. He knew that it would be dark by the time she reached his ranch and that she would have to stay all night. A sneering smile flicked across his face as he said, "Trust a girl to get you in trouble and leave you there. They scream and faint if a mouse even wiggles his tail. 'Tis a pity they can't faint before they have time to scream. But girls are girls. However lucky for, me this one will be gone out of the way. It sure will be easy sailin' now."

He rode boldly on as the girl had disappeared in a hollow. He left his horse well hidden in the forest near Old Sawyers' ranch house. He waited until about midnight and then stole cautiously to the house and slipped along to a window where he listened intently. He quietly raised a window and dropped softly inside. He was now in the same room with the safe. It was a big room and the safe stood on the opposite side almost straight across from him. This he knew because he had been in the house many times when he was a child. That seemed years and years ago although he was hardly more than a boy now. He was happy and contented then. What fun he and Old Sawyers' daughter had had together and now they no more than spoke. Old Sawyers had been very good to him, in fact treated him like a son. He had been a life long friend of Jack's father and here he was stealing from him! Had he sunk so low? No, he would not think of such things. It was all the fault of others that he was what he was. He would just get even with all he could. He would get their money first and if that did not satisfy him he touched his gun significantly. However he must get busy because if he had forgotten how to open the safe it would probably take time to open it.

Jack crossed the room, carefully avoiding chairs, and knelt before the safe. He turned it as he remembered and the door swung open. As he did not have any light he had to feel for the money he expected to find there. He felt in several shelves and then his fingers touched the money. There was three rolls of bills with bands around them. He pulled it toward him with a greedy sigh of content.

Suddenly the room was flooded with light as a figure stepped out from behind the safe. It was a strange masked cowboy. He was holding a deadly gun straight at Jack, who, being overcome with surprise, leaped to his feet clutching the money as if it meant freedom instead of otherwise.

The cowboy's look went straight into Jack's soul reading his whole life. It seemed to Jack that he could stand it no longer but must scream aloud when the look turned to pity and the cowboy pointed upward with a silent hand. He then turned, but still keeping jack under cover of his gun, and pulled a roll of bills from his own pocket, and after placing them in the safe, closed the door.- - - - - - - - - - - He then waved a hand toward the door of the room and they both went out leaving a dark and silent room behind.

When they were under cover of the forest the cowboy ordered Jack to halt. He turned on a light which he had with him and took the roll of bills from Jack. He pulled off the bands and heaped the bills on the ground. To Jack's utter astonishment he saw that they were simply black slips of paper. He lit a match and held the flame to them. They quickly went up in smoke and, after tramping the ashes, he raked a few leaves over them. He stood looking down at them for some time and then raised his head and faced Jack with a look of mingled sorrow, pity, and pleading.

The cowboy said, "You are weak, a weakling. You let temptation rule you. Be strong, brave, and true like a man should be. After all you are a man. You have a man's place in the world. Why not take it? Why not be somebody worth while? Why not live, be happy and free, instead of exist, and be unhappy and unfree? Reform. Yes, build your life over. Leave out the bad part. Forget the past. Live as you should live. You are not alone in the world. Will you brace up and be a man? I don't intend to punish you. You had not the money. That is not why I done this. Don't promise. A promise is easily made but mighty hard to keep. And a broken promise is worse than no promise. Do it. Prove it. Live right and you will need no promise."

Jack listened to all this and in his heart knew it was all true and resolved to be better. He said, "Several times I have been on the point of giving up this hateful way of life for it is not pleasant, I live in unrest and may any time wake up and find myself caught, and you know where the end is. Every time I would be about to go right someone would turn me down for what I am and I couldn't see that it wasn't their fault for my condition. I see it all now and much, much more. However tell me three things and I will live right the rest of my life and make up for this. As you wish I will not promise but I will prove it. I will.

"I hope so. I was sure you had some good in you, man enough to go right. But what three things do you wish to know."

"First, how did you know I was going to get the money?"

"I saw you ride behind a clump of trees and disappear. Sometime later I saw you ride out from the same bunch and turn south instead of continuing east. Knew you were headed this way and I also knew that Old Sawyers had a lot of money on hand. I easily guessed the rest."

"Alright, I see. And second, how did you get the money and place the blank paper in its place?"

"I went to the house before you arrived, slipped in and changed places with the rolls of bills."

"Yes, and third, why did you do it? If you want me caught which you say you don't, why don't you take me, why change bills?"

"As I said I do not want you punished and I changed bills because I did not wish to see you as an actual thief. I did it to save you. I wanted to restore your faith in mankind."

"You have restored my faith in man but never in woman. Now if a woman would of have helped me but I am done with them. If I had faith in them I would be wholly right again. But, how did you know all about my life?"

"Why", laughed the cowboy as he pulled his mask and hat and long brown hair fell about his shoulders. "I am, as always, your friend Julia Sawyers."

Jack saw to his bewilderment that she was right. He afterwards lived a good life and had friends everywhere. He also found after the restoration of faith in both man and woman by Julia, that his heart was not sore at all from his college experience. He had left all past events of his life behind and had risen far above them to stay forever.

He also found that Julia Sawyers was as good a pal as ever.

You can guess the rest of it.

Teachers note: "Poor ending"

English II
Nov. 10, 1921

SCHOOL SPIRIT

It was only one more day until the great athletic contest. Every scholar was excited for the marrow, which was Saturday, that they could hardly study. They felt sure that their school would have won the belt of honor and the purse of money if the well known athletic, Robinson, wasn't entering the contest. There were murmurs all over the room such as; "Oh, if he hadn't come—or—if he will only have lost some of his strength and ability." The school wanted the honor of winning also the money to remodel their gymnasium. They had it all planned as how they were going to have it fixed.

Some time ago the school had held an athletic contest and Dan having won was the one to be in the contest against the neighboring school.

Dan was a tall, rather slender, quick, strong, of great endurance, never giving up handsome lad. His arms and face were a beautiful healthy tan of the wonderful outdoor life. Under his brawny skin rippled large powerful muscles as strong as steel. Everyone seemed so worried and excited but Dan, who, as the old saying is was as cool as a cucumber.

There was a large crowd gathered, eager to watch the contest which began about eight o'clock. There was to be a fight between the athletic winners of each school, which was Dan and Robinson. When they came out there was a great applause and the people waited breathlessly to see who would win. The combatants leaped at each other like furious wild animals. Around and around they went so fast it almost made one dizzy to watch them. Robinson seemed to be winning and suddenly when they neared the corner Dan Slipped and nearly fell which gave Robinson the advantage and he threw Dan.

The school was very sorry and all looked with downcast faces while Dane rose to his feet and he and Robinson and the judges talked earnestly for a few moments. Then to the surprise of everyone the two combatants were back on the field fighting more furiously than ever.

For a spell of minutes every one listened, watched, and waited breathlessly. Robinson seemed to be gradually failing until he became so weak that Dan with his last efforts managed to throw the huge bulky fighter off his feet.

A great applause followed which echoed ad re-echoed from one side of the crowd to the other. A bunch of the school boys carried their exhausted champion on their shoulders thru the crowd to the judges stand. It was finally decided that Dan should get the belt of honor and Robinson the purse of money. Of course the judges didn't know how badly the school wanted the money. However, when the school heard Dan Tell Robinson that he would trade with him if he would trade they made him promise not to trade because they had decided that they would rather have him keep the belt than have the money.

A person from the other school stood upon a platform and seized a megaphone thru which he shouted, "There is to be a surprise if you people will consent. If you will let us practice in your gymnasium we will give you the money which we gained as our share of the prize, to remodel and make larger your gymnasium." They all agreed to this and two schools were the best of friends.

English II
Dec. 5, 1921
Theme

THE DUCKING TRADGEDY

One fine bright morning, I, Jack, and my cousin, John, decided to take our lunch and go down the river fishing. We were very happy boys when we went trudging down the dusty road with our fishing pole, bait, and lunch, and my chum's dog frisking ahead. When we came to the river we decided to take turns fishing and carrying the lunch.

We fished until noon when I said, "Lets have dinner, for I am getting hungry. Aren't you?"

"I sure am", said John, " I feel as though I could eat an elephant."

We sat in the green grass on the bank of the river under the cool shade trees and ate our lunch. We both enjoyed it very much and declared it the best lunch we had ever eaten.

"I think we made a fine catch," commented John, swelling up with pride.

"So do I", I replied pride fully. Those dozen trout ought to make us both a good meal. I am sure there's as many as each of us can eat."

After eating we played with my chum's dog. He would wade in the water about a foot deep after sticks which we threw in and bring them back to us.

"Let's throw him in where he will have to swim," suggested John.

I agreed and so we went up the river a little further where the water was about three feet deep. There was a slick sloping bank and after we gained as we thought a firm foothold John called the dog. He came bounding and barking joyously and didn't seem in the least bit afraid.

John cried excitedly, "Jack you grab him by the collar and hold him and I will throw him in."

"All right", I responded enthusiastically. "Be sure you get him in where it's deep."

Our plan was going very nicely until John tried to throw the dog in. Instead of jumping in the water he leaped for a small island in the river. The sudden leap unbalanced John and I held on with a life and death grip which caused the three of us to fall in the water and get a good ducking.

We were very wet and cold when we climbed upon the bank, but the dog wasn't nearly as wet as we. He didn't seem to care at all while both of us were very cross and disagreeable as we trudged home with our lunch basket filled with fish and our fishing pole. Each of us was thinking of the punishment our mothers would give us when we reached home, and not about the glory of the trout.

English II
Oct 27, 1921
Theme

THE LUMBER CAMP

There were great sawmills and sawdust burners along a wide river, and broad sawdust covered streets in the town. We walked down one of the side streets to a long wooden bridge which rested on pins shaped upstream like the prow of a boat, in order to withstand the battering of the logs. It was a long bridge and beneath it the swift oily leaden water of the current slipped by smoothly as glass. The stream was divided into many channels by means of great broad poles, some of which were partly filled with logs. Men were moving here and there over the logs, armed with long pike-poles as a means of separating them. Down stream as far as we could see were huge mills flanked by lumberyards, the masts of their laden ships, their black sawdust burners, and above all the pure white triumphant banners of steam that shot straight to the gray sky.

We crossed the bridge and walked between tall leaning stacks of lumber, piled crosswise so the air could blow between the boards. The green pitch gave it the smell of pine.

We went thru many sawdust covered alleys, with stacks of lumber such as this on each side forming high walls which seemed to be frowning down at us. At last we came to a side street which offered full view of the sun. We turned down this street a few feet and found ourselves standing over the inlet of the lake.

Then for the first time we realized that we had been walking on "made ground". The water chugged restlessly against the uneven ends of slabs, thousands of them, laid side by side, down to and below the waters surface. These formed a structure upon which the sawdust had been heaped.

We retraced our steps to the street on which we had started. There we found a steep stairway and by it mounted to the tramway above, along which we walked for some distance looking and wondering at the streets and by ways of the lumber yard. Once we stepped aside to give passage to a large powerful black horse and his train of cars loaded with lumber. A little further on we came to a couple of men unloading similar cars and passing the boards down to other men below who piled them. They wore leather aprons and a square piece of leather strapped across the inside of their hands in protection against splinters.

We walked along a high narrow platform, overlooking the waterfront, to the mill. There we saw a great water rich with logs. From this there was a place leading up to the second story of the mill. Up this came an endless chain armed with teeth which took hold of the logs and slowly carried one right behind the other up to the saws.

It was rather dusky as we entered the saw room but in an instant we saw the glitter and whine of the two huge saws, moving silently but with a menace of a great spear. There were pulleys, belts, machinery and men, all which helps to get the logs to the saws, which with a shriek, eat through them instantly. We went on through the mill and out to the broad open tramway. Here we saw the finished lumber trundled out on rollers to be transferred to the cars.

We went to the boarding house. In the dining room was a long table, covered with red oilcloth, and pine benches worn smooth and shiny by long and constant use. They used thick cookers and served steaming hearty well-cooked food.

At one side by the window stood a small table on which was spread a red cloth with a white pattern. It was for the bosses, owners, and clerks, and possessed real chairs.

We were told that the logging was carried each day by careful organization of the laborers. They were divided into swampers, roadworkers, choppers, sawyers, loaders, and teamsters. The logs were hauled out of the forest, by log roads to the river, down which they were driven, during high water, by the "Rivermen".

However we didn't have time to visit that section of the camp as it was getting late and we had quite a distance to cover before dark.

Dec 12, 1921
English II
Theme

THE SECRET LETTERS

Little Dorthy was a very beautiful little girl with sweet smiling red lips, rosy cheeks, golden curls, and dancing blue eyes. She probably never would have thought about reading her older sister, Ruth's, letters had she not been so secret about them, for whenever she received one she ran upstairs and locked herself in her room to read it. When she came back she would be very red in the face but seeming ever so happy.

One day Dorthy was in Ruth's room and saw a small nick in one of the dresser drawers. Being as her sister had always kept them locked Dorthy decided to investigate. Presently she discovered a beautiful pink box which she opened and found to be filled with letters. Surely these were her sister's secret letters, so she determined to find out what they contained. Very carefully she pulled each one from the envelope and read them with a puckered brow and many guilty glances bestowed upon the door. She was ready at a minutes notice to put them back and be standing looking out thru the window. However, she finished reading them undisturbed and very carefully placed them back and stole from the room.

That very evening Ruth received a letter and started gaily up the stairs looking very happy when Dorthy called after her, forgetting that she was telling on herself. "I don't see anything in your old letters to be so happy and secret about."

Ruth stopped and looked at her in bewilderment, saying inquiringly, "What did you say, child?"

She always called Dorthy "child" which made her very angry so she retorted stamping her feet, "There's nothing in your old letters but words longer than my arm and I can't pronounce nor understand 'em." They are all signed your loving friend Bill! Bill! Bill! Bill! Why, I just hate that horrid old name and I'd tell 'im so if I were you and he could just say what he pleased for all I'd care."

Ruth came quickly down the stairs and very angrily seized her sister by the shoulder and gave her a good shaking. "Do you mean to tell me that you read my letters?" she demanded.

Dorthy confessed and received a good hard whipping, and gave a promise never to do such a thing again.

Jan. 24, 1922
English II
Semester Theme

THE SNOW STORM

Dan Hale mounted his big black stallion and started on his perilous journey home. Dan was a tall slender boy with rich brown eyes, brown hair, a square chin, and firm yet smiling deep red lips. His horse, Captain Jack, was a powerful, deep chested, lanky, shining black, with a white spot on his forehead, and a long silken, wavy black main and tail.

Dan had come over to Bonneville early in the morning to get some medicine and help for his mother who was sick. He had hunted for some woman who would go and take care of her, but was unsuccessful in the attempt. Now he was returning late in the afternoon, in spite of the protests of the people for they told him that he could never reach his home. There had been much snow when he came over, but during the day a terrible snow storm had come up and now the snow was two feet deep in Bonneville. They knew it would be twice that much on Mt. Bonny over which lay the twenty-five mile trail home.

Dan knew that his mother needed the medicine and that if anyone could travel the dangerous snow-covered trail after dark that it would be Captain Jack. He touched Captain Jack lightly on the flank with his spurs which sent him in a long untiring lope out over the snow-packed trail. It was about five miles to the foot of Mr. Bonny which were fairly good going for the trail had been broken and the land was nearly level.

Dan pulled Captain Jack down to a walk when they reached the unbroken trail that started the steep, difficult climb up Mt. Bonny. The snow was almost four feet deep, but, nevertheless, Captain Jack started bravely up. Progress was slow for breaking the trail thru the deep snow took time and strength. When they reached the top both were breathing hard so they rested for a short time. Then they started down the steep, slick, dangerous decent. Dan held the reins loosely and let Captain Jack pick his way very carefully. They went fairly good until about halfway down. Here the trail was very, very, narrow, and the mountain almost perpendicular. The trail wound back again about fifty feet below. When about half way along the trail it suddenly gave way and Dan and Captain Jack were sliding at a terrific rate down the mountain which all appreared to be level because of the white blanket of snow that covered all the rocks and bushes. Captain Jack gained his feet when he reached the trail for although it was covered with snow it formed a place for his sharp hoofs to catch.

Both horse and rider were cut, bruised, and scratched, but not dangerously hurt although it was rather painful. They reached the foot of the mountain without further mishap and started out across the now open and hilly country. They could go faster now but they couldn't go faster than a walk because of the snow. By this time it was as dark as possible and Dan let Captain Jack take the direction he wished for he knew that he would never miss the trail or get in the drifts and washouts.

They were crossing a small valley or hollow when suddenly the long, shrill, piercing cry of a horse in agony broke the silence. Before the cry, there was no sound save the crunch, crunch, crunch of the snow and the labored breathing of Captain Jack as he made his way through the deep snow. The cry frightened both horse and rider for Dan gave a shudder and grasped the reins tight in one hand while the other went to the pistol at his hip, which he always wore in case of need. Captain Jack gave a swift leap forward and stopped dead still. Well! They both knew what that cry meant, that some horse and rider had lost their way and were perishing in a snow drift or washout.

Dan thought maybe he could save the rider, so he turned Captain Jack in the direction from which the sound came, and touched him lightly on the flank with his spurs and urged him into a labor some lope thru the deep dangerous snow.

Presently they could see directly thru the darkness a dark form struggling to rise. A moment more and they came upon it and found that it was a horse in a snow drift. Dan leaped off and found that the horse's leg was broken and that he was breathing his last. He looked around for the rider whom he presently saw nearby. Much to his astonishment he found it to be a beautiful girl. She was lying unconscious in the snow where she had been thrown when her horse fell. She was tall and slender with brown hair.

As Dan picked her up and with numb hands wrapped his heavy coat around her, she awoke, her light blue eyes dancing and a row of white even teeth flashed between her deep red smiling lips when she laughed.

Dan climbed on Captain Jack and with her in his arms started out on a lope for home. He kept urging Captain Jack on for he was becoming colder and colder. Also, he knew that he must hurry if he were to save the girl's life for he didn't know how long she had lain in the snow. He thought that she had probably got lost when darkness came down and had wandered around until her horse had fallen.

When they reached the ranch Captain Jack came to a halt before the ranch house door and the two unconscious forms slid from his back into the snow. Instantly the door opened and the white anxious face of Mr. Hale appeared in the door. When he saw the exhausted riderless horse standing in the snow with drooping head, he had to catch the door to keep from falling. Then, realizing that Captain Jack would never leave his master, he walked over to him and found Dan and the girl. He carried them in and cared for them. In a few days they were almost as well as ever.

It turned out that the girl's name was Daisy Riley and that she was looking for work when she got lost in the darkness and the snow storm.

She stayed and took care of Mrs. Hale who soon recovered under her skillful care. She was so good and kind and willing to do things that Mrs. Hale wanted her to stay longer. She decided to stay all the coming summer and help with the work. Daisy and Dan had many glorious rides and good exciting times together. Before the summer was over, Dan and Daisy fell deeply in love with each other and were promised to be married.

English II
Nov. 23, 1921
Thanksgiving
Theme

TWO THANKSGIVING GIFTS

One cold windy snowy Thanksgiving Day a poor ragged crippled blind beggar woman was standing shivering beside the road in hope someone would give her some money to buy some food and fuel.

The first passerby was a tall warmly dressed person who only gave the poor woman a mere look. She thought that maybe the next person would be kind and have pity on her.

Presently she heard a rumble of chariot wheels and the governor came by on his way to the city for a Thanksgiving dinner. When he saw the old woman he stopped the carriage and put his hand out thru the door and gave her some money. He saw that he had a gold piece and decided to change it for a piece of silver. As he started to pull his arm in his sleeve caught and jerked the money from his hand and it fell at her feet. Being as he didn't want to get out he told her to pick it up and drove on wishing he hadn't given so generous a gift. She knelt and fumbled in the snow trying to find the gold piece.

When the first passerby reached his large beautiful home where the fire was burning very brightly, he warmed his numbed hands and feet and began to think of the old woman in the snow. He thought how cold she must be with her ragged scanty wet clothing and how hungry and uncomfortable. He decided to give her a surprise and after telling the cook to prepare dinner for two he went in search of her. He came upon her still seeking for the money. After giving it to her he lead her to his home where after she was warm and dry he gave her the most, welcome, wonderful and happy Thanksgiving dinner she had had for many a day.

High school report cards (1922–24)

RECIPES & REMEDIES

From Aunt Mary's Cookbook

(The spelling is Mary's)

Mary Baimbridge's recipe book was written by hand in pencil in a small notebook. It is in the care of the Douglas County Museum.

Note that the recipes do not mention temperatures required for baking. Mary baked in a wood-burning range that had no thermostat. Temperature was regulated by adjusting the fire in the firebox. Cooks learned to put their hand in the oven and "feel" if the temperature was right.

She apparently felt that in some cases the ingredient list was sufficient.

The following are from Aunt Mary's book:

RECIPES

Ginger Bread

1 cup sugar
1 cup molasses
1 cup sour milk
½ cup melted butter
1 tablespoon ginger
1 teaspoon soda

Flour enough to make it a little thicker than griddle cakes but not so stiff but that it will smooth itself without the aid of a spoon. No eggs at all. Baked in a small sized dripping pan moderate oven it will be light but not dry. Let the cake remain in the pan and cut out as you want for the table that will keep from drying up.

Crackers

Butter one cup
Salt one teaspoon
Flour two quarts

Mock Angle [Angel] Cake

1 cup Sugar
1 cup Flour
3 Teaspoon baking powder
1 pinch salt

Sift 3 times

1 cup scalded milk

Add slowly and beat till smooth then fold in the whites of six eggs beaten stiff. Bake in a moderate oven for about 35 minutes.

Coffee Cake

1 cup cold coffee
1 cup sugar
1 cup molasses
1 cup butter
5 cups flour
1 cut ground fruit
1 teaspoon cream of tarter
1 teaspoon soda
Spice to tastes

Ginger Snaps

1 cup sugar
2 cups molasses
1 cup butter
2 teaspoons soda
2 teaspoons Ginger
3 pints flour

Yellow or Gold Cake

1 cup sugar
½ cup butter
2 egg yokes
1 whole egg
½ cup sweet milk
1 teaspoonful of baking powder
1 ½ cups of flour

REMEDIES

White Liniment

1 pt of strong vinegar
½ teacupful of turpentine
3 eggs
2 Tablespoonfuls of laudanum (A form of opium)
2 tablespoonfuls of whiskey

Put all together and shake well.

Bed Bug

Turpentine   1 pint
Denatured Alcohol   1 pint
Carrosine Sublimate   2 oz

Keep away Lagrippe

Put a teaspoonful of Sulpher in each shoe sole and you wont take the gripe.

(Mary's sister, Sarah, died of "La Grippe" leaving two small daughters, Leah, 2 ½, and Mildred, 3 months. Mary raised the girls and lived with Mildred until she had to be moved to a nursing home. She passed away in 1955.)

MAPS

Mildred Kanipe Memorial Park

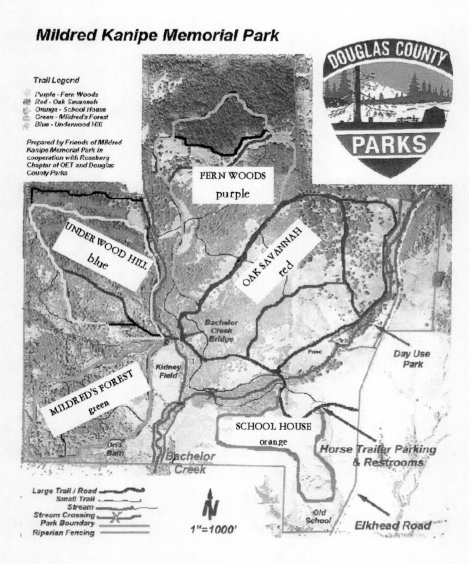

Trail Legend
Purple - Fern Woods
Red - Oak Savannah
Orange - School House
Green - Mildred's Forest
Blue - Underwood Hill

Prepared by Friends of Mildred
Kanipe Memorial Park in
cooperation with Roseburg
Chapter of OET and Douglas
County Parks

DOUGLAS COUNTY
PARKS

FERN WOODS
purple

UNDER WOOD HILL
blue

OAK SAVANNAH
red

Bachelor
Creek
Bridge

Pond

Day Use
Park

Kidney
Field

MILDRED'S FOREST
green

Drill
Barn

SCHOOL HOUSE
orange

Horse Trailer Parking
& Restrooms

Bachelor
Creek

Large Trail / Road
Small Trail
Stream
Stream Crossing
Park Boundary
Riparian Fencing

N
1"=1000'

Old
School

Elkhead Road

Kanipe Park Trail Map

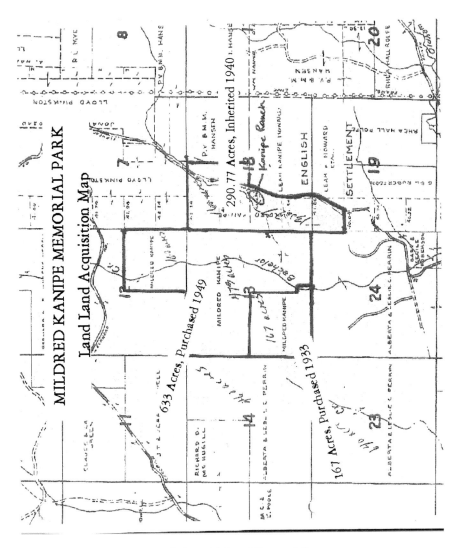

Land Acquisition History Map

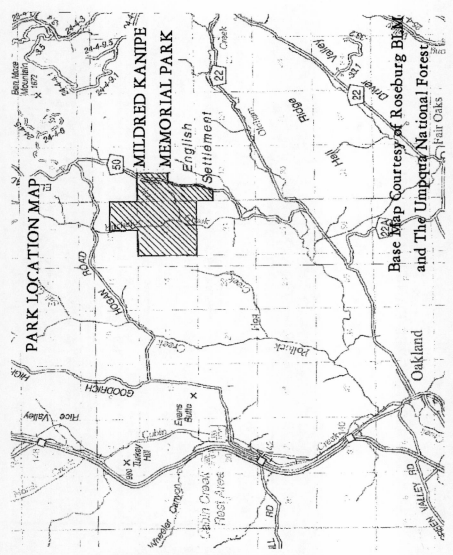

Directions to Mildred Kanipe Memorial Park

THE NATIONAL REGISTER OF HISTORIC PLACES

How to Apply

The listing of a property in the National Register of Historic Places is testimony to the historic importance of a site and/or building to the nation, the state, or the locality where it is. The process of getting a property approved is an exacting one, requiring an estimated 150 hours to complete.

One does not need to be the owner in order to prepare a nomination. However, owner consent is required for submittal and review of any nomination of a private property. Public properties do not require owner consent, but in the interest of goodwill and positive public relations, it is advisable to at least notify public entities of the intent to nominate a publicly-owned property.

In Oregon, the applicant must first apply to the State Historic Preservation Office, (SHPO), for preliminary evaluation. If this office determines that the property is eligible, they will advise in the preparation of the final forms.

To complete the application, extensive research is necessary to provide the historic detail and context required to support the historic significance of the resource. All sections of the form must be completed. Specific photos must be included and sent in the correct format. Until recently photos had to be printed from black and white negatives, but just in time for these applications it was decided that digital photos would be acceptable. They must be printed on specified archival quality paper with specified ink—in black and white.

When the application is complete it is submitted to the State Advisory Committee on Historic Preservation for their formal review.

They will sometimes ask for revisions, corrections, or additional information to be included when they approve an application.

When the final document is complete, the State Historic Preservation Office forwards the nomination to the Keeper of the National Register in Washington DC, who has 45 days to review and approve or deny the nomination.

Much helpful information is available on the internet. The Oregon SHPO link to the National Register program is http://egov.oregon.gov/OPRD/HCD/NATREG/index.shtml. The federal National Register program website is HTTP://www.nps.gov/history/nr/.

The final applications, (forms only—no photographs), for the two Mildred Kanipe Memorial Park properties are included here. They are of interest because they have additional historical information that is not included in the body of this book. In addition, anyone thinking of applying for a National Register listing may find it useful to review them as examples of successful applications.

Keep in mind that I submitted the original applications. Then, SHPO added to what I had to make the applications more complete. The Farmstead application, which was complicated by the size of the area and the number of buildings, had additional help. Liz Carter, Historic Preservation Consultant, graciously donated her services to complete a fine application.

ENGLISH SETTLEMENT SCHOOL

17455 ELKHEAD RD., OAKLAND, DOUGLAS COUNTY, OREGON

Tax Lot 300 =33.84 Acres, 1 acre (plus or minus) included in nomination for National Register

The English Settlement School was placed on the National Register of Historic Places September 4, 2007.

The first English Settlement School was built in 1855 and was located southeast of this site on Oldham Creek. This building is estimated to have built around 1910. The school was closed and the district merged with the Oakland School District in 1934.

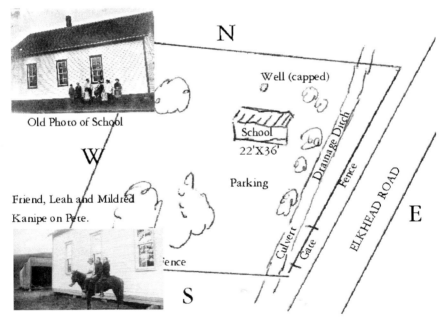

Old Photo of School

Friend, Leah and Mildred Kanipe on Pete.

N

Well (capped)

School 22'X36'

Drainage Ditch

Fence

ELKHEAD ROAD

W

E

Parking

Culvert

Gate

Fence

S

Mildred Kanipe and her sister, Leah, both attended this school. Leah taught here for two years after graduating from Oakland High School.

English Settlement School site sketch

NPS Form 10-900
OMB No. 10024-0018
(Oct.1990)

United States Department of the Interior

National Park Service

National Register of Historic Places Registration Form

This form is for use in nominating or requesting determinations for individual properties and districts. See instruction in How to Complete the National Register of Historic Places Registration Form (National Register Bulletin 16A). Complete each item by marking "x" in the appropriate box or by entering the information requested. If an item does not apply to the property being documented, enter "N/A" for "not applicable." For functions, architectural classifications, materials and areas of significance, enter only categories and subcategories from the instructions. Place additional entries and narrative items on continuation sheets (NPS Form 10-900a). Use a typewriter, word processor, or computer, to complete all items.

1. Name of Property

historic name _____ English Settlement School _____

other names/site number _____

2. Location

street & number 17455 Elkhead Road _____
_____   not for publication

city or town __Oakland_____
_____ vicinity

state _Oregon_____ code _OR___ county _
Douglas____ code _____ 019 _ zip code _97462_

_____

3. State/Federal Agency Certification

As the designated authority under the National Historic
Preservation Act, as amended, I hereby certify that this ____
_X___ nomination _____ request for determination
of eligibility meets the documentation standards for
registering properties in the National Register of Historic
Places and meets the procedural and professional
requirements set forth in 36 CFR Part 60. In my opinion,
the property _X__ meets _____ does not meet the
National Register criteria. I recommend that this property
be considered significant _____ nationally _____ statewide _
_X__ locally.

Signature of certifying official/Title - Deputy SHPO
        Date

 Oregon State Historic Preservation Office

 State or Federal agency and bureau

4. National Park Service Certification

I hereby certify that the property is: Signature
    of the Keeper   Date of Action

_____ entered in the National Register

See continuation sheet.

_____ determined eligible for the National Register

See continuation sheet.

_____ determined not eligible for the National Register

removed from the National Register

_____ other (explain):

OMB No. 10024-0018

English Settlement School
Douglas Co., OR

Name of Property

County and State

5. Classification

Ownership of Property   Category of Property
    Number of Resources within Property

(check as many as apply)   (check only one box)

(Do not include previously listed resources in the count)

_____ private   __X_ building(s)

Contributing Noncontributing

  _X__ public - local   ___ district

_____1_____ buildings

_____ public - state   _____ site

_____ sites

_____ public - Federal   _____ structure

_____ structures

_____ object

_____ 1_____ objects

1_____ 1_____ Total

Name of related multiple property listing
Number of contributing resources previously
(enter "N/A" if property is not part of a multiple property listing)
listed in the National Register

_____ N/A _____

0_____

---

6. Function or Use

Historic Functions
Current Functions
(enter categories from instructions)
(Enter categories from instructions)

EDUCATION: School _____
VACANT/NOT IN USE _____

_____
_____
_____
_____
_____
_____
_____
_____
_____
_____

7. Description

Architectural Classification
Materials
(Enter categories from instructions)
(Enter categories from instructions)

NO STYLE
foundation: STONE: Basalt

walls: WOOD: Weatherboard

roof: METAL: Aluminum

Other:

Narrative Description
(Describe the historic and current condition of the property
on one or more continuation sheets)

See continuation sheets.

English Settlement School
Douglas Co., OR

Name of Property
County and State

8. Statement of Significance

Applicable National Register Criteria
Areas of Significance
(Mark "x" in one or more boxes for the criteria qualifying the property
(Enter categories from instructions)
for National Register listing).

EDUCATION
__X__ A Property is associated with events that have
ARCHITECTURE
made a significant contribution to the broad

patterns of our history.

_____ B Property is associated with the lives of persons

significant in our past.

__X__ C Property embodies the distinctive characteristics

of a type, period, or method of construction or
Period of Significance
represents the work of a master, or possesses
__1910-1930__
high artistic values, or represents a significant and

distinguishable entity whose components lack

123

_____

individual distinction.

_____ D Property has yielded, or is likely to yield,
Significant Dates
        information important in prehistory or history.
        _1910, 1930_____

_____

_____
Criteria Considerations
(Mark "x" in all the boxes that apply)

Property is:
Significant Person

(Complete if Criterion B is marked above)
_____ A owned by a religious institution or used for

_____
        religious purposes

_____ B removed from its original location
Cultural Affiliation

_____ C a birthplace or grave
        _____

_____
_____ D a cemetery
_____

_____ E a reconstructed building, object, or structure

Architect/Builder
_____ F a commemorative property
_____

_____
_____ G less than 50 years of age or achieved
significance   _____

Within the past 50 years

Narrative Statement of Significance
(Explain the significance of the property on one or more continuation sheets)
See continuation sheets

_____

9. Major Bibliographical References

Bibliography (Cite books, articles, and other sources used in preparing the form on one or more continuation sheets) See continuation sheets

Previous documentation on file (NPS):   Primary location of
additional data:

___ preliminary determination of individual listing (36CFR67)   __X__ State
Historic Preservation Office
    has been requested   __X__
Other State agency
___ previously listed in the National Register   ____
Federal agency
___ previously determined eligible by the National Register   __X__ Local
government
__ designated a National Historic Landmark   ____
University
__ recorded by Historic American Buildings Survey   __X__
Other
__ recorded by Historic American Engineering Record   Name of repository:
Douglas County Historical Society

OMB No. 10024-0018

English Settlement School
        Douglas Co., OR
Name of Property
        County and State

_____

10. Geographical Data

Acreage of Property _____1 acre_____

UTM References
(Place additional UTM references on a continuation sheet)

1 _10_ _481931_ _4813071_____
3 ____ _____ _____
   Zone   Easting   Northing
   Zone   Easting   Northing

2 ____ _____ _____
4 ____ _____ _____

Verbal Boundary Description
(Describe the boundaries of the property on a continuation sheet) See
Continuation Sheet

Boundary Justification
(Explain why the boundaries were selected on a continuation sheet) See
Continuation Sheet

11. Form Prepared By

name/title _ Lois Eagleton, Chair, and Oregon State Historic
Preservation Office staff_____

organization Friends of Mildred Kanipe Memorial Park
Association, Inc. date _ March 1, 2007_____

street & number _ PO Box 105_____
telephone _(541) 459-9397_____

city or town _Oakland_____ state_
_ OR_____ zip code _97486__

Additional Documentation

Submit the following items with the completed form:

Continuation sheets

Maps: A USGS map (7.5 or 15 minute series) indicating the property's location.
    A sketch map for historic districts and properties having large acreage or numerous resources.

Photographs: Representative black and white photographs of the property.

Additional items (check with the SHPO or FPO for any additional items)

Property Owner

name _____ Douglas County Park Department _____

street & number __ PO Box 800 _____
telephone _(541) 440-4500 _____

city or town _Winchester _____
state _OR___ zip code _97495 _____

maintaining data, and completing and reviewing the form. Direct comments regarding this burden estimate or any aspect of this form to the Chief, Administrative Services Division, National Park Service, PO Box 37127, Washington, DC 20013-7127; and the Office of Management and Budget, Paperwork Reductions Project (1024-0018), Washington, DC 20503.

SUMMARY:

The English Settlement School is located in the vicinity of the City of Oakland among the region's rolling hills and prairies. The building itself is a simply adorned rectangular, one-story, wood-frame, front-gabled, one-room schoolhouse resting on a foundation of basalt field stones. Openings include regularly placed four-over-four double-hung windows and two wood-paneled doors. The interior consists of a single room with a vestibule and two cloak rooms set to the east end, which are finished with bead-board wainscot, siding, and ceiling boards.

SETTING:

The English Settlement School is located at 17455 Elkhead Road in rural Douglas County, approximately eight miles northeast of the City of Oakland. Situated in flat east-sloping area in a ravine between the region's rolling hills, the schoolhouse sits in its original location aligned on an east-west axis. The entry faces east toward the outside bend of a prominent curve on Elkhead Road. A seasonal creek runs on the east side of the lot between the school and the road among a lightly-treed camas-flower prairie. The south façade of the building features two heritage rose bushes, daffodils, and other period foundation plantings. A fence of metal posts, woven-wire field fence, and barbed wire runs along the east and south property lines, and a modern metal gate hung on wood posts is situated on the southeast corner to control access to the gravel drive from Elkhead Road. A non-contributing historic well lies approximately 35 feet north of the schoolhouse, and is capped with modern fittings. No other buildings, structures, or objects are located on the property. Views from the school include pastured hills rising on all sides and Elkhead Road to the immediate east.

EXTERIOR DESCRIPTION:

The English Settlement School building is a rectangular, one-story, wood-frame, front-gabled, one-room schoolhouse. Measuring 22' by 36', the schoolhouse is supported by its original system of wood girders and floor joists set on hand-placed field stones with the exception of the foundation on the north and west sides that were replaced with pressure-treated dimensional lumber and concrete footings. Mill-sawn tongue-and-groove flooring laid on an east-west axis complete the floor structure. The frame is balloon construction with a truss roof system. The building is covered with a medium-pitch front-facing gable roof clad in corrugated-aluminum sheets.

Mill-sawn shiplap siding, corner boards and frieze boards finish the exterior. The shiplap cladding exposure is 5". The mostly knot-free siding is nailed to the balloon-framed structure approximately 24" on center with round-head wire nails. The corner boards are approximately 6" wide and are attached with earlier square nails, thus suggesting that the builder ran short of the round-head nails toward the end of construction. The corner boards on the southwest corner are missing. The barge board encircling the roof line measures approximately 1" by 12" and is overhung by boxed eaves. The exterior of the schoolhouse was originally painted white, but it is now almost devoid of paint and the siding is weather-worn.

Three wood double-hung four-over-four windows measuring 28" wide by 68" tall are symmetrically placed on the north and south facades, each with a decorative crown molding. Glass panes measure 16" by 12"; however, much of the original glass and parts of the muntins are missing. A modern one-over-one window is located on the northeast corner of the north facade. The main entrance is centered on the front-gabled east façade, with a 6' x 2' rough-cut basalt field stone placed as a step. The four-panel door with tall rectangles placed over smaller square panels has decorative crown molding, and a single hopper window is placed over the top. On the south façade above the east-most window there is a round opening, apparently for a chimney pipe, cut through the siding. A rectangular metal plate with a semicircle cut out to accommodate the pipe is placed on the top half of the opening. The pipe is no longer present, leaving the space open to the elements. On the west façade there are two rectangular openings in the siding. One at the gable cuts through the siding. The other is set to the north side and has been boarded from the interior. A horizontally placed board approximately 5' in length is placed above it. The purpose of the openings and the board are not clear. On the same side, the remnants of electrical wire and a ceramic insulator are present. A two panel door is set on the southwest corner. The two-panel door has a single rectangle placed over a smaller square panel. The door lacks the decorative crown molding present on the main entry.

INTERIOR DESCRIPTION:

The building's interior consists of a large classroom with a small entry vestibule and two cloak rooms placed on the east end of the building. The main door on the east façade swings inward and opens to a vestibule measuring 10'6"x7'9". On the west wall of the vestibule are two wood-plank doors with overhead openings. The doors open in toward the vestibule and provide access to the classroom, which measures 28' 3" x 22' 0". A cloak room measuring 7' 9" and separated by a 7' partition is placed on each side of the vestibule. The plank doors for each cloak room open into the space from the main classroom. Although its placement is still evident by nail marks and missing paint, the partition between the north cloak room and the vestibule has been removed. Evidence of electrical lighting installed after the building's original construction is demonstrated by four equally-spaced ceramic light fixtures placed on the ceiling of the classroom and another centered in the vestibule.

Interior finishes include a vertical bead-board wainscot measuring 3 1/3" wide and extending approximately 3' from the floor. The wainscot is topped with a 2 ¾" decorative chair rail. The chair rail in the northwest corner of the building is missing. Walls above the wainscot are clad in horizontally placed bead board and the same material is used to enclose the rafters, but it is placed on an east-west axis in contrast to the flooring that is set on a north-south axis. Quarter round molding finishes the floor and the ceiling. Windows are trimmed with 3 ¾" x 1" molding and have 3 ½" sills. Nail marks and missing paint on the north wall between the two west-most windows indicate a 5 1/2' partition once divided this area from the rest of the room. Windows on the south side of the building have attachments for window shades, but the coverings are not present. An opening for a chimney for a wood stove is centered in the main classroom, but apparently was removed. On the west wall a large 2"x6" board is nailed diagonally across the wall to support it, and there is evidence of a now missing shelf along the west wall. A nailed square piece of plywood covers an opening on the same wall.

DATE OF CONSTRUCTION:

Although the Douglas County Historic Building Inventory lists the building's construction date as sometime after 1870, this is apparently incorrect as it references an earlier school building. Local historian Larry Moulton compiled a book on Douglas County school history and indicates that the first school for the English Settlement community was constructed of hand-hewn timbers or log in 1854 or 1855. The building was located one mile to the south of this school on Oldham Creek. Moulton speculates that a second school, probably board-and-batten style, was built around 1875 "north of Power's barn" on the other side of Elkhead Road, which was later moved to a hill north of Wilber on Highway 99.[1] However it is unclear whether such a building was ever constructed or where it may have been located. No documentary evidence has yet been found that definitively dates the current English Settlement School; however, a thorough examination of the building's construction by Oregon State Historic Preservation Office staff and local oral histories indicate that this particular school was built around 1910.[2]

ALTERATIONS:

Sometime during the building's history electricity was installed as evidenced by the remains of four screw-in light bulb sockets on the ceiling and exterior electrical equipment. Other

---

1) Larry Moulton, "Douglas County Schools: A History Outline" (Oakland, OR.: self published, nd.)
2) Harbour, Terry, "Douglas County Cultural and Historical Reousrce Inventory" (Douglas County, 1982), 2. Exhaustive research by the applicant and SHPO staff has not produced definitive evidence of a second school or the exact date of construction of the subject of this nomination.

evident additions that presumably occurred during the building's use as a school includes the additions of a wood stove pipe, a single one-over-one double-hung window on the northeast corner, and several cutouts made on the west façade. Archival photos available at the Douglas County Museum show that a woodshed and privy were located behind the school during its operation. These were removed at an unknown time and the exact locations of these sites cannot be determined due to ground disturbance by cattle. Other alterations include the removal of a partition on the north wall and a shelf on the west wall. Last used as a school in 1930, the building has since been vacant, with domestic animals using it for a shelter and wild animals as a home. Within the last two decades plywood was placed over the windows and the main entrance, leaving the rear door for access. Presumably the shingle roof was removed and the building was clad in corrugated aluminum sheets in the same period. During this process the original corbelled brick chimney was removed.[3] In 2005 the recently formed Friends of Mildred Kanipe Memorial Park Association cleaned out the animal manure from the inside of the school and secured the back door with a lock. The organization also cleaned out the weeds and brush around the building and the grounds. In the same year the Douglas County Parks Department removed deteriorated siding on the lower 1' of the building on the north, east, and west sides, replaced rotten foundation joists, and leveled the building on new cast-concrete block foundation. Several of the original foundation stones and much of the original foundation still supports the building. The removed siding was not replaced. As part of the repair work the County installed a French drain along the north and west sides of the building approximately 15' from the foundation to carry away the winter seepage that caused the structural problems. A historic well on the property has been caped with modern fittings, and thus is considered a non-contributing feature.

SUMMARY

The one-room school building completed and opened for use as the English Settlement School in rural Douglas County, Oregon stands approximately eight miles northeast of the City of Oakland among the region's rolling hills. Built in approximately 1910 during the height of production farming in the Oakland area, the building served as the only school in the English Settlement community and the school district until 1934 when the district combined with the nearby Oakland school system. The building itself is a modest interpretation of high-style schoolhouses promoted by reformers and state education officials from the mid-eighteenth through the early twentieth centuries. Although deteriorated after years of use as a livestock shelter, the building is little altered since its construction. As such, it physically demonstrates the materials and workmanship common to one-room schools as well as the guiding philosophies of construction that shaped building design, setting, and location. The building is eligible for the National Register of Historic Places under Criteria A for its association with educational practices in early twentieth-century rural Douglas County and

---

3) Statements concerning the buildings original appearance and historic outbuildings based on archival photographic evidence available at the Douglas County Museum. See photo continuation sheet.

Criterion C as an example of the distinctive physical characteristics of an early twentieth-century American one-room schoolhouse and contemporary methods of construction.

THE FOUNDING OF OAKLAND AND ENGLISH SETTLEMENT

Initially explored in 1811, Euro-American settlement began in Douglas County in the 1840s. Movement into the area accelerated with the opening of the "Applegate Trail" in 1846. Although not incorporated until decades later, towns such as Oakland, Wilbur, Winchester, and Drain formed in the 1840s and in the 1850s Sutherlin, Yoncalla, Myrtle Creek, and Roseburg became established. In order to encourage rapid settlement the U.S. government offered settlers 320 acres per individual or 640 acres per family of free land for those willing to meet a four year residency requirement through the Donation Land Claim Act of 1850. The offer of land and the discovery of gold led to a population surge, and Umpqua County was organized 24 January 1851.[4] The Donation Land Claim Act was amended several times, and was eventually replaced by the Homestead Act of 1862 that gave settlers up to 160 acres of land. Federal subsidy of railroad companies through the 1866 Oregon and California Railroad Land Grant and other initiatives encouraged the establishment of prosperous farming communities throughout the county.

Paralleling the settlement of the valley, early pioneers began to arrive in the Oakland/English Settlement area in 1846. Oakland itself was laid out in 1849; however the first residents did not arrive until 1850. Although never a large town, with the arrival of the railroad Oakland developed into an important commercial shipping center for the rich farmlands that surrounded it. By 1907 the town served as a major distribution point for agricultural produce between Portland and San Francisco. In that year 175 carloads of livestock were shipped, with turkeys being one of the area's major crops. Other products such as grains, dried fruits, wool, venison and salmon were also shipped from Oakland.[5]

The farming area known as English Settlement, which was five to eight miles east and northeast of Oakland was settled by a group of farmers from Derbyshire and other English provinces drawn to the region by the lure of free land under the Donation Land Claim Act. Early English settlers to the Oakland area include George Shambrook, W.H.B. Deardorf, and Langley Hall who arrived in the early 1850s and earned their living as farmers and

---

4) On January 7, 1852, the territorial legislature created Douglas County from the eastern part of Umpqua County. In 1853 Umpqua County lost its northern part to Lane County. Finally, in 1862, the remainder of Umpqua county was incorporated into Douglas County.

5) The town had been established to the north of its current location twenty years before, it was moved in order to take advantage of the economic possibilities the railroad offered, Douglas County Historical Society, 13; Harold Avery Minter, *Umpqua Valley Oregon and its Pioneers* (Portland: Binfords & Mort, Publishers, 1967), 130 -132; Joseph M. Quinn and Terranc J. Parker, "Oakland Historic District" " nomination to the National Register of Historic Places (Salem, OR.: Oregon State Historic Preservation Office, 1978), Section 8, page 1.

stock raisers.[6] Census data from 1870, 1880, 1900, and 1910 show that a number of the residents were either themselves English or had one or more parents who were. The majority of these émigrés arrived in the mid-nineteenth century. Many of these families farmed the land, but some worked in trades.[7] Often newcomers came to the area upon the advice of friends and relatives. Thomas and Emily Baimbridge moved to the region because they already had friends and at least one relative who had come before them.[8] Although commonly known as English Settlement, the families in the area were always outnumbered by their American neighbors, and by 1910 the English population had largely married into the local population that hailed from states in the U.S. Midwest and East.[9] Although the community never established its own town, the residents did see to the education of their children and the community continuously operated its own school district until 1934.[10]

AMERICAN SCHOOLING

From the eighteenth century until WWII, most communities, especially rural areas, educated their own children in local schoolhouses. Standard texts in the mid and late nineteenth century were *McGuffy's Eclectic* readers and the standard teaching method was rote memorization and recitation. By the 1880s most states required that teachers be at least sixteen years of age and be certified, which involved taking a one day test administered by the County Superintendent. No other training was required, but some teachers had other credentials. Generally men were preferred because they were thought to be able to handle the farm boys better than women. Administration of the schools was the responsibility of the School Superintendent, often an elected official, who organized teacher education and testing, supervised teachers, and provided supplies. By the mid-nineteenth century several separate Progressive efforts to standardize state-level education were underway, including teaching methods, teacher education, and building design. One aspect of these reforms was a push toward skills-based training. Another target of the reformers was the country school, which was thought to be backward. In 1908, then President Teddy Roosevelt pushed school consolidation as an answer to the "rural school problem" of poor teacher preparation and inadequate facilities. The debate continued through the next two decades with many educators, civic leaders, and state school superintendents proposing consolidation. Many State School Superintendents provided architectural plans for the "model" rural school to promote this shift. Encouraged by political pressure and a shift of the rural population to cities, consolidation began in earnest in the 1930s and continued through the early 1960s.[11]

6) J.V. Chenoweth, *The Making of Oakland* (Oakland, OR.: Oakland Printing Company, 1970), 42-44.
7) U.S. Census Bureau, Census of 1870, 1880, 1900, and 1910. (Ancestry.com, April 2007) <www.ancestry.com>.
8) Douglas County Historical Society, 64-65.
9) U.S. Census Bureau, Census of 1870, 1880, 1900, and 1910.
10) Moulton, Nd.
11) Andrew Gulliford, *America's Country Schools* (Washington DC: The Preservation Press, 1984), 36-45; Paul Rocheleau, *The One-Room Schoolhouse* (New York: Universe, 2003), 12-26.

EDUCATION IN THE STATE OF OREGON

Schooling in the West was highly valued and seen as the path to the future, and Oregon's Territorial and State governments took an active role in creating and administering schools. Providing adequate schools was one of the first priorities of the Oregon Territorial Legislature. A year after the U.S. Congress granted the northwest region territory status, the Oregon's Territorial Legislature created its public school system in 1849. Oregon's public education system became enshrined in the state constitution, which assigned the legislature the responsibility of establishing such a system and provided for an elected state superintendent of instruction.[12] Seeing the need and advantage of an organized and uniform public education system, larger communities throughout the state began forming school districts in the 1850s. The size and boundaries of the individual districts took into consideration that students either walked or rode ponies to school, often over crude roads and in all types of weather.[13] Public education was mostly a local matter throughout the last years of the nineteenth century. Following national trends, this changed as the State began to require that County School Superintendents submit annual reports. The Superintendents based their reports, in part, on written Teacher's Reports that were sent in by the instructor at each school.[14] The documents show that while larger communities such as Portland, Roseburg, Medford, and Baker City had large populations of school children, well-developed educations systems, and a number of multi-room school houses, that the majority of the State's population attended small one-room school houses staffed by a single teacher through most of the early twentieth century. Teacher's education level and salary was higher in larger urban school districts, and often much lower in rural areas; thus reflecting the relative wealth of the communities the schools served.[15] Despite the widespread use of one-room schoolhouses, in 1914 the Oregon State Department of Education began pushing Progressive education reforms by encouraging standardization of teacher training, texts, and school design through various publications. By the 1930s school consolidation accelerated due to consistent pressure by the State and advances in transportation, such as the wide-spread adoption of automobiles and the extension of highways, reduced the need for local community schools. [16]

12) Sarah K. Hahn, "Lowell Grange," nomination to the National Register of Historic Places (Salem, OR.: Oregon State Historic Preservation Office, 2005), Section 8 page 2-3.
13) Oakland School District, Records of the English Settlement School District, Number 26.
14) Joni Nelson and Rosalind Keeney, Mary Gallagher, May Dasch, "Rock Hill School, nomination to the National Register of Historic Places (Salem, OR.: Oregon State Historic Preservation Office, 1992), Section 8, Page 18.
15) Oregon State Department of Education, Annual Reports of the County Superintendents, 1910-1930; Statements based on a generalization developed by sampling records for the State of Oregon at five year intervals beginning in 1900.
16) Nelson, Keeney, Gallagher, and Dasch, Section 8, page 3.

EDUCATION IN DOUGLAS COUNTY

Early residents of Douglas County endeavored to ensure that their children received a basic education, and as the communities grew so did their education efforts. During the early settlement period most children were educated at home by their parents or were sent to a nearby home where a teacher, also an early settler, taught basic reading, writing, and arithmetic. One of the first school buildings in the region was the Roseburg Academy in Roseburg, Oregon, which was constructed in the 1850s. Beginning in the 1860s, almost a decade after the larger towns, smaller communities began establishing school districts and building their own schoolhouses. Most rural students received an eighth-grade education in single-room buildings made of rough lumber with a wood-burning stove for heat. Those who wished to continue their education attended institutions in larger towns and cities such as nearby Roseburg or Eugene to the north.[17] It was common for area residents to be very involved in their schools as school board members or in other capacities. The clerk, for instance, was responsible for keeping the records of the school district, including the number of school-age children, ages four to twenty, in the district. The County attempted to standardize the education students received by proscribing what was taught. It was also required that all eighth-grade students pass a standardized test before receiving their diploma. To ensure the quality of instruction, the County held annual *Teachers' Institutes*. For instance, attendees at the August 1889 institute received instructions on new teaching methods and subject matter.[18]

Standardized record-keeping, which began in 1900, allows for a more comprehensive look at the school system. For the period between 1900 and 1932 county-wide school attendance varied between four and five thousand students, with most between the ages of six and fourteen. At the beginning of this period most of the county's school districts had only a single school house, many of these were one-room schoolhouses. This changed as the county's population grew, but by 1925 ninety-six teachers still presided over one-room schoolhouses and many districts still maintained only a single school. As school districts grew, so did the length of the school year. In 1900 the school year in Douglas County averaged only 130 days, but by the 1930s it had lengthened to over 150 days. Reflecting national and state trends, few teachers had training beyond the county certification in the early part of the century, but by 1910 many had formal training. Teachers in urban areas were paid more, and women received about twenty percent less for their work than men.[19]

---

17) Chenoweth, 14. Douglas County Museum Staff, "Early School Days in Douglas County: (Douglas County Historical Society: City?, 1985), 1. Chenoweth, 14.
18) "Programme[sic] of the Teacher's Institute for Douglas County, Oregon" (Roseburg: 1889), located at the archive of the Oakland School District, Oakland, OR.
19) Oregon State Department of Education, Annual Reports of the County Superintendents, 1910-1930

EDUCATION IN ENGLISH SETTLEMENT

The second English Settlement School, and the subject of this nomination, was built on the Donation Land Claim of Joseph Deardorff, who sold his claim sometime in the 1850s to Winslow Powers, who had a Donation Land Claim adjacent to the east. Powers rented his then 640-acre ranch to Thomas and Emily Baimbridge in June, 1872 and sold it to them a few years later. When Thomas and Emily Baimbridge passed away, their land was divided among their six children. Their daughter Sarah, inherited the land that the farm buildings were on. The site of the school was inherited by Sarah's sister Mary. Sarah's husband, John Kanipe, bought back the land parcels that had been part of the original ranch, effectively restoring the parcel Thomas Baimbridge had purchased in the 1870's. When John Kanipe died in 1940, the land on the east side of Elkhead Road, what had been Winslow Powers Donation Land Claim, was left to his daughter Leah Kanipe. Her younger sister Mildred Kanipe received that part of the original Deardorff Land Claim that included the house and farm buildings and the English Settlement School. Although never married, Mildred Kanipe ran the family farmstead until she passed away in 1983. After her death the property was provisionally deeded to Douglas County for a park.[20]

Like their neighbors, the residents of English Settlement valued education as evidenced by the early organization of a school district and construction of their first log schoolhouse in 1860.[21] Originally organized as School District Five, the area's residents raised $50 by private subscription to run the school, and received $62.68 from the County. For the year ending in 1861 only eight weeks of school were held. The twenty-eight students in attendance were taught spelling, math, and grammar by a single teacher. In November 1875 the community discussed building a new schoolhouse in another location, but it is unclear if this was ever done.[22] On 30 October 1886 residents organized School District Twenty-Six. It is unknown what prompted this, but the new district was far from School District Five, which suggests that the action was a response to changing settlement patterns.[23] Records from School Districts Five and Twenty-Six for the period between 1860 and 1899 are unavailable, and most information about this time is anecdotal and based on local recollections as recorded in community history books. However, it is clear that the area's residents were actively involved in raising money for the school and making decisions about how best to educate their children.[24]

Like other small districts in Douglas County, the English Settlement school district continued to be a small rural district with a single one-room schoolhouse and teacher in

---

20) Douglas County Clerk, Title Records, various dates.
21)Chenoweth, 17; U.S. Census Bureau, Census of 1870, 1880, 1900, and 1910; School attendance rates were counted as part of the census.
22) Chenowenth, 17
23) Oakland School District, Records of the English Settlement School District, Numbers 5 and 26.
24) Chenoweth, 17

through the early twentieth century. Reflecting local trends, the community took an active role in education their children with many of the residents serving as teacher, clerk, or school board member. For instance, the Kanipe family was very involved with the district. In addition to sending their children to the school, Sarah Alice Kanipe served as the district clerk from 1903 and 1907, and her husband John Kanipe served as the Chairman of the School Board in 1926. The family also donated land for the building's construction around 1910, the building's estimated date of construction. Throughout the period one to sixteen school-age children lived in the district, but not all attended school. Those who did were taught the general county curriculum, including reading, writing, arithmetic, as well as topics in the sciences and humanities. Through 1911 most teachers had only a second or third grade school education, but beginning in 1912 the community's instructors had at least one year of training at the state school. Despite an increasing level of education, there was a fairly high turnover rate among the community's teachers, with most working only a year. This is perhaps because the district paid its teachers less than the average county salary. These trends continued for the next two decades. Records show that in 1930 the English Settlement School served eight children, was still taught by a single teacher, and was supported by a modest $516.88 in local annual taxes. [25]

Like many small school districts in the nation and state, improved transportation led to school consolidations in Douglas County and the closing of many one-room school houses, including the English Settlement School. School consolidation began in Douglas County around 1930 due to improved transportation and rural depopulation. In the Oakland, area consolidation was contentious, as many small communities resisted losing their individual identity and control over the education of their children. However, with the exception of the Umpqua School District, the surrounding communities merged their schools with the Oakland School District.[26] Reflecting this regional shift, English Settlement School District began sending their children to Oakland Schools in 1930, and in 1934 the school was closed and the area was officially annexed by Oakland Schools.[27]

SCHOOLHOUSE ARCHITECTURE

From the beginning of the eighteenth century to the middle of the twentieth rural schooling in the United States was "invariably" tied to the one-room schoolhouse with almost half of all American school children attending such an institution as late as 1913. Far from an aesthetic choice, the one-room schoolhouse was a practical design that reflected the financial resources of the nation's rural communities, and was built large enough for the number of pupils expected to attend but was no larger than the maximum distance that a single teacher's voice could carry across a room. As Historian Andrew Gulliford

---

25) Oregon State Department of Education, Annual Reports of the County Superintendents, 1910-1930.
26) Chenoweth, 14.
27) Oregon State Department of Education, Annual Reports of the County Superintendents, 1930-1935.

notes, rural schoolhouse architecture is "above all, an architecture based on limitations."[28] Although these vernacular buildings often reflected local ethnic building traditions, their form, detailing, and shape were limited by available local materials, the know-how of the builder, and the economic resources of the community. In most cases the buildings were purely functional as style was "an extra that was seldom affordable."[29] A community's first schoolhouse was often built using volunteer labor and easily available materials, and was intended as an easy-to-build inexpensive temporary structure.[30] As with most early buildings during Oregon's settlement history, these schools were small log or rough-sawn buildings with brush roofs.[31] Reflective of this reality, the first English Settlement's school was reported to be made of "hand-hewn" timber, "probably log."[32] Most communities upgraded from this first structure to a "second generation" frame building as time and finances allowed.[33]

The third building, or "third generation" schoolhouse was often larger and more decorative that reflected a community's growing wealth. These date to the last decades of the nineteenth and early twentieth century. Architectural historian Fred Schroeder divides these into two main categories. The first Schroeder calls "vernacular" and differentiates between "folk vernacular," buildings that show strong local or ethnic building traditions, and "mass vernacular," types that reflect popular design trends and are built from milled lumber and commercial products. The second type are architect-designed schoolhouses which are uncommon in rural areas. Most rural one-room schoolhouses are "eclectic" in that they use the commercial construction products seen in mass vernacular types, but are adapted by local builders to accommodate their ability and available materials.[34] These eclectic vernacular buildings resembled rural homes or small country churches in their size, scale, materials, and construction methods. Most rural schools are rectangular or square one-story buildings with a gabled roof. The interior was commonly divided into a single classroom and a vestibule with cloak rooms for each sex. Efforts were made to give the inside a finished appearance. White was the most popular exterior color and green, red, blue, and brown were popular trim colors. More ornate buildings often had a round or square bell tower. Third-generation buildings were often influenced by Revival, Queen Anne, Richardsonian Romanesque, Bungalow, Mission, and International styles; however, the vernacular aesthetic often asserted itself as local builders created simplified interpretations of popular high styles.[35]

---

28) Gulliford, 160; Rocheleau, 47-48.
29) Ibid.
30) Ibid; Rocheleau, 50.
31) Philip Dole, "Buildings and Gardens" in *Space, Style and Structure,* vol. 2, Thomas Vaughan, ed. (Portland: Oregon Historical Society, 1974.) 81-82.
32) Moulton, nd.
33) Gulliford, 166.
34) Fred E. H. Schroeder, "Schoolhouse Reading: What You Can Learn from Your Rural School" *History News,* April 1981; Rocheleau, 47-48, 50.
35) Gulliford, 159, 167.

Rectangular schools, the most popular form of eclectic mass vernacular school buildings, were balloon-frame buildings with a simple gabled roof. Hipped roofs became popular in the twentieth century. The type generally had a single entrance on the short side of the building, which was sometimes sheltered by a porch or portico, but was often open to the elements. Entry doors usually faced south or east. Many buildings had separate entrances for boys and girls, although more practical-minded communities often installed only a single door to cut costs. Many had three to four widely spaced small-pane windows set in a double-hung sash, often on the north and south sides of the building to provide the best possible light. Almost all were clad in mass-produced roof shingles and clapboard siding, as these products were inexpensive and widely available. Before 1870 most vernacular schools were unpainted, but the introduction of linseed oil paints and manufactured pigments made painting affordable. Most schools were painted white. Wood stoves were the most common heating method, thus brick chimney's and metal stove pipes were often added. School yards were simple. Paths through unkempt grass were at times cut to outhouses, but were otherwise not mowed. Interior spaces were similar to other third generation schools. At times attempts were made to plant the school grounds with ornamental plants.[36]

The remarkable similarities between schoolhouses, especially for third-generation buildings, are in part a result of the proliferation of pattern books written by educational reformers beginning in the 1830s and through the early twentieth century. In an attempt an to improve the educational process reformers produced designs for "ideal" schools that addressed setting, materials, design, and the layout of the interior space. In 1831 Educator William A. Alcott published an essay entitled, *An Essay on the Construction of School-Houses*. In it Alcott called for the arrangement of desks in rows to allow for the circulation of students and the teachers, large windows for light and ventilation, and space to store teaching aids. He also suggested that an area be left around schools to allow children to play. Revolutionary for its time, Alcott's design was widely adopted across the nation. The most influential among the school designers was educator, Connecticut legislator and U.S. Commissioner of Education Henry Barnard. Barnyard's *School Architecture*, first published in 1832, called for stylized buildings set in pleasant semi-rural settings, which Barnard thought encouraged learning. The plans also addressed adequate lighting, circulation, and ventilation. Other architects and reformers continued to refine these ideas through the nineteenth century, through the Progressive-Era push to standardize school design.[37] Plans issued in the early 1900s by State governments during the school reform movement, such as those made available by the Oregon Department of Education, were based on popular styles of the period such as the Bungalow Style and generally featured hipped instead of gabled roofs. The more traditional designs continued in rural areas for many years.[38]

---

36) Ibid, 172, 174, 176.
37) Ibid, 167-168.
38) Hahn, Section 8, page 3.

THIRD GENERATION ONE-ROOM SCHOOLHOUSES IN OREGON

Despite local differences in material, setting, and style, Gulliford states that one-room schoolhouses "nonetheless constitute a distinctive building type" that is recognizable across the nation.[39] Beginning as crude temporary buildings during the initial settlement period, schoolhouses "became more functional as they moved West with the Frontier."[40] With the aid of schoolhouse plan books, such as Henry Barnard's *School Architecture* published in 1831 and the cultural template in the minds of the pioneer builders, these traditional vernacular school buildings were transported to the West Coast in the 1870s and 1880s. The common features of the folk-inspired and plan-book derived buildings include rectangular shape, large windows, open interior space, bell tower (when it could be afforded), rural setting, and since wood was the most available building material in Western Oregon, frame construction.

In Oregon, six one-room rural schoolhouses are listed on the National Register of Historic Places. These include the Soap Creek School, Adir Village vicinity, Benton, Co; Victor Point School, Silverton vicinity, Marion Co., Parker School, Independence vicinity, Polk Co.; Dry Creek School, Summerville vicinity, Union Co.; Briedwell School, Amity vicinity, Yamhill Co.; and Rock Hill School, Sheridan, Yamhill Co. The structure of a seventh schoolhouse was incorporated into the Lowell Grange in Lowell, Grant Co. Of the six schools, one building has been converted into a private residence, leaving only 5 representatives of this particular building type with both their interior and exterior intact. Each of these resources are rectilinear third-generation eclectic mass-vernacular schoolhouses constructed in the late nineteenth or early twentieth centuries. In most cases the buildings are constructed using fieldstone foundations, balloon frame construction, a gable-front roof, and make use of bead board, shiplap, double-hung windows, and panel doors for finishing materials. Most are set in picturesque rural settings and were painted white. Interior layout is similar with one or two entrances, vestibules, and cloak rooms.[41] All six are located in the northern Willamette Valley. The principal difference between the resources is in stylistic details. For instance, built in 1889 the Victor Point School's architecture is described as a vernacular adaptation of "late Victorian" architecture or "Rural Gothic."[42] Similarly, the

---

39) Gulliford, 171.

40) Ibid, 182.

41) Information abstracted from the following National Register of Historic Places nominations: Vicki Correll, "Dry Creek School," nomination to the National Register of Historic Places (Salem, OR.: Oregon State Historic Preservation Office, 2000);Lauren Cram, "Briedwell School," nomination to the National Register of Historic Places (Salem, OR.: Oregon State Historic Preservation Office, 1988); Lorna Grabe, "Soap Creek School," nomination to the National Register of Historic Places (Salem, OR.: Oregon State Historic Preservation Office, 1991); Nelson, Keeney, Gallagher, Dasch, 1992; Richard Robertson and Cathy Robertson, "Parker School," nomination to the National Register of Historic Places (Salem, OR.: Oregon State Historic Preservation Office, 1989); Carol Walker and Bruce Duerst, "Victor Point School,: nomination to the National Register of Historic Places (Salem, OR.: Oregon State Historic Preservation Office, 1996).

42) Walker, Section 3, Page 1.

Briedwell School, constructed in 1895, also mirrors contemporary Victorian styling.[43] Both buildings have bell towers. Built during the same period, the Dry Creek School does not reflect a particular architectural style and does not have a bell tower, but exhibits "classical detailing."[44] The Rock Hill school does have a bell tower, but this 1910 building lacks distinctive ornamentation.[45] The 1914 Parker School and the 1935 Soap Creek School both feature a bell tower and are constructed to resemble the craftsman style, which the Oregon State Department of Education proposed during this time period.[46] The imitation of specific architectural styles or the inclusion of a bell tower indicates that these schoolhouses are high-style interpretations of the building type. Only relatively wealthy communities, such as those of the Willamette Valley, would have been able to construct such buildings. Thus the collection does not accurately reflect the geographic and stylistic variety of this resource type in the state.

THE ENGLISH SETTLEMENT SCHOOLHOUSE

The builder of the English Settlement School is unknown, but it is evident through the attention to detail that this school was built with skill and experience. The building retains its original interior and exterior features. It is exceptionally intact and possesses integrity of design, materials, workmanship, setting, and location. It embodies the distinctive characteristics of an American rectilinear eclectic mass-vernacular schoolhouse, a folk design common from the beginning of the eighteenth century through the middle of the twentieth Century. The English Settlement Schoolhouse also exemplifies the characteristics of a third-generation schoolhouse, which typically began with a crude log school building, followed by a small frame schoolhouse, followed by a larger, stylized schoolhouse. Available records show that this building is possibly the third schoolhouse in the English Settlement. The building was likely built around 1910, and was operated until 1930.

The setting of the English Settlement School in an open picturesque area in close proximity to a major road among the farms of English Settlement reflects the historic placement of schools, but also the ideals proposed by pattern books. The placement in a relatively flat lightly-treed camas prairie with views of the surrounding rolling hills, yet tucked out of the prevailing winds suggests attention to contemporary wisdom that education buildings should be set in an beautiful and healthful atmosphere conducive to learning. The historic landscaping on the south side of the building shows intentional efforts to beautify the area and enhance the building beyond the natural environment. Placement of the school on the major local highway is a logical choice, and fits the historic pattern of locating schools so that no one family had to send their children too far from home. As was the accepted

43) Cram, Application, Section 7, Page 1-2.
44) Correll, Application, Section 7, Page 1-2.
45) Nelson, Application, Section 7, Page 1-4.
46) Grabe, Application, Section 7, Page 1; Robertson, Application, Section 7, Page 1-2.

wisdom for choosing a school location, English Settlement School is aligned on an east-west access to allow the windows to be placed on the north and south facades, which was thought to be optimal for providing adequate light and ventilation.

Although not remarkable, the building's construction is representative of similar schools. Like other Oregon examples, the building is placed on readily available field stones and constructed with the light and versatile balloon-frame and truss system. Using existing physical evidence and historic photos, it is clear that as originally built the school made use of mass-produced building materials such as wood shingles, shiplap siding, dimensional-lumber corner boards, wire nails, red brick, and bead board and decorative moldings for the interior. Lumber for construction no doubt originated from one of the county's numerous lumber mills. Other materials were most likely obtained locally or shipped in by rail to Oakland.[47] Although the original roof and chimney are no longer present, sufficient historic material still exists to demonstrate the clear departure from the more crude construction and limited building materials of first and second generation buildings, and demonstrates English Settlement's rising economic fortunes during Oakland's heyday as an important shipping point for agricultural goods.

Interior finishes and the building's design likewise demonstrate the community's wealth and common educational practices. Although the building's design is not attributable to a specific architectural style, attention to finish details and a vague classical styling are demonstrated by the decorative crown moldings over the doors and windows, enclosed eaves, and frieze boards. The interior shows similar attention to detail with the use of moldings and the alternating direction of the bead board used throughout the interior. These details show the community's efforts to provide the best possible school for their children and emulate the designs popularized by pattern books. In the interior, separate entries from the vestibule into the main classroom and closets for each sex mirror the belief in separating boys and girls in the education process. Although no longer present, the rear shelving and partition are modest attempt to provide the storage areas for teaching aids proposed by Alcott. Still, the limits of the community's finances are also evident in the building's construction and layout. The simple exterior decoration, mix of square and wire nails, use of knotted lumber, lack of a bell tower or porch, and a single one-door main entry show that even while emulating high-style schoolhouses, the community made practical compromises. The interior shows similar patterns in the use of only a few finish materials.

CONCLUSION

Despite some deterioration, the English Settlement School is an excellent and well-preserved example of the rectilinear third-generation eclectic mass-vernacular

---

47) The presence of lumber mills in the area and the importation of finished goods in Douglas County is well established. See Chenoweth, *The Making of Oakland*; Douglas County Historical Society, *Historic Douglas County, Oregon*, 1982.

schoolhouses built in Oregon in the late nineteenth and early twentieth centuries. The building's setting, location, design, materials, and workmanship are representative of other contemporary buildings, and the school physically demonstrates the ideologies that shaped American education. However, this building is distinct from other Oregon one-room schools in the National Register in that it is a simplified adaptation of common construction practices reflective of the relative wealth of the small community it served. The building also reflects a once common, and important trend in American education. The pattern of a local community schoolhouse every few miles disappeared in the mid-twentieth century as improved methods of transportation and rural depopulation made the consolidation of school districts appear beneficial from an administrative, economic, and possibly educational and political standpoint. The closure of the English Settlement School in 1930 and the dissolution of the district in 1934 illustrates this trend. The English Settlement School is eligible for the National Register of Historic Places under Criterion A for its association with educational practices in early twentieth-century rural Douglas County. The building is also eligible under Criterion C as an example of the once-common American one-room schoolhouse because the building still conveys the feeling of a small community and its school in the early-twentieth century due to its high degree of integrity of design, materials, and workmanship.

BIBLIOGRAPHY:

Baimbridge, Thomas. 1870 Diary. Douglas County Museum.

_____. Diary/Account book, 1872. Douglas County Museum.

Bancroft, Hubert Howe. *The Works of Hubert Howe Bancroft Volume XXX, History of Oregon Vol. II 1848-1888.* San Francisco: The History Company, Publishers, 1888.

Beckham, Stephen Dow. *The Land of the Umpqua: A History of Douglas County, Oregon.* Roseburg, Oregon: Douglas County Commissioners, 1986.

Benjamin, Asher. *The Practice of Architecture; containing the five orders of architecture and an additional column and entablature, with all their elements and details explained and illustrated, for the use of carpenters and practical men.* New York, New York: DaCapo Press, 1972 [c1833].

_____. The American Builder's Companion. New York, New York: DaCapo Press, 1972 [c1806].

Bureau of Land Management, General Land Office Records. http://www.glorecords.blm.gov/. Accessed July 2007.

Chenoweth, J.V. *The Making of Oakland.* Oakland, Oregon: Oakland Printing, 1977.

Dole, Philip. "Farmhouse and Barn in Early Lane County." *Lane County Historian* X no. 2 (Aug. 1965).

_____. "Farmhouses and Barns of the Willamete Valley," in *Space Style and Structure*, Thomas Vaughan, editor. Portland, Oregon: Oregon Historical Society, 1974.

Douglas County Historical Society, *Historic Douglas County Oregon 1982.* Roseburg, Oregon: Douglas County Historical Society, 1982.

Douglas, County of. County Clerk's Office records, Roseburg, Oregon.

Douglas, County of. Surveyor's Records. http://www.co.douglas.or.us/surveyor/sars/default.asp. Accessed July 2007.

Eagleton, Lois. "English Settlement School," National Register Nomination Form, on file at the Oregon State Historic Preservation Office. 2007.

Gallagher, Mary K. et al. *Historic Context: The Barns of Linn County, Oregon 1845-1945.* Albany, Oregon: Linn County Planning Department, 1997.

Harbour, Terry R. and Stephen Dow Beckham. Douglas County Cultural and Historic Resource Inventory, 1981-82. Revised 2002. On file with Douglas County Planning Department, Roseburg and Oregon State Historic Preservation Office, Salem.

Kadas, Marianne. "Roseburg Downtown Historic District," nomination to the National Register of
Historic Places. Salem, OR.: 2003.

Kanipe, Leah. "Settlement Began in Early Forties," manuscript loaned to Douglas County Museum by Mrs. Homer Trusty, January 1975, n.d.

Kanipe, Mildred. Diary. Douglas County Museum.

Kniffen, Fred. "Folk Housing: Key to Diffusion," *Annals of the Association of American Geographers*, Vol. 55, No. 4 (December 1965), pp. 549-577.

Minter, Harold Avery Minter. *Umpqua Valley Oregon and its Pioneers.* Portland, Oregon: Binfords & Mort, Publishers, 1967.

Moulton, Larry. "Douglas County Schools: A History Outline." Oakland, OR.: self published, nd.

Oregon State Archives, Oregon Historical County Records Guide, "Douglas County History." http://arcweb.sos.state.or.us/county/cpdouglashome.html. Accessed July 2007

Oregon Genealogical Forum. "Genealogical Material from Oregon Donation Land Claims." Portland, Oregon: Genealogical Forum(?), 1957. http://www.ancestry.com. Accessed July 2007.

Oregon State Historic Preservation Office. Statewide Inventory of Historic Sites and Buildings.

Powers, James W. *Frontier Days: The Life of Winslow Powers and the Early Settlement of Eastern Oregon.* Wallowa, Oregon: Bear Creek Press, 2004.

Quinn, John M. and Terrence J. Parker. "Oakland Historic District," National Register Nomination Form, on file at the Oregon State Historic Preservation Office, 1978.

Speulda, Lou Ann. *Oregon's Agricultural Development: A Historic Context 1811-1940.* Salem, Oregon: Oregon State Historic Preservation Office, 1989.

Sutherlin Sun Tribune, (Oregon) 7 October 1976.

United States Census records, 1850-1950. http://www.ancestry.com. Accessed July 2007.

Thomas Vaughan, editor. *Space Style and Structure: Building in Northwest America*. Portland, Oregon: Oregon Historical Society, 1974.

Walling, Albert G. *History of Southern Oregon, comprising Jackson, Josephine, Douglas, Curry and Coos countries, comp. from the most authentic sources.* Portland, Oregon: A.G. Walling, 1884.

Winterbotham, Jerry. *Umpqua, The Lost County of Oregon.* Brownsville, OR.: Creative Images Printing, 1994.

NPS Form 10-900-a

        OMB Approval No. 1024-0018

United States Department of the Interior
National Park Service

National Register of Historic Places Continuation Sheet

Section number   <u>10</u>   Page   <u>1</u>

Verbal Boundary Description:

The proposed property, located at T 24S R 04W, Sec 19 includes the southeast corner of tax lot 4460.01, with the boundary measuring 208.7 feet from the east and south lot lines.

Boundary Justification:

Lacking easily defined legal or geographic boundaries, the proposed boundary has been drawn to include the subject resource, heritage foundation plantings, and one acre of lightly-treed pasture and camas-flower prairie in order to preserve the building's original immediate setting.

THE BAIMBRIDGE-KANIPE FARMSTEAD

Tax Lot 200 14.21 Acres plus Tax Lot 500 4.40 Acres = 18.61 total Acres

MILDRED KANIPE MEMORIAL PARK

16513 Elkhead Rd., Oakland, Douglas County, Oregon

This land was originally settled by the Yoncalla tribe, the southernmost band of the Kalapuya Indians. In 1853 it was part of a Donation Land Claim acquired by Joseph Deardorff. He sold his claim of 327 acres to neighbor Winslow Powers in 1859 who in 1872 rented both claims to Thomas and Emily Baimbridge and several years later sold the then 647 acre ranch to them. They were Mildred Kanipe's maternal grandparents. This property was in the family until Mildred passed away in 1983 and left her total almost 1,100 acre ranch to Douglas County for a park. Milred had purchased 167 acres in 1930 and inherited just over 290 acres, which included this site, when her father died in 1940. She then purchased the Underwood ranch of 633 acres which tied the other two parcels together.

In February of 2007, the Friends of Mildred Kanipe Park applied for this historic site to be included on the National Registry of Historic Places. This was approved in October, 2007

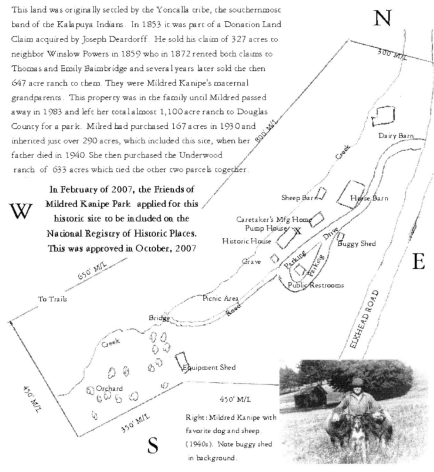

Right: Mildred Kanipe with favorite dog and sheep. (1940s). Note buggy shed in background.

Farmstead site sketch

BAIMBRIDGE-KANIPE FARMSTEAD NATIONAL HISTORIC DISTRICT
Placed on the National Register of Historic Places January 29, 2008

HOUSE

When John Kanipe passed away in 1940, Mildred Kanipe inherited this part of the land. She already had 167 acres she had purchased ten years before but the two were not connected, so she

DAIRY BARN

It is estimated that the first part of this house was built about 1865 by Winslow Powers. The kitchen addition (shorter roof on right) was added by Thomas Baimbridge, Mildred Kanipe's grandfather, after he rented the ranch from Powers in 1872 and then purchased it.

Sarah Baimbridge, Mildred Kanipe's mother, was born in the house in 1876. After she married John Kanipe, they had Leah, born in 1905, and Mildred, born in 1907. Both were born in this house.

The house was never significantly remodeled. It never had a bathroom, and water and electricity were added when the house was about 100 years old.

ran a dairy for eight years in this building and used the money earned to buy the 633 acre Underwood farm which connected the two parcels. She then owned the almost 1,100 acres that make up the present park land.

SHEEP BARN

The Sheep Barn was built in 1935 by Mildred's brother-in-law Romie Howard. Sheep were always an important part of the ranch.

HORSE BARN

The buggy shed was turned at one time. Early photos show it facing east-west and leaning. Look at the back side. You can see slanted boards.

BUGGY SHED

John Kanipe, Mildred Kanipe's father, raised percheron horses and sold them as trained teams. Note beautiful tie stalls in this barn.

When Mildred and Leah were children they rode their pony, Pete, back and forth in the side shed of the barn in rainy weather.

EQUIPMENT SHED

Farmstead buildings

S

Baimbridge-Kanipe Farmstead
ORCHARD
Douglas County, Oregon

From Mildred Kanipe's notes
found at the Douglas County
Museum. Many of the trees
are gone in 2007. Numbered
trees remain.
(Does not include trees on
west side of creek)

E

W

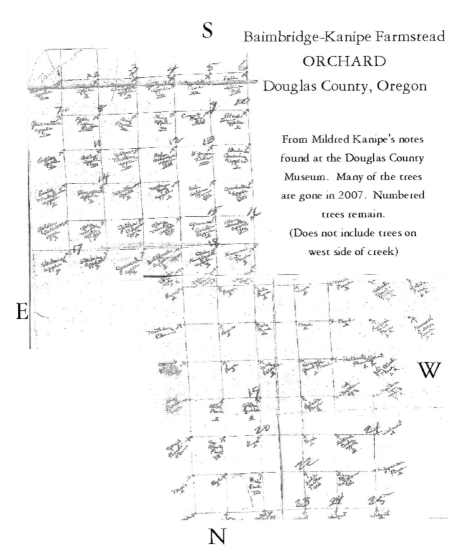

N

Farmstead orchard

151

Baimbridge-Kanipe Farmstead

ORCHARD

Douglas County, Oregon

The following are the varieties of fruit and nut trees that Mildred Kanipe identified on a map she drew of the orchard. Of the 82 trees she listed, only 25 remain. All of the many peaches are gone, but they are short lived trees so that is not surprising. It is also possible that some of the trees were planned and never planted. The varieties she listed may or may not be correct. One pear tree was listed as an "apple", and a pear tree she listed as a "Golden Jubilee" appears to be a local wild pear. Observation when the trees remaining bear fruit will help to verify accuracy of the identification.

The descriptions below were obtained from *"A" is for antique apples* by Patricia B. Mitchell and David L. Mitchell found on the Internet at *http:www.foodhistory.com/foodnotes/leftovers/antiqueapples.htm*.

The article begins, "In 1972 James Beard wrote that 'a number of the old-fashioned varieties (of apples) we used to know are in short supply or have disappeared entirely.....The great Gravensteins and Spitzenbergs seem to have vanished' "

Both of these varieties are represented in this orchard and Spitzenbergs are readily available today from some nurseries.

1. TRANSPARENT apple: (AKA Yellow Transparent, Early Transparent, Russian Transparent). Transparent apples are medium in size, with fragrant, juicy, firm, tender, crisp flesh. Satisfactory eaten out of hand, they make marvelous pies, applesauce and apple butter and are first-rate fried. Our ancestors particularly appreciated Transparents because, being early summer apples, they provided the

152

first fresh fruit in many months, and are also disease resistant. The variety originated in Russia, and was introduced in 1870.

2. BALDWIN apple: (AKA Butters, Woodpecker). The Baldwin is a medium to large yellowish or greenish apple mottled with red, and a slightly tart taste; the flesh is crisp, firm, rather tender, and juicy. It is good for dessert and cooking. It ripens in autumn. The seedling originated in Lowell, Massachusetts, around 1740. By 1852, it had become the most widely planted apple in the U.S. until the late 1920's.

3. SUMMER CHAMPION apple

4. SPITZENBURG apple: (AKA Esopus Spitzenburg, Esopus Spitsenberg, Esopus Spitzenburgh, True Spitzenburg) A medium to large, orangey-red, oblong fruit that is crisp, firm, juicy, somewhat tender, sweet, and spicy, perfect to eat out of hand (and also wonderful cooked). The flavor is akin to pineapple, the fragrance is, when cut, like cinnamon. It was the favorite apple of Thomas Jefferson. This fall variety originated in New York. (Some think that this apple is EXTINCT!)

5. BARTLETT pear

6. FALL PIPPIN apple, (AKA Autumn Pippin, Cathead, Cobbett's Fall, Cobbett's Fall Pippin, Concombre Ancien, Holland Pippin, Pound Pippin) This large yellow winter apple is enjoyable eaten raw or used in cooking. It has been confused with the Holland Pippin, but ripens later and is of better quality.

7. GRAVENSTEIN apple: (AKA Early Congress, Gravensteiner) Gravenstein was brought from Germany in 1790, though it originated in Italy in the 1600's. This all-purpose apple is crisp, juicy, and tart, superb both for cooking and eating fresh. The medium to large fruit is predominately yellow with areas of green and red. In spite of James Beard's comment of despair over the loss of Gravensteins, it is reported that "some still survive as orchards in Northern California". And, here is one in Douglas County, Oregon.

8. FALL PIPPIN apple, (AKA Autumn Pippin, Cathead, Cobbett's Fall, Cobbett's Fall Pippin, Concombre Ancien, Holland Pippin,

Pound Pippin) This large yellow winter apple is enjoyable eaten raw or used in cooking. It has been confused with the Holland Pippin, but ripens later and is of better quality.

9. CANUT PEAR

10. **BLACK BEN** apple, (AKA Black Ben Davis, Gano) This late-ripening, medium-to-large fruit is juicy, firm, and moderately crisp. It is said to have originated around 1800 on the Washington County, Arkansas, farm of a Mr. Black.

11. **ORTLEY** apple: (AKA Detroit, Golden Pippin, Greasy Pippin, Warren Pippin, White Bellflower, White Detroit, Woolman's Long Pippin, Yellow Pippin) this medium-size conical, light-green-yellow variety ripens in late fall. It was introduced in 1825, originating in New Jersey.

12. **PEAR** (list says "apple")

13. **D'ANJOU** pear

14. **STAYMAN** apple (AKA Stayman Winesap)
Firm apples with a complex sweet-tart flavor, prized for cooking, eating, and storing. Their primary color is deep crimson, with touches of green. They are fall apples. They began as a seedling of Winesap; originated in Kansas; and were introduced in 1866.

15. **GRIMES GOLDEN** apple, (AKA Bellflower (in Arkansas). Grimes Golden Pippin). A man in what is now Brook County, West Virginia, found the first Grimes Golden growing wild there sometime before 1800. The yellow-gold, medium-sized apples are crisp and juicy with a spicy taste. They are excellent eaten fresh, tops for cider, frying, and baking, and smell good, too. Coriander-scented.

16. **GLORIA MUNDI** apple

17. **STARKING** apple

18. **KING DAVID** apple: This tree was first found in Washington County, Arkansas, in 1893. The medium-size apple has light green coloring overshadowed by a bold dark red. Its tangy flavor resembles

that of a Winesap, and it is firm, crisp, and juicy. Excellent all-purpose apple.

19. PEAR (Looks like wild pear. List says "Golden Jubilee)

20. ITALIAN prune

21. ENGLISH walnut

22. SEEK-NO-FURTHER apple: (AKA Rambo, Cooper, and Scribner) Introduced in America ca. 1640 by Swedish settler Peter Gunnarsson Rambo. This apple was later known as Johnny Appleseed's (John Chapman's) favorite apple.

23, 24, 25. ENGLISH walnut

NPS Form 10-900
OMB No. 10024-0018
(Oct.1990)
United States Department of the Interior

National Park Service

National Register of Historic Places Registration Form

This form is for use in nominating or requesting determinations for individual properties and districts. See instruction in How to Complete the National Register of Historic Places Registration Form (National Register Bulletin 16A). Complete each item by marking "x" in the appropriate box or by entering the information requested. If an item does not apply to the property being documented, enter "N/A" for "not applicable." For functions, architectural classifications, materials and areas of significance, enter only categories and subcategories from the instructions. Place additional entries and narrative items on continuation sheets (NPS Form 10-900a). Use a typewriter, word processor, or computer, to complete all items.

1. Name of Property

historic name **Baimbridge-Kanipe Farmstead Historic District**

other names/site number _____

2. Location

street & number **16513 Elkhead Rd.** _____ not for publication

city or town **Oakland** _____ vicinity

state Oregon   code OR

county Douglas   code   019   zip code 97462

---

3. State/Federal Agency Certification

As the designated authority under the National Historic Preservation Act, as amended, I hereby certify that this ____ X___ nomination _____ request for determination of eligibility meets the documentation standards for registering properties in the National Register of Historic Places and meets the procedural and professional requirements set forth in 36 CFR Part 60. In my opinion, the property _X_ meets _____ does not meet the National Register criteria. I recommend that this property be considered significant _____ nationally _____ statewide _X_ locally.

Signature of certifying official/Title - Deputy SHPO
           Date

Oregon State Historic Preservation Office

State or Federal agency and bureau

---

4. National Park Service Certification

I hereby certify that the property is: Signature
    of the Keeper   Date of Action

____ entered in the National Register

_____ See continuation sheet. _____

_____ determined eligible for the National Register   _____

_____ See continuation sheet. _____

_____ determined not eligible for the National Register   _____

_____ removed from the National Register _____

_____ other (explain):   _____

OMB No. 10024-0018

Baimbridge-Kanipe Farmstead
Douglas Co., OR

Name of Property

County and State

5. Classification

Ownership of Property   Category of Property

Number of Resources within Property

(check as many as apply)   (check only one box)

(Do not include previously listed resources in the count)

_____ private   _____ building(s)

Contributing Noncontributing

__X__ public - local   __X__ district

____6____   ____3____ buildings

_____ public - state   _____ site

____1____   ____2____ sites

_____ public - Federal   _____ structure

__1__   ____2____ structures

_____ object

_____ objects

8 _____ 7_____ Total

Name of related multiple property listing
Number of contributing resources previously
(enter "N/A" if property is not part of a multiple property listing)
listed in the National Register

_N/A_____
None_____

_____
_____

6. Function or Use
_____

Historic Functions
Current Functions
(enter categories from instructions)
(Enter categories from instructions)

_DOMESTIC: single dwelling_____
_VACANT/NOT IN USE_____
_AGRICULTURE/SUBSISTANCE:_____
_AGRICULTURE/SUBSISTANCE:_____
_____animal facility_____
_____animal facility_____
_____agricultural outbuilding_____
_____agricultural outbuilding_____
_____agricultural field_____
_____agricultural field_____
_____
_____
_____
_____

_____
_____

7. Description

Architectural Classification
Materials

(Enter categories from instructions)
(Enter categories from instructions)

NO STYLE
foundation: STONE

walls: WOOD: droplap and board and

batten

roof: METAL

Other:

Narrative Description
(Describe the historic and current condition of the property on one or more continuation sheets)

OMB No. 10024-0018

8. Statement of Significance

Applicable National Register Criteria
Areas of Significance
(Mark "x" in one or more boxes for the criteria qualifying the property
(Enter categories from instructions)
for National Register listing).

AGRICULTURE
  _X_ A Property is associated with events that have
 SETTLEMENT
             made a significant contribution to the broad

             patterns of our history.

_____ B Property is associated with the lives of persons

             significant in our past.

_____C Property embodies the distinctive characteristics

             of a type, period, or method of construction or
Period of Significance
             represents the work of a master, or possesses
 c. 1865-1957
             high artistic values, or represents a significant and

             distinguishable entity whose components lack

_____

individual distinction.

_____ D Property has yielded, or is likely to yield,
Significant Dates
          information important in prehistory or history.
   _None_____

_____

_____

Criteria Considerations
(Mark "x" in all the boxes that apply)

Property is:
Significant Person

(Complete if Criterion B is marked above)
_____ A owned by a religious institution or used for
_None_____
          religious purposes

_____ B removed from its original location
Cultural Affiliation

_____ C a birthplace or grave
      _None_____

_____

_____ D a cemetery

_____

_____ E a reconstructed building, object, or structure

Architect/Builder
_____ F a commemorative property
_Unknown_____

_____

_____ G less than 50 years of age or achieved
significance   _____

Within the past 50 years

Narrative Statement of Significance
(Explain the significance of the property on one or more continuation sheets)

9. Major Bibliographical References

Bibliography (Cite books, articles, and other sources used in preparing the form on one or more continuation sheets) See continuation sheets

Previous documentation on file (NPS):

additional data:

___ preliminary determination of individual listing (36CFR67)

Historic Preservation Office

      has been requested

State agency, OR State Library

___ previously listed in the National Register

Federal agency

___ previously determined eligible by the National Register

government

___ designated a National Historic Landmark

University, University of Oregon Library

___ recorded by Historic American Buildings Survey

___ recorded by Historic American Engineering Record

Primary location of

__X_ State

____ Other

____

__X_ Local

____

____ Other

Name of repository:

OMB No. 10024-0018

Baimbridge-Kanipe Farmstead
Douglas Co., OR

Name of Property

County and State

10. Geographical Data

Acreage of Property __18.61__

UTM References
(Place additional UTM references on a continuation sheet)

1	10	482225	4814444
3	10	482219	4814140
	Zone	Easting	Northing
	Zone	Easting	Northing

2	10	482314	4814426
4	10	481940	4814204

Verbal Boundary Description
(Describe the boundaries of the property on a continuation sheet)

Boundary Justification
(Explain why the boundaries were selected on a continuation sheet)

11. Form Prepared By

name/title __Lois Eagleton, Chair, Friends of Mildred Kanipe Memorial Park Association, Inc.; Liz Carter, Historic Preservation Consultant; Oregon SHPO Staff__

organization __Friends of Mildred Kanipe Memorial Park Association, Inc.__   date __March 1 2007__

street & number __PO Box 105__
telephone __(541) 459-9397__

city or town __Umpqua__
state __OR__   zip code __97486__

Additional Documentation

Submit the following items with the completed form:

Continuation sheets

Maps: A USGS map (7.5 or 15 minute series) indicating the property's location.
A sketch map for historic districts and properties having large acreage or numerous resources.

Photographs: Representative black and white photographs of the property.

Additional items (check with the SHPO or FPO for any additional items)

Property Owner

name Douglas County

street & number PO Box 800
telephone (541) 440 4500

city or town Winchester
state OR   zip code 97495

Paperwork Reduction Act Statement: This information is being collected for applications to the National Register of Historic Places to nominate properties for listing or determine eligibility for listing, to list properties, and to amend existing listings. Response to this request is required to obtain a benefit in accordance with the National Historic Preservation Act, as amended (16 U.S.C.460 et seq.).

Estimated Burden Statement: Public reporting burden for this form is estimated to average 18.1 hours per response including time for reviewing instructions, gathering and maintaining data, and completing and reviewing the form. Direct comments regarding this burden estimate or any aspect of this form to the Chief, Administrative Services Division, National Park Service, PO Box 37127, Washington, DC 20013-7127; and the Office of Management and Budget, Paperwork Reductions Project (1024-0018), Washington, DC 20503.

INTRODUCTION

The Baimbridge-Kanipe Farmstead is located at 16513 Elkhead Road, Oakland, Douglas County, Oregon, approximately eight miles northeast of the town of Oakland, and twenty miles north of the county seat of Roseburg. The farmstead is situated in an area of large farms called English Settlement, so named for the number of English emigrants to the area.

The almost 1,100 acre farm was left to Douglas County by its last and longtime owner, Mildred Knipe, on her death in 1983, on the stipulation that it be used as a public park; the farm is now known as the Mildred Kanipe Memorial Park. The nominated area consists of 18.61 acres (tax lots 200 and 500) and contains eight (8) contributing resources, including the house (circa 1865), two barns (pre-1900), a sheep shearing shed (circa 1935), a small buggy shed (pre-1900; repairs 1980s), an equipment shed (pre-1900), livestock chute (post-1930) and the historic orchard (no date). The nominated area includes all of these contributing resources and some of the farm fields surrounding the group.

There are seven (7) non-contributing resources, including a manufactured home (caretaker's residence) and wood shed (1987), the paved parking lot (1980s), new public restroom facilities (1988), a newer wooden footbridge, and Mildred Kanipe's grave (1983). A railroad flatcar auto bridge was installed in 2007.

The period of significance for the group is circa 1865-1957, which corresponds to the approximate construction date of the house through the end of the fifty-year age guideline for listing of properties on the National Register. The farm is eligible for listing in the National Register under criterion A for association with the settlement and agricultural development of the Oakland area.

SETTING

The Baimbridge-Kanipe Farmstead is located in northern Douglas County in a region of rolling hills traversed by several streams that drain into the Umpqua River. Several miles northeast of the community of Oakland, this area was historically used as farmland, and it continues to function as an agricultural community. In 1884, A.G. Walling described the English Settlement area as

A tract of land six miles long by two wide [that] lies eight miles north of Oakland, and is called English Settlement because of the nationality of its first occupants. Three creeks, Oldham, Bachelor and Pollack, traverse it, the land along the streams being level, while that between is rolling prairie. The best of grain, fruit and vegetables are produced, and the valley is stocked with fine breeds of cattle, horses, sheep, and swine.[48]

Most of the farms remain in pasture or hay fields, grazing cattle and/or sheep. The Baimbridge-Kanipe Farmstead buildings are situated on the west side of Elkhead Road, in a north-south draw just east of an unnamed tributary to Bachelor Creek. The creek, until recent years, flowed year round and teemed with fish, mainly cutthroat trout. The creek now runs dry during the summer months after the headwaters were logged. Trees line the creek, and from the farm group the land opens into grass fields to the south.

The buildings of the multi-unit farm complex arranged in a linear fashion along the creek, utilizing the available level space in the flood plain; the outbuildings string out to the north and east from the house. The current paved drive off of Elkhead Road, winding down between the horse barn and carriage house follows the original dirt or gravel lane to the house; the lane continues beyond the current parking lot, across the creek to the land beyond. The landscape in the immediate vicinity of the farm group consists of expanses of grass and trees, with little formal landscaping. Foundation plantings around the house include some annual and perennial plants, roses and other ornamental plants around the historic house and the caretaker's residence. Of particular note are five mature cedar trees planted around the farmhouse: two pairs located off the southeast and southwest corners of the building at ten-foot intervals, and another by the porch at the east elevation.[49] Mildred Kanipe's grave is located south of the house and is surrounded by a picket fence.

Review of aerial photographs from 1939 through 1982 indicate that the landscape of the nominated area remained virtually unchanged during that period. Circulation and land-use patterns, vegetation and building arrangements established by previous generations remained intact throughout Mildred Kanipe's ownership of the farm. (Figures 1 – 4)

Intrusions on the historic setting are primarily associated with the conversion of the site from working farm to public county park. The placement of the Caretaker's residence between the house and the horse barn encroaches on the historic landscape visually and physically. The grading and paving of the historic lane and the creation of a paved parking lot encircling a public restroom facility intrudes on the visual and physical integrity of the open meadow immediately outside the front door of the house. Other small changes on the landscape

---

48) A.G. Walling, History of Southern Oregon..., (Portland, Oregon: A.G. Walling 1884), 441.
49) These trees were reportedly taken from nearby Ben Moore Mountain and transplanted by Thomas Baimbridge sometime before the turn of the century.

– addition of picnic tables, new flat span foot- and auto-bridges, and an irrigation pond located outside of the nominated area - do not negatively impact the physical or historic integrity of the setting, feeling or design of the farm group.

HOUSE DESCRIPTION

House Exterior

The Baimbridge-Kanipe house is a good example of the type of vernacular buildings that were constructed during the settlement era in rural Oregon. The one-and-a-half story house is irregular in plan and sits on a stone pier and hewn beam and log foundation. The building was constructed in phases with a hewn frame and vertical and horizontal plank walls. The main volume of the house measures approximately 25 foot by 44 foot, and appears to have been the first phase of construction. This was followed by the smaller kitchen addition to the north. (Photos 2 and 4) Exact dates of construction for the house, kitchen addition and woodshed have not been definitively established, but appear to fall in the range of circa 1865-1880. (Photos 18 and 19)

The house displays a variety of sidings, including vertical board and batten (west elevation and northernmost addition), horizontal droplap siding (south and east elevations) and flush horizontal boards (east side kitchen wall and east addition). The original siding appears to have been board-and-batten (as seen on the east elevation), given the condition of the siding and the depth of the window trim reveal. (Photo 1 through 5) At some point the battens on the south and east elevations were removed and a secondary layer of horizontal drop-lap was applied.

Fenestration is irregular, and the primary window type is six-over-six double hung wood sash with simple flat board surrounds. There are three exterior doors – two on the front porch and one from the kitchen - and a fourth that now opens onto an unfinished addition on the east elevation. (See floorplan) The side-gable roof has approximately 18 inch eaves with exposed rafters and purlins, and is covered in corrugated sheet metal roofing over older wood shingles and wide waney-edge skip-sheathing. The house has one fireplace and three flues.

Decorative features include a wide frieze board on all elevations of the original portion of the house and simple flat board door and window surrounds. Stylistic categorization of the house is difficult; from the exterior it exhibits no clear leaning toward either the Classical Revival or the Gothic Revival styles that were sometimes employed during the early years of Oregon settlement.

The front, or east elevation of the house is marked by a recessed corner porch supported by a newer four-by-four post which replaces the original hewn post. (Photo 3) A section of the smooth-sawn porch ceiling boards is patched, which may indicate the location of a former stair or ladder providing access to the attic space. Within the porch are contained two entrance doors - both with paired vertical recessed panels - one opening into the living room and the other into the dining room, which likely served as the kitchen prior to the construction of the kitchen addition. The kitchen door is a four-panel wood door that has been altered to accommodate a half-light. Windows are six-over-six double hung wood sash, many with original or very early glass. Siding consists of horizontal drop-lap (main house), horizontal board (kitchen) and newer board-and-batten (northernmost addition).

The north elevation is dominated by the kitchen, a storage room addition to the north of the kitchen, and an open wood shed; according to family recollections, the storage room and woodshed were constructed prior to 1920.[50] Due to the setback of the kitchen section, a portion of the gable end of the original house is visible, displaying the wide frieze/bargeboard and a partially obstructed six-over-six window. Siding is secondary drop-lap.

The west elevation has board-and-batten siding; windows are six-over-six double hung wood sash, with a smaller fixed four-pane window in the pantry, adjacent to the kitchen. Near the center of this elevation is a 1960s addition that was reportedly to be made into a bathroom, but was never completed (the house currently has no indoor bathroom facility). The addition is set on a pier block foundation, clad in horizontal board siding and has no windows.

The south elevation displays the gable roof with wide frieze/bargeboard detail. Siding is secondary horizontal drop-lap, and there is a six-over-six double hung window in the living room and the attic. The fireplace box, constructed of stone and repaired with red brick, is exposed on this elevation, though the red brick chimney stack itself is on the interior, piercing the roof just east of the ridge.

House Interior

The older portion of the house consists of three rooms divided by single-wall construction: a living room with fireplace, a small bedroom to the west, and a dining room to the north. The dining room likely served as the kitchen prior to the construction of the kitchen addition. The kitchen addition, attached to the north wall of the main house, consists of one room from which there is access to the root cellar (under the main house) and attic sleeping rooms. There is a small pantry on the north wall of the kitchen. The woodshed is attached to the north end of the kitchen, with access from the exterior of the building. There are exterior doors from the living room, dining room and kitchen. (Figures 5 and 6)

The living room has a secondary narrow-width fir floor that is severely buckled due to

50) John Howard to Lois Eagleton, personal communication, August 2007. John Howard is Mildred Kanipe's nephew (her sister Leah's son), and was born in 1930.

foundation settling. Original flooring was probably wider. The walls are hewn frame clad on the interior with varying width (approximately 12 to 20 inches) rough sash-sawn boards set vertically, and covered with muslin and wallpaper. There are no baseboards. Window and door surrounds are simple flat boards with no molding. On the center of the south wall is a fireplace flanked by a closet and cupboard on one side, and a six-over-six window on the other. (Photo 6) The fireplace and storage design and detailing is typical of those found in settlement-era houses of the 1840s through about 1865, which often displayed Classical Revival stylistic tendencies. The hearth, firebox walls and firebox lintel are stone, and the back of the firebox is brick. The wood surround and mantel display simple but elegant pilaster and molding designs reminiscent of those found in builder's guides of the period. The wall above the fireplace is finished with vertical painted wood board-and-batten paneling – probably a later application - which was subsequently covered with wallpaper. The ceilings are smooth-sawn, tightly fitted painted boards that were also later covered with wallpaper.

A small bedroom to the west of the living room is similarly finished. The partition wall separating the living room from this bedroom is about one inch thick.

The dining room has a narrow-width fir floor, laid perpendicularly to that in the living room. Walls are finished in either varying width smooth-sawn painted vertical boards or vertical board-and-batten paneling. The ceiling consists of smooth-sawn, tightly fitted painted boards. In the southeast corner is a paint shadow indicating the former location of a large cabinet, possibly the one that is now in the kitchen. On the west wall is a six-over-one window and a raised panel door with two vertical panels. Based on the patch pattern around the window, it appears that this was original the location of an exterior door. The doorway into the kitchen is framed with a slightly peaked door head, and includes a four-panel door with a wide lock rail.

To the north of the dining room is the kitchen addition. (Photo 7 and 8) The hewn-frame is covered with horizontal planks of regular dimensions, or horizontal board-and-batten paneling, either painted or displaying remnants of wallpaper or linoleum. The kitchen floor displays wider plank fir floors, and very wide base- or mop-boards. The ceiling is clad in painted drop-lap siding similar to the secondary siding on the exterior of the building.

A flue indicates the former location of the stove on the west wall. A tall wood cabinet, which may have originally been in the dining room, is now in the kitchen, and may be original to the house. A circa 1960s counter, sink with running water, cabinets and built-in ironing board are the newest additions to the kitchen. The wood doors have four recessed panels and rimlocks (or shadow lines of rimlocks) and windows are six-over-six double hung. Surrounds are flat wood boards with either flat or slightly peaked door and window heads.

Access to the root cellar and the attic are provided through the kitchen, which also has an exterior door to the east and a doorway into the pantry on the north.

Wooden stairs provide access down to the root cellar, which is constructed of dirt only, and is partially collapsed. The attic is reached via a narrow wooden staircase, which leads to a small landing. The partially blocked window on the north wall of the original house is visible from the staircase. Several steps up from the landing is the larger attic sleeping area in the attic of the original house, which is lit by a six-over-six window in the south wall. (Photo 9) The smaller area over the kitchen was originally lit by the window in the south gable end, which was later covered by the woodshed addition. The upstairs is completely unfinished. The hand-hewn plates with mortis-and-tenon joinery held with large wooden pegs are visible. The roof structure consists of a combination of poles and rough-sawn rafters covered with waney-edge wide-board skip-sheathing.

Alterations

The house retains a high degree of historical integrity, in spite of its poor physical condition. Exterior alterations to the original house include the addition of the kitchen, the north woodshed addition, addition of an exterior stove chimney in the living room (unknown date), a rear unfinished addition (unknown date), corrugated metal roofing (1980s), and application of secondary droplap siding (unknown date). Interior alterations include application of board-and-batten paneling (post-1878), installation of electricity (date unknown), a kitchen counter and sink with running water (c. 1960), and a built-in ironing board (c. 1960). None of these changes significantly affect the building's historic integrity.

CONTRIBUTING FARM BUILDINGS

Dates for most of the outbuildings are elusive, and many are based on materials and structural analysis of each building. All of the subject buildings appear on aerial photographs in 1939, the earliest air photos available for this area.

Buggy Shed

The gable roofed buggy shed measures 12 foot by 20 foot with two 4-foot wagon doors in each gable end for "drive through" ease of parking. (Photo 10 and 20) This building was the subject of a major renovation by the Douglas County Park department in 2001. Work included rebuilding the entire structural system and then re-installing the historic board and batten siding and doors on the new frame. The roof rafters metal roof are also new. These changes have not sufficiently compromised the building's integrity to warrant categorization as a non-contributing resource. Individually, the building retains integrity of location, setting, association, feeling, design and much of the original material. Perhaps more importantly the buggy shed contributes to the overall sense of completeness of the farm group as a whole, and its removal or a less sensitive rehabilitation would negatively impact the physical and historic integrity of the farmstead. Historic photos show that the building's orientation was changed from an east-west orientation to a north-south orientation at an unknown time. (Photo 20)

Horse Barn

The Horse Barn is the largest building in this grouping. It has a medium-pitched asymmetrical gable roof oriented north-south, and measures 76 feet by 54 feet. (Photos 11, 12, and historic photo 21, Figures 7 and 10) Built on stone foundation piers, the hand-hewn frame has mortise-and-tenon joinery with wood pegs. It appears to have been constructed as a transverse plan with six bays, the two central bays being slightly narrower; the floor consists of heavy wood planks. The northern and southern ends of the barn interior contain several stalls with narrow hay lofts above. The central section, which may have originally been used as a threshing floor, now combines open space with grain/feed binds, and is covered with a hay loft.

Dirt-floored sheds run longitudinally along the east and west sides of the barn. The building is clad in wide1 inch by 8 inch circular-sawn planks set vertically. The barn contains a mixture of wooden pegs, hand wrought nails, square machine made and wire nails. There is one remaining wrought gate hinge remaining on one of the posts.

The construction date of the barn is unclear. The interior framing configuration and a circa 1930 historic photograph showing the barn with a lower roof pitch both suggest a construction date prior to 1900, possibly as early as the 1860s.[51] (Photo 21 and Figure 10) Alterations to the barn include complete replacement of the roof, including rafters. Based on analysis of aerial photographs and the building itself, it appears that the east side shed was added sometime between 1939 and the mid-1950s; it is likely that the roof pitch was also changed at this time.[52] Throughout the building various deteriorated hewn frame members have been replaced or have newer members married to them. The original floor plan configuration is difficult to discern due to changes made over time to accommodate a diversity of uses. The barn is currently being used as a shop and storage by the property caretaker; the south end stalls are being developed as a ranch museum display.

---

51) Referring to the categories listed in Mary Gallagher's work on Linn County (Oregon) Barns (Table 4: Distinctive Characteristics of Linn County Barns 1850-1945, pp 38-40), the Baimbridge-Kanipe horse barn retains many characteristics that place it in the 1850-1899 time bracket. In addition, the 1870s Thomas Baimbridge diary alludes to farm activities that would require a barn on the property, though specific discussion of the barn design is not included.
52) A 1938 aerial photograph seems to show the barn with an asymmetrical roofline, the longer slope being the west slope. By 1952 the roof appears to have been altered, and the alignment of the drive from Elkhead Road appears to have been altered slightly to accommodate the wider barn.

The changes to the horse barn occurred within the historic period, and reflect continued but changing uses on the farm. These alterations do not detract from the significance of the barn or from the overall integrity of the farm group.

Sheep Shearing Shed

The Sheep Shearing Shed was built circa 1935 by Romie Howard (Mildred Kanipe's brother-in-law), and is located approximately 25 to 30 feet west of the horse barn.[53] (Photo 13) The rectangular building measures 20 foot by 40 foot and was used for handling sheep when they were brought in for shearing. The shed sits on a wood post foundation, has sawn lumber framing and a gable roof which is covered with corrugated metal sheets. The exterior walls are clad in 12 inch rough-sawn vertical boards, with 24 to 36 inch opened screened section of the building in the upper section of the walls. There are sliding doors on the north and south ends of the building to facilitate the movement of animals through the building. The interior space has wood floors, and is divided into pens and work areas by low wood partitions. Local tradition holds that the building may also have been used as a chicken house at some time in its history.

Dairy Barn

The large Dairy Barn is the northernmost building in the farm group. The construction date is unknown, but is presumed to be pre-1900. The barn measures approximately 55 feet long by 49 feet wide. It has a medium double-pitch gable roof oriented east-west, with a hay hood on the east gable end; the north and south sidewall eaves are very low to the ground. (Photos 14, 15, historic photo 22, and Figure 8) The building is framed with a combination of rough hewn-log and pole framing, with some more finished hand-hewn elements and sits on a field stone foundation. Log post supports are visible on the exterior of the north elevation. The sash-sawn 1inch by 8 inch board siding is set vertically on the gable ends and the north elevation, and 12 inch boards are applied over vertical boards on the south elevation.

The barn has a longitudinal plan with a central dirt floor wagon drive flanked by a row of stalls with stanchions and deteriorated wood floors on one side, and stanchions, feed bins and storage space on the other.

The framing of the barn is very deteriorated, and many of the original structural components appear to be missing, as evidenced by notches and mortises with no corresponding pieces attached. The roof structure is newer, with sawn rafters and skip-sheathing covered with corrugated metal.

---

53) John Howard to Lois Eagleton, personal communication, August 2007.

Mildred Kanipe ran a dairy from about 1941-1948, and circa 1940 she built a 14' by 20' addition on the southwest corner of the barn for use as a milk room. This small addition has a post and stone pier foundation with a poured concrete floor. It is framed with dimensional lumber and has aluminum panels applied to the interior of the framing for ease of cleaning. The upper 12 to 24 inchs of the wall is screened for ventilation. Access to and from the barn is provided through a door at the end of the south aisle of the barn. Equipment in the milk room includes a chiller, metal sinks, a water heater and storage racks.

As with the horse barn, this building was altered during the historic period, and these changes also reflect evolving activities and needs on the farm. The changes do not detract from the significance of the individual building or negatively affect the overall integrity of the farmstead.

Equipment Shed

The Equipment Shed is located approximately 200 yards south of the house, away from the primary grouping. The shed measures approximately 60 feet long and 25 feet wide. The building is rectangular in plan, with structural framing consisting of rough hewn vertical posts, poles and dimensional lumber; the building has a gable roof. (Photo 16) The north and west walls are open, and the south and east walls are clad in random-width, circular-sawn vertical boards. The building currently houses an interpretive display of horse-drawn equipment that was used on the farm, and there is an associated fenced area to the north of the building that displays two farm machines. The date of construction of the equipment shed is not currently known, but it does appear on 1939 aerial photographs.

Orchard

The remnants of the historic orchard are located south and west of the farm buildings. (Photo 17) The orchard consists of a number of fruit trees arranged in rows aligned on a north-south axis. As planned and planted the orchard had approximately eighty-two trees, including apples, peaches, prunes and nut trees and spread on both sides of the creek.[54] Although a few trees remain on the west side of the creek, the plan of the orchard is most evident on the east side where several rows are still evident. Approximately 20 trees are extant; the age of the trees is not currently known. However, the orchard does appear in fragmented form on both sides of the creek in aerial photographs from 1939. By the 1950s some newer infill trees on the east side of the creek are clearly visible in air photos, and these – both older and infill - remain in place today.[55]

---

54) Orchard Map, Personal Papers of Mildred Kanipe, Douglas County Historical Society, nd. Map does not indicate when trees were planted or who planted them.
55) Aerial photographs 1939-1982, University of Oregon Knight Library, Aerial Photography Collection.

Lost and Non-contributing Resources

At least one outbuilding has been lost due to deterioration. The Rabbit Shed was located north of the Sheep Shed, and the outline of its location is still visible. An outbuilding (perhaps an outhouse) is visible near the house in historic photographs, but is now gone. All historic wooden fencing around the house and outbuildings has also been removed.

Non-contributing features on the property are largely related to the County's ownership and operation of the property as a public park. These resources include the caretaker's house and pump house, the parking lot, the public restroom facility, a large irrigation pond, and two bridges across the creek.

FUTURE PLANS

The Douglas County Parks Department in cooperation with the Friends of Mildred Kanipe Memorial Park Inc. are currently assessing the needs of the property in order to take steps to stabilize the buildings. The intention is to further develop the park as an outdoor museum. Currently, interpretive panel displays are placed around the park and in several building describing the history of the property, and the equipment shed houses a collection of historic horse-drawn farm implements.

INTRODUCTION

The Baimbridge-Kanipe Farmstead is locally significant under National Register criterion A for its association with the settlement and agricultural development of Douglas County. With initial development starting in the 1850s, the farm was in continuous active agricultural use until 1983 when it was deeded to Douglas County for use as a public park by the last owner, Mildred Kanipe. The period of significance for the farm group is circa 1865-1957, which corresponds to the probable construction date of the current house to the fifty year mark, and includes all of the historic resources in the farm group. These resources include the house, horse barn, dairy barn, sheep shearing shed, carriage house, implement shed, livestock chute, historic orchard and circulation patterns. These features collectively represent a timeline of the history and variety of agricultural activity on the site over a period of over one-hundred years.

The Baimbridge-Kanipe Farmstead retains a high degree of integrity of location, materials, design, feeling and association as evaluated within its defined period of significance. The site's integrity of setting is largely intact, though it has been compromised by the siting of a manufactured home between the house and the horse barn, and by nearby park improvements including construction of restroom facilities and the creation of a circular paved drive and parking lot. Within the period of significance, integrity of workmanship is largely intact; many of the outbuildings were altered over time (within the period of significance) as needed to allow for continued farm uses. Many of the buildings have been re-roofed with metal roofing. (See Figures 1-4)

The house is virtually intact, and remained without electricity or running water until the 1960s. The horse barn roof was altered sometime after 1930 to its current configuration, but does not appear to have been altered since. The dairy barn was most recently altered circa 1940, and has not sustained any obvious alterations since. Other buildings or structures have been updated and repaired as necessary and as expected for working farm buildings. Historic landscape features include the orchard and circulation features (roads). The historic fencing and the rabbit hutch seen in historic photographs have been removed.

EARLY DOUGLAS COUNTY HISTORY

The Umpqua/Douglas County region was initially explored by members of the Northwest Company an others in the early 1800s, and McKay's Fort is generally accepted as having been the first non-native structure built in the region.[56] The Hudson's Bay Company (HBC) later established Fort Umpqua along the Umpqua River in 1836, and maintained this post as a trade center until the early 1850s, in spite of the fact that the British had ceded their interests in the region in the mid-1840s.

American settlement of the area now known as Douglas County began in the 1840s, encouraged by the Organic Act (1843) and the Donation Land Claim Act (1850), which initially granted up to 640 acres of land for a husband and wife who lived on and worked their claim for four years. Early settlement buildings throughout western Oregon included an initial log cabin, constructed quickly to provide shelter, usually followed by a barn, and later a hewn log or perhaps a sawn-lumber house. The construction of the barn often preceded that of the permanent frame house.[57]

In 1846 the Oregon-California Trail, a portion of which was also known as the Applegate Trail, was established by Levi Scott, Lindsay and Jesse Applegate and others. The wagon road extended from southern Oregon north through the Willamette Valley, and was inspired by the need for a route less treacherous than the Columbia River or the Barlow Road. With improved access to the region, settlement in Douglas County (initially known as Umpqua County) began in earnest. While some emigrants came directly to the Umpqua Valley area, many made initial claims in the Willamette Valley before selling and re-moving south into the northern portion of the county.

---

56) Terry R. Harbour and Stephen Dow Beckham, *Douglas County Cultural and Historic Resource Inventory* (1981-82), 2.
57) Under the Donation Land Claim Act of 1850 single men could obtain 320 acres, while single women were not eligible to receive land. Other conditions also applied.

The low-lands of the Willamette Valley were settled first, with later settlers forced to take up claims in the foothills or adjacent smaller valleys. Small communities grew around milling operations or commercial centers which served the needs of the new settlers. Enclaves of extended families, religious, or ethnic groups often gravitated in to neighborhood groupings. "More than half of Oregon's pioneers were accompanied by relatives or former neighbors and examples of clan migrations are numerous."[58]

Although not incorporated until decades later, communities such as Oakland, Wilbur, Winchester, and Drain formed as early as the 1840s, followed by Sutherlin, Yoncalla, Myrtle Creek, and Roseburg in the 1850s. The offer of "free" land and the discovery of gold led to a population surge, and Umpqua County was organized January 24, 1851.[59] "Douglas county, named after Stephen A. Douglas, was created January 7, 1852 out of that part of Umpqua county which lay east of the Coast Range. In 1864 the remainder of Umpqua county was joined to Douglas, and Umpqua ceased to be.[60] The county of Douglas as we know it today was established in 1915 after several debates and boundary changes.[61]

As the available land diminished, the Donation Land Claim Act was amended several times, and was eventually replaced by the Homestead Act of 1862 that gave settlers up to 160 acres of land. Federal subsidy of railroad companies through the 1866 Oregon and California Railroad Land Grant and other initiatives continued to encourage the establishment of prosperous farming communities throughout the County.

OAKLAND AND ENGLISH SETTLEMENT AREA

The community of Oakland is located in northern Douglas County about 20 miles north of Roseburg, along old Highway 99. Prior to the arrival of the early settlers, the area was occupied by the southernmost band of the Kalapuya Indians. Diseases brought by European and American explorers in the late-eighteenth and early- nineteenth centuries, and later skirmishes between the natives and the first settlers and trappers had already greatly reduced the native population by the 1850s. In 1855, treaties were negotiated with the remaining Kalapuya villages giving the land to the United States government. The Kalapuya were forcibly moved to the Grand Ronde reservation in Western Polk and Yamhill Counties in 1856.

A few early and short-lived residences in the Oakland area appeared in the 1840s, but

---

58) Lou Ann Speulda, *Oregon's Agricultural Development: A Historic Context 1811-1940*. (Salem, Oregon: Oregon State Historic Preservation Office, 1989), p. 7-8.
59) On January 7, 1852, the Territorial Legislature created Douglas County from the eastern part of Umpqua County. In 1853 Umpqua County lost its northern part to Lane County. Finally, in 1862, the remainder of Umpqua county was incorporated into Douglas County.
60) Hubert Howe Bancroft, *The Works of Hubert Howe Bancroft Volume XXX, History of Oregon Vol. II 1848-1888* (San Francisco: The History Company, Publishers, 1888), p. 711.
61) "Douglas County History," Oregon Historical County Records Guide, http://arcweb.sos.state.or.us/county/cpdouglashome.html, accessed July 2007.

more permanent settlers came in the early 1850s. One of the first was Dr. Dorsey S. Baker, who established a grist mill along Calapooya Creek in 1851. Reason Reed and L.H. Crow were other early land claimants in the vicinity. Soon a hotel, stores and a school were built. "Development of the town continued until 1872 when the Oregon and California Railroad bypassed the site. Aware of the potentials of drawing merchants and investors to a location on the rail route, A.F. Brown purchased several different land parcels, including the Donation Claims of L.H. Crow and Reason Reed, to lay out a 'new' Oakland."[62] Many of the original buildings of old Oakland were relocated to the new town site, and were joined by new buildings housing depots, warehouses, livery stables and numerous other business and industrial enterprises. As a result of this strategic move, Oakland developed into an important commercial shipping center for the rich farmlands that surrounded it.

> A wilderness settlement in the 1850s...Oakland grew slowly as a
> market and supply center for the area's farmers and ranchers. With
> its relocation in 1871-1872, planned and promoted by Alonzo Brown
> (whose home remains), more rapid growth occurred. By the time
> Oakland was incorporated as a city in 1878, several passenger trains
> stopped there each day... With new markets open to them, farmers
> diversified their plantings to such cash crops as barley and hops, and
> sheep, cattle, turkeys and other livestock were shipped to distant
> regions on Oakland's new avenue of trade. [63]

As a railroad town Oakland became, in the words of a turn-of-the-century reporter, a 'civilized community.' It served the varied needs of a broad area, providing goods from furniture to fencing, and services from those of the church to those 'of the evening.'[64]

Oakland was the terminus of the railroad for six months, and then it was put through to Roseburg in 1872, and finally completed on to the California border in 1887. By the 1880s Oakland was a prominent community in northern Douglas County, and continued to grow economically and agriculturally. Farmers " '...came from all around to Oakland to get their mail and do some trading. They nearly always had eggs and butter to trade for groceries. They didn't need much, as they had gardens, dairy products and fruit, and they took their grain to the grist mill to have the wheat made into flour and graham...' " [65] A large portion

---

62) Stephen Dow Beckham, *Land of the Umpqua: A History of Douglas County, Oregon* (Roseburg, Oregon: Douglas County Commissioners, 1986), p. 132.
63) Joseph M. Quinn and Terrence J. Parker, Oakland Historic District National Register Nomination Form (Oregon State Historic Preservation Office, 1978), Section 8.
64) Ibid.
65) Beckham, *Land of the Umpqua*, 134.

of the area's wealth came from sheep farming, and in "...1880 Douglas county shipped a million pounds of wool...and sold 27,000 head of sheep...."[66]

The town of Oakland was heavily damaged by a fire in 1899, an event that caused a stall in the community's development. Agricultural production did not seem to diminish, however. By 1907 the town served as a major distribution point for agricultural produce between Portland and San Francisco. In that year 175 carloads of livestock were shipped, with turkeys being one of the area's major crops. Other products such as grains, dried fruits, wool, venison and salmon were also shipped from Oakland.[67] By the 1930s Oakland was known for its turkey exports, and through the 1950s lumber was a thriving industry. Ranching, particularly sheep ranching, was and continues to be a major factor in the local economy.[68]

The English Settlement area is located several miles north and east of Oakland. It is not known when this name began to be attached to the region, but the English Settlement is named and described in Walling's 1884 *History of Southern Oregon* as "...a tract of land six miles long by two wide [that] lies eight miles north of Oakland, and is called English Settlement because of the nationality of its first occupants." Early settlers – of English extraction and others - included Sid Oldham, the Halls, Winslow Powers, and William Hanna, soon followed by the Deardorffs, James Smith, Elizabeth Johnson and others. Most arrivals to this area settled their claims between 1853 and 1854.[69]

The prime soils and rolling hills of the English Settlement area made it excellent farm and ranch land. Agricultural pursuits in the 1850s consisted of subsistence farming for the family's consumption, and small-scale wheat production. Stock raising soon followed as did crops (vegetable and grain) for sale at market. Sheep raising was popular and successful early on. Sheep were introduced in the Oregon Territory by the Hudson's Bay Company; starting in the mid-1840s settlers were also importing and began successfully breeding sheep in western Oregon.[70] By the arrival of the railroad in the 1870s the area's agricultural production potential had been clearly established. Although the English Settlement community never grew to a town, the residents did maintain their own continuously operating school district, from the 1860s until 1934.[71]

66) Hubert Howe Bancroft, *The Works of Hubert Howe Bancroft Volume XXX, History of Oregon Vol. II 1848-1888* (San Francisco: The History Company, Publishers, 1888), p. 711.
67) *Historic Douglas County, Oregon* 1982, 13; Harold Avery Minter, *Umpqua Valley Oregon and its Pioneers* (Portland: Binfords & Mort, Publishers, 1967), pp. 130 -132; Quinn and Parker, "Oakland Historic District," Section 8.
68) Quinn and Parker, "Oakland Historic District," Section 8.
69) "Genealogical Material from Oregon Donation Land Claims" (Portland, Oregon: Genealogical Forum (?), 1957), www.ancestry.com, accessed July 2007
70) Charles H. Carey, General History of Oregon (Portland, Oregon: Binfords & Mort Publishers, 1971), 684-687.
71) Larry Moulton, "Douglas County Schools: A History Outline,"(Oakland, Oregon, nd).

AGRICULTURE IN NORTHERN DOUGLAS COUNTY

While settlement agriculture in Oregon began with the arrival of Europeans and European-Americans in the 1830s, these activities were largely limited to the Willamette Valley, and were often short-lived due to the hardships of isolated living. Once the "problem" of land ownership in the Oregon Territory was resolved politically, settlement of the fledgling state began in earnest.

The richness of the alluvial soils of the Willamette, Umpqua and Rogue Rivers meant that early agricultural activity was primarily focused in the Willamette Valley and the Umpqua and Rogue Valleys of southwestern Oregon. Initially engaging in subsistence farming for survival, early settlers relied heavily on hunting and the foraging of wild food for much of their early sustenance. Cereal crops such as wheat, barley, oats and corn provided grain for flour, feed for livestock and currency for the purchase of additional seed or supplies.[72] Most harvesting in the mid-nineteenth century was done by hand labor; cutting, binding, threshing (or "thrashing") and fanning were all often accomplished without the use of machinery. Threshing floors were created either outside by pounding a selected piece of ground smooth and hard, or under cover by laying heavy planking in a section of the barn.[73]

Barns were among the earliest buildings to appear on the agrarian landscape. Although stock animals usually free-ranged, the use of the barn for feed, equipment storage and sometime-shelter for stock was critical to the survival and success of the emigrant families. Early barns served these multiple purposes until more specialized buildings such as equipment sheds, hay barns, chicken, sheep and dairy barns, fruit dryers and other building types were added to the farmstead. For the first years settlers were focused on establishing homes and communities on the frontier, more concerned with survival than profit.

The discovery of gold in California (and later in Oregon and regions northeast) created a market for agricultural goods (as well as lumber), and helped transform this subsistence agriculture into one of production for export. As grist- and sawmills appeared and transportation routes were established, much-needed supplies were shipped to the California mines. This in turn encouraged greater diversification in agricultural pursuits.

The Hudson's Bay Company had brought livestock to Fort Umpqua in the 1830s, and subsequent settlers increased both sheep and cattle herds, making stock raising a dominant undertaking in Douglas County. Again, mines both to the south and north provided ready markets for sheep, wool and cattle exports. Dairying as an industry first

---

72) Speulda, 6-10; Beckham, *Land of the Umpqua*, 208-209.
73) Beckham, *Land of the Umpqua*, 209; Philip Dole, "Farmhouses and Barns of the Willamette Valley," *Space, Style and Structure: Building in Northwest America*, Vol 1 (Portland, Oregon: Oregon Historical Society, 1974), 89-90; Mary Gallagher et al, *Historic Context: The Barns of Linn County, Oregon 1845-1945* (Albany, Oregon: Linn County Planning Department, 1997), pp. 9-10.

became lucrative in the northwestern Oregon counties, but individual farms commonly had dairy cows which provided products for family consumption and local sale of milk, cheese and butter. "Horse raising was tied to the production of farm work, oxen were favored into the 1850s, with draft horses, such as Clydesdales and Percherons more useful to pull the field machinery of the later periods."[74] Honey bees appeared in Oregon in 1850s. Seth Luelling was the first to successfully import grafted fruit trees to Oregon in 1847, and soon fruit was being grown in the Willamette, Umpqua and Rogue River valleys and sold in both local and California markets.[75] Prunes and apples were dominant orchard crops in the region, and by 1919 prunes were "...the largest industry in the county."[76] Agricultural production in northern Douglas County was abundant enough by 1860 to hold the first annual Umpqua Valley Agricultural Society meeting in Oakland that November.

Toward the end of the initial phase of settlement, the population increases and transportation improvements contributed to agricultural growth. "Connection by rail to the national marketplace established a consistent demand for Oregon products. In the counties west of the Cascades, the widely dispersed family farm was being encroached upon by commercial centers, forcing the intensification of farm lands for specialized crops."[77]

> In 1867 Alonzo Brown purchased a Marsh Harvester... The machine was primarily a horse-drawn mower, which cut the grain stacks, leaving the grain head and short stock for hand-binding... The equipment imported by Alonzo Brown ... heralded the dawning of a new era in Douglas County farming. In the 1870's farmers, in order to compete, rushed to purchase laborsaving devices. The advent of this machinery and the use of the steam-powered tractors in the 1870's and the 1880's signalled that commercial farming had commenced in Douglas County. The prospect for its success seemed bright when in 1872 the O&C Railroad [Oregon and California] reached Roseburg.[78]

Farm machinery continued to improve, and through the first twenty years of the twentieth century horses continued to be used as the primary "engine" of the farm until they were eventually displaced by motorized equipment. As farm production increased and diversified, so did farm buildings. Barns that were initially used for multiple purposes were altered, moved or razed and replaced with buildings designed for specific functions such as carriage houses, sheep sheds, implement sheds, dairy barns and horse barns.

---

74) Speulda, 10.
75) Speulda, 8-9.
76) "Umpqua Valley, Oregon," promotional pamphlet (Roseburg, Oregon: Roseburg Chamber of Commerce, 1919), 13.
77) Speulda, 13.
78) Beckham, *Land of the Umpqua*, 210.

Northern Douglas County farms continued to produce grains and livestock for market, and fruit and vegetable production increased. Hops were a lucrative crop in Oregon between the mid-1860s and the early 1900s; the Calapooya Creek watershed was particularly productive, and hop dryers and warehouses began to appear on the landscape.[79] In 1884, A.G. Walling wrote "As a fruit region, the Umpqua valley shares with the Rogue river region the honor of producing the finest quality and greatest abundance of Oregon fruit. Apples, pears, plums, cherries, peaches, apricots and grapes grow in profusion."[80]

As mechanized equipment became more commonplace, horse raising diminished, but cattle continued to be a common undertaking. Sheep and wool production in Douglas County preceded the establishment of the railroad, and persists today as a significant industry.

> In 1865 Douglas County had 48,507 sheep and produced 109,826 pounds of wool. Three years later...17 wagon loads of wool [were shipped] to Scottsburg for export to San Francisco. Although wool growers attempted to organize in 1873, their permanent association emerged in 1931 when they began sponsoring the Douglas County Fat Lamb and Wool Show. These growers took advantage of the abundant, well-watered grass of the Umpqua region."[81]

After the turn of the century, turkeys raising emerged as an important industry, augmenting the already-successful sheep and cattle industries. "Between approximately 1920 and 1950, turkeys were one of the most important agricultural products in Douglas County. Oakland...hosted the Northwest Regional Turkey Show in the 1930s and 1940s."[82]

With only nineteen people per square mile, it is clear that northern Douglas County continues to be dominated by agricultural, range and timber lands.[83] Recent economic success has centered around timber and winemaking.

THE BAIMBRIDGE-KANIPE FARMSTEAD

Ownership History

The Baimbridge-Kanipe Farmstead, with its arrangement of historic buildings dating from circa 1865 to circa 1935, represents a continuum of agricultural development and activity

---

79) Beckham, *Land of the Umpqua*, 212.
80) Walling, 395-96.
81) Beckham, *Land of the Umpqua*, 214; Alfred Lomax, "History of Sheep Husbandry in Oregon," Oregon Historical Quarterly Vol. XXIX No. 2 (June 1928), 142. Lomax cites sheep population in 1864 at 80,000 head. Regardless, by the mid-1860s sheep farming was a successful undertaking in Douglas County.
82) Fred Reensjerna, *Life in Douglas County, Oregon: the western experience*, (Roseburg, Ore.: Douglas County Museum, 1993), 14.
83) 2000 Census data, http://quickfacts.census.gov/qfd/states/41/41019.html, accessed August 2007.

in Douglas County. Located in Township 24S Range 4W Section 18, the farm group is sited on the west side of County Highway 50, also known as Elkhead Road, in a draw along an unnamed creek.

Deardorff Ownership 1854-1859 / Occupancy 1854-c1868

The site was first occupied by Euro-Americans with the arrival of Joseph and Elizabeth Deardorff in 1854.[84] Records indicate that Joseph came from Indiana or Iowa, and his wife Elizabeth from Illinois. The two were married in Iowa in 1840, and by the time they arrived in Oregon they had seven children, aged one through eighteen years. They settled their claim in 1854, a parcel that consisted of almost 328 acres.[85] The claim does not appear on the General Land Office maps, but the road that would later become Elkhead Road/County Road 50 is visible and terminates at the site of this farm in 1855.

In 1859, the Deardorffs sold the claim to neighbor Winslow Phelps Powers for the sum of $1,000. However, it appears that the Deardorffs may have continued to live on the claim, as they are listed in the area in 1860 U.S. Census, where Joseph's occupation was that of a farmer; $500 of personal property is indicated, but no real property value is listed for them. In 1865 Elizabeth died, several months after the birth of the couple's last child.[86] Joseph remarried to Emma Day in 1868 or 1869 in Douglas County, and by 1870 the Deardorffs had left Douglas County, and were listed in census records as living in Pleasant Hill, Lane County, Oregon.[87] The family then moved to a ranch along Deardorff Creek in Grant County sometime around 1872.[88]

Powers Ownership 1859-1880

Winslow Powers, who was born in 1821 in Vermont, came to Oregon in 1847, settling on a claim in the Willamette Valley. Not long after his arrival, he traveled to the California mines, and ultimately removed to the Oakland area sometime in 1853.[89]

---

84) This date is derived from a combination of sources including "Genealogical Material from Oregon Donation Land Claims" (Portland, Oregon: Genealogical Forum (?), 1957), www.ancestry.com, accessed July 2007; 1860 U.S. Census records that indicate a 7-year-old child born in Iowa (hence born around 1853),and a five-year-old child born in Oregon (born circa 1855), from U.S. Census, District 5 Umpqua County, Oregon, 1860, page 30. Additional genealogical data at http://www.gencircles.com/users/familyhunter2/5/data/48508. Accessed July 2007.
85) "Genealogical Material...," accessed July 2007.
86) Kanipe Collection, Douglas County Museum, Roseburg, OR; Douglas County Land Records, Douglas County, Roseburg, OR; Interviews of Kanipe family members John Howard, Cathryn Howard Weathers, Oakland, OR.
87) James Burke (great-great-grandson of Emma McDaniel Day Deardorff), personal communication, July 24-28, 2007; U.S. Census records 1860-1880; General Land Office Donation Land Claim records; "Genealogical Material...." Emma Day's brothers-in-law Nicholas and Henry had adjoining land claims along the Umpqua River, several miles west of the Deardorff claim.
88) James Burke, personal communication, July 24-28, 2007; http://www.gencircles.com/users/junesmelser/1/data/5716, accessed July 2007.
89) "Genealogical Material..." accessed July 2007; Powers, James W, *Frontier Days: The Life of Winslow Powers and the Early Settlement of Eastern Oregon* (Wallowa, Oregon: Bear Creek Press, 2004), p. 18. Powers settled his claim in November 1853.

Deciding that he preferred farming and stock raising to mining, Powers passed on to the Umpqua Valley where he took a donation land claim... Here he erected a log house, cultivated the soil and surrounded himself with various kinds of stock... In 1853 he met an amiable young girl Miss Harriet N. [Newell] Tower who had crossed the plains with her parents in 1852 and was now located within four miles of Powers' home.[90]

Genealogical data indicates that he married Harriet Tower in December of 1854 in Umpqua County, and their first child was born one year later.[91] Powers' house is mentioned in government surveyor's notes from 1855, and he apparently "...constructed a sawmill in the English settlement east of Oakland. He built the first frame house in the area from lumber cut at his mill."[92] Based on the surveyor's description, it appears that the house mentioned is on the southern part of Powers' original claim (prior to his purchase of the Deardorff claim).

It seems unlikely that the Powers' ever lived on the Deardorff claim, since census and genealogical data indicates that the Deardorffs were still living in the vicinity – presumably on their claim southeast of the subject property – until the mid-1860s.

Sometime between 1871 and 1874 the Powers family moved to Wallowa County, Oregon, renting the subject farm (the old Deardorff claim) to Thomas and Emily Baimbridge. Baimbridge family documents indicate that Powers was renting the property to the Baimbridges by June of 1872, and sold it to them in 1880.

Baimbridge Tenancy c 1872-1880 / Ownership 1880-c1902

The Baimbridge family emigrated from Derbyshire, England in 1870. "George Hall, who owned a ranch east of Oakland [in English Settlement], was a relative and they first wintered in a cabin on his ranch. They then leased the Thomas place in near-by Driver Valley..." [93] By 1872 they were renting and living on the land owned by Winslow Powers; they purchased the farm in 1880.[94] One source states that the purchase price was "...$3,000 and 1,000 young ewe sheep...," which suggests that the land was used for sheep ranching from at least the 1870s.[95] The family resided there until both Thomas and Emily had passed away, in 1891 and 1896 respectively, at which time the farm (that portion

90) James W. Powers, *Frontier Days...*, p. 18.
91) U.S. Census, 1860; genealogical data from www.ancestry.com and http://www.gencircles.com/users/eburgblue/1/data/7. Accessed July 2007.
92) Harold Avery Minter, *Umpqua Valley Oregon and It's Pioneers* (Portland, Oregon: Binfords & Mort, 1967), p. 131; County Surveyor's Record, Douglas County Oregon, Subdivisions of T24S, R4W, page 3051. Douglas County Surveyor's documents online, accessed July 2007.
93) Mildred Kanipe, "The Family History of the Baimbridges & Kanipes," *Historic Douglas County, Oregon 1982* (Roseburg, Oregon: Douglas County Historical Society, 1982), 64.
94) Baimbridge Diary/Account book, Douglas County Historical Museum files; Douglas County deed records, W.P. Powers & wife to Thos. Baimbridge, 13 March 1880, page 322.
95) Kanipe Collection, Douglas County Museum, Roseburg, OR; Douglas County Land Records, Douglas County, Roseburg, OR; Interviews of Kanipe family members John Howard, Cathryn Howard Weathers, Oakland, OR.

including the house and outbuildings) was inherited by their youngest daughter Sarah, who was born in 1876.[96]

Kanipe Ownership c 1902-1983

Sarah married John A. Kanipe around 1902, and together they had two daughters, Leah and Mildred. John Kanipe was born in either North or South Carolina around 1871, and was living in Tennessee in 1880 before moving to Oregon with his parents sometime between 1880 and 1900.[97]

According to Mildred Kanipe,

> About 1876 the Kanipes with their only son John [Mildred's father], aged 5, came to Oakland, Oregon, for a new start in ranching. They raised grain on different ranches in the area and about the time John got old enough to do a man's work they rented the Doc Hall place east of Oakland where my father [John] raised grain and Percheron horses. He would raise the colts and break teams to work and sell them.
>
> About 1902 John Kanipe and Sarah Baimbridge were married. They lived on the original W.P. Powers claim. John Kanipe bought the adjoining farm from Mary Baimbridge [Sarah's sister] and she lived with them. He later bought most of what had been the Baimbridge ranch. He owned a share in and helped run a threshing machine; it was powered by a J.I. Case steam engine and he used his teams of horses to pull the water wagon. He continued raising horses and grain but in later years turned mostly to sheep. John and Sarah Kanipe had two children, Leah and Mildred.[98]

Sarah died in 1907, and John and their two young daughters continued to live on the property along with Mary Baimbridge until John's death in 1940. Census records indicate that the family farmed the land (listed as "general farmer" in 1920, and "stock farmer" in 1930). John Kanipe was locally known for breeding and training Percheron horses for use on area farms. It is likely that the alterations to the horse barn were done around the turn of the century by John, to accommodate his horses.

Mildred, who never married, "inherited just over 290 acres of the Deardorff land claim in 1940 when her father died. Her Aunt Mary lived with Mildred until she passed away in

96) Mildred Kanipe, "The Family History..." (1982), 64.
97) U.S. Census records 1870-1900. www.ancestry.com accessed July 2007.
98) Mildred Kanipe, "The Family History..." (1982), 64.

1955."[99] Augmenting her holdings by purchasing the adjacent Underwood farm, Mildred ultimately owned nearly 1,100 acres that included the Deardorff and Powers donation land claims. She was the sole owner and operator of the farm for over forty years, and continued to raise sheep and cattle, grow hay for winter feed, and keep goats, rabbits and poultry in a manner much as those before her had done. She worked the farm until poor health forced her to leave the land in 1980, and she died in 1983.

Agriculture was the primary endeavor of most of the settlers coming to Oregon in the mid-nineteenth century. On arrival, construction of shelter and subsistence farming was as much as a family could handle. After several years, production increased and marketable crops in the form of grain, fruits, livestock, poultry, wool and dairy products became the economic foundation of these rural communities. This appears to be the pattern of development on the Baimbridge-Kanipe farmstead as well. This property has always functioned as a working farm; all owners and occupants of the property are listed in various census records as farmers, from 1860 to 1930. The variety and span of age of the buildings are evidence of its continuing and varied use over its 150 year life.

CONSTRUCTION HISTORY

The sequence of construction of buildings on the Baimbridge-Kanipe farm is difficult to discern. Dating of the outbuildings is particularly difficult due to the heavy use the buildings are subject to, and the subsequent deterioration, repair and remodeling to accommodate new uses. All buildings appear on the earliest aerial photograph available for the area, taken in 1939.

It seems likely that the house, probably the oldest building in the farm group, was built either during the ownership of the Deardorffs (1854-1859) or the earlier years of the Powers' ownership (1859-1880), perhaps as late as 1870. While this area (T24S R4W) was surveyed and documented by the General Land Office in the years 1856, 1860 and 1897, no land claims are indicated on any of these maps for the section (Sections 18 and 19) in which the Baimbrige-Kanipe farm is located. Further, no survey notes were found for claims owned by either Deardorff or Powers, although Powers' house is mentioned as a point of reference in another survey.

Two clues suggest the existence of a house (though not necessarily the current one) here in the 1850s. First, the 1856 GLO map shows the terminus of the future Elkhead road at this farm site. Second, Joseph and Elizabeth Deardorff did submit a notification for their

---

99) Kanipe Collection, Douglas County Museum, Roseburg, OR; Douglas County Land Records, Douglas County, Roseburg, OR; Interviews of Kanipe family members John Howard, Cathryn Howard Weathers, Oakland, OR. . The land inherited by Mildred was part of the original Deardorff Donation Land Claim; the land inherited by her sister Leah was the Powers Donation Land Claim, located on the other side of Elkhead Road; Mildred Kanipe already owned 167 acres at the time she inherited the land. The parcels were unconnected until the purchase the Underwood Farm.

claim, and a certificate for the claim in their name was issued in 1866.[100] Requirements for receiving a certificate on a claim included living on and working the land for at least four years from the time of notification. The fact that the Deardorffs did not receive a certificate until 1866 does not necessarily suggest that the farm or any part of it did not exist until that date. It seems that most certificates were not issued until the mid-1860s.

Once settlers had filed their notices of entry for ... claims, they were extremely slow to take title. The reluctance of the pioneer generation to procure a record of ownership for their lands was that once the land was patented, it was subject to taxation. As long as it was registered as a claim at the land office in Winchester or Roseburg, however, the property was protected as theirs. The only inducement to move a parcel toward patent was if the "owner" wished to subdivide or dispose of the lands. In many instances donation land claims and "preemption" lands in Douglas County did not go for patent until the original settler died.[101]

Regardless, land ownership records and the location of the house do not support the contention that the house was built as early as 1851-52 by Powers as suggested by Kanipe family and local lore. Most arrivals to the English Settlement area settled claims in 1853-54, and Powers did not own the land until 1859. Further, it is likely that the initial residence was a log cabin, followed later with a more substantial house. The physical features of the Baimbridge-Kanipe house coupled with land records and genealogical information support a potential construction period of perhaps the late 1850s to mid-1860s, though no direct historical documentation to confirm a specific date of construction has been found. For the purposes of this document, the construction date is set at circa 1865.

The few pages of the 1872 diary/account book available from the Baimbridge family clearly suggest the existence of an established farm by that time. Payment of rent to W. Powers implies there is a house; sale of livestock, hay and grain suggest not only that the farm is producing these things but that there may also be a barn on the property. Dates extrapolated from newspapers on the walls of the house suggest that some portion of it may have been built prior to 1878. This construction – if it occurred as late as the mid-1870s - was likely either an addition (kitchen), a remodel or an interior refinishing project. This contention is supported by Leah Kanipe-Howard, Mildred Kanipe's sister who in her personal memoirs said that her grandfather, Thomas Baimbridge, completed the addition.[102]

Of the five outbuildings on the property, the horse barn appears to be the oldest. (See Figure 7) This transverse-plan barn contains mortise-and-tenon hand-hewn framing of a configuration that suggests an early construction date – perhaps as early as pre-1870s – and the Baimbridge diary entries 1872 do suggest the existence of a barn though the

100) Bureau of Land Management, General Land Office records for "Deardorff, Joseph," http://www.glorecords.blm. gov/. Accessed July 2007. Notification number 639, Certificate number 802; no claim number has been found.
101) Beckham, *Land of the Umpqua*, 162.
102) Kanipe, Leah. "Settlement Began in Early Forties," manuscript loaned to Douglas County Museum by Mrs. Homer Trusty, January, 1975, n.d.

barn roof has since been altered.[103] Hand-wrought nails and remnant hand-wrought gate hardware also support this dating. While the current roof pitch points to a later construction date – possibly as late as 1920 - a historic photograph shows the barn in the background with a lower pitch roof than the current configuration.[104] This same photo also shows wood fencing and the Buggy Shed. (See Figure 10).

The only building for which there is a somewhat definitive construction date is the Sheep Shearing Shed. According to the recollection of John Howard, Mildred Kanipe's nephew, the Shed was built in 1935 or 1936 by Mr. Howard's father Romie Howard.

COMPARATIVE ANALYSIS

According to the Cultural and Historic Resource Inventory of Douglas County, a survey initially conducted in 1981-82 and revised in 2002,

> Historic resources associated with agricultural pursuits are distributed
> throughout most valleys in the County. The few early surviving
> resources such as barns and houses are located in the broad valleys
> that were taken by Donation Land Claimants in the late 1840's and the
> first half of the 1850's. Some early farm buildings have survived with
> buildings from a later period, but none have survived in the company of
> another from the same period.[105]

For the purposes of the 1981-82 survey two types of farms were identified: the basic farm was comprised of "...at least one surviving house and barn or other major agricultural building. A multi-unit farm was made up of the basic house and barn, plus at least one other historic resources such as a second barn, granary shed..." etc.[106] The Baimbridge-Kanipe Farm, with its eight contributing features, falls into the latter category.[107]

According to preliminary analysis of Oregon State Historic Preservation Office historic inventory data for Douglas County, twenty-two (22) multi-unit farms were identified in the County survey. Of these twenty-two, twelve (12) included at least one main building (usually the house or a barn) constructed prior to 1900, and only seven (7) included at least one main building constructed prior to 1880.

While integrity was not evaluated in the survey, condition of the resources is indicated.

---

103) Entries refer to barley, hay, oats and existence of livestock, all of which would require the use of a barn in some fashion for shelter, storage, threshing, etc.
104) Gallagher et al, 38-40; Dole, 89 and 120.
105) Harbour and Beckham, 6. The Baimbridge-Kanipe Farm may in fact be a farm with a house and barn that are contemporaries. While both barns have been altered, the framework of the horse barn could to date to approximately the same period as the house.
106) Harbour and Beckham, 6.
107) The Baimbridge-Kanipe Farm was not included in this survey, or in the 2002 update of the survey.

The Baimbridge-Kanipe Farm is perhaps unusual in that it retains such a variety of buildings each intended for a specific agricultural use. The horse barn, dairy barn, sheep shearing shed, equipment shed and buggy shed each illustrate distinct activities or functions that were integral to farm operations, and they collectively tell a story of life on the farm. The house, which is probably the oldest of the buildings on the property, remains virtually unchanged from the time of its last major addition (the kitchen) which was over one-hundred years ago. This fact adds to the significance of the farm group as it enhances authenticity of the site as a true pre-1900 farm.

Oregon Statewide Inventory - Douglas County – Multi-Unit Farms built prior to 1899

Name/Location	# of Resources	Date(s)	Condition
Redfield, John, Farm Azelea-Glen Road, Glendale	8 (house, 2 barns, 5 sheds)	c 1856-57	Good condition
Krogel, Charles F., Farm Dixonville Rd., Roseburg	3 (house, barn, dam)	c 1865	Good condition
Dunnavin, James S., Farm N. Myrtle Creek Rd., Myrtle Creek	3+ (house, granary, barn, other outbuildings)	c 1870	Fair-poor condition
Hurst, David, Farm Fort McKay Rd., Sutherlin	3 (house, 2 barns)	c 1870	Good condition; NR listed
Long, Robert W., Farm John Long Rd., Oakland vic	3 (house, barn, other outbuilding)	1872	Good condition/ altered

Oregon Statewide Inventory - Douglas County – Multi-Unit Farms built prior to 1899 Cont'd

Name/Location	# of Resources	Date(s)	Condition
Weaver, Adam Jr., Farm Tiller Trail Hwy., Canyonville	4 (house, summer kitchen and dining room, 2 barns)	c. 1873	Good-poor condition

Springer, Rudolph, Farm Azelea-Glen Rd., Glendale	4 (house, barn carriage house, irrigation ditch)	c 1885	Fair condition
Clough, Joseph L., Farm Days Creek Cutoff Rd., Canyonville	6+ (house, barn, wash house, bunkhouse, smokehouse, orchard, other outbuildings)	c 1885; c 1922	Good condition
Douglas County Poor Farm Melqua Rd., Roseburg	5 (housing, school, granary, barn, ferry site)	c 1886-95	Good condition
Kemp Farm Iverson Rd., Umpqua	3 (house, 2 barns)	1894	Good condition
Quine, George, Farm Canyonville-Riddle Rd., Riddle	8 (house, cooler house, wood shed, shop, garage, 2 prune dryer furnaces, orchard)	c 1895	Good condition

Few other documented farms in northern Douglas County retain the collective integrity and breadth of resources found on the Baimbridge-Kanipe property. Having operated nearly continuously from the mid-1850s to 1980 as a working farm, the property presents a unique window on agricultural development over 100+ years in northern Douglas County. Little change seems to have occurred here, other than the addition or alteration of outbuildings to suite changing needs. In fact, the group of outbuildings seems to have been updated and augmented with more regularity than the residence. Each building, with its specified purpose, represents an aspect of the farming life that endured on this property for over one-hundred years; these activities continue today on surrounding farms in the area. Visitors to the site have the unusual opportunity to see many of the elements of an early farm, and the progression of agricultural growth and diversity all confined to a single site.

CONCLUSION

The Baimbridge-Kanipe Farmstead is an excellent example of an early pioneer farmstead and is locally significant under National Register Criteria A as it was one of the earliest remaining intact farms in northern Douglas County. It retains a high level of integrity in its buildings and landscape in spite of recent intrusions that facilitate its use as a County park. It is unusual in that few farms in Douglas County that date to the settlement era contain the number and age range of buildings that are found on this farmstead; it retains representative buildings from many of the predominant agricultural endeavors that took place in Douglas County from the 1850s to the present day.

BIBLIOGRAPHY:

Baimbridge, Thomas. 1870 Diary. Douglas County Museum.

_____. Diary/Account book, 1872. Douglas County Museum.

Bancroft, Hubert Howe. *The Works of Hubert Howe Bancroft Volume XXX, History of Oregon Vol. II 1848-1888.* San Francisco: The History Company, Publishers, 1888.

Beckham, Stephen Dow. *The Land of the Umpqua: A History of Douglas County, Oregon.* Roseburg, Oregon: Douglas County Commissioners, 1986.

Benjamin, Asher. *The Practice of Architecture; containing the five orders of architecture and an additional column and entablature, with all their elements and details explained and illustrated, for the use of carpenters and practical men.* New York, New York: DaCapo Press, 1972 [c1833].

_____. The American Builder's Companion. New York, New York: DaCapo Press, 1972 [c1806].

Bureau of Land Management, General Land Office Records. http://www. glorecords.blm.gov/. Accessed July 2007.

Chenoweth, J.V. *The Making of Oakland.* Oakland, Oregon: Oakland Printing, 1977.

Dole, Philip. "Farmhouse and Barn in Early Lane County." *Lane County Historian* X no. 2 (Aug. 1965).

_____. "Farmhouses and Barns of the Willamete Valley," in *Space Style and Structure*, Thomas Vaughan, editor. Portland, Oregon: Oregon Historical Society, 1974.

Douglas County Historical Society, *Historic Douglas County Oregon 1982.* Roseburg, Oregon: Douglas County Historical Society, 1982.

Douglas, County of. County Clerk's Office records, Roseburg, Oregon.

Douglas, County of. Surveyor's Records. http://www.co.douglas.or.us/surveyor/sars/default.asp. Accessed July 2007.

Eagleton, Lois. "English Settlement School," National Register Nomination Form, on file at the Oregon State Historic Preservation Office. 2007.

Gallagher, Mary K. et al. *Historic Context: The Barns of Linn County, Oregon 1845-1945.* Albany, Oregon: Linn County Planning Department, 1997.

Harbour, Terry R. and Stephen Dow Beckham. Douglas County Cultural and Historic Resource Inventory, 1981-82. Revised 2002. On file with Douglas County Planning Department, Roseburg and Oregon State Historic Preservation Office, Salem.

Kadas, Marianne. "Roseburg Downtown Historic District," nomination to the National Register of
Historic Places. Salem, OR.: 2003.

Kanipe, Leah. "Settlement Began in Early Forties," manuscript loaned to Douglas County Museum by Mrs. Homer Trusty, January 1975, n.d.

Kanipe, Mildred. Diary. Douglas County Museum.

Kniffen, Fred. "Folk Housing: Key to Diffusion," *Annals of the Association of American Geographers*, Vol. 55, No. 4 (December 1965), pp. 549-577.

Minter, Harold Avery Minter. *Umpqua Valley Oregon and its Pioneers.* Portland, Oregon: Binfords & Mort, Publishers, 1967.

Moulton, Larry. "Douglas County Schools: A History Outline." Oakland, OR.: self published, nd.

Oregon State Archives, Oregon Historical County Records Guide, "Douglas County History." http://arcweb.sos.state.or.us/county/cpdouglashome.html. Accessed July 2007

Oregon Genealogical Forum. "Genealogical Material from Oregon Donation Land Claims." Portland, Oregon: Genealogical Forum(?), 1957. http://www.ancestry.com. Accessed July 2007.

Oregon State Historic Preservation Office. Statewide Inventory of Historic Sites and Buildings.

Powers, James W. *Frontier Days: The Life of Winslow Powers and the Early Settlement of Eastern Oregon.* Wallowa, Oregon: Bear Creek Press, 2004.

Quinn, John M. and Terrence J. Parker. "Oakland Historic District," National Register Nomination Form, on file at the Oregon State Historic Preservation Office, 1978.

Speulda, Lou Ann. *Oregon's Agricultural Development: A Historic Context 1811-1940.* Salem, Oregon: Oregon State Historic Preservation Office, 1989.

Sutherlin Sun Tribune, (Oregon) 7 October 1976.

United States Census records, 1850-1950. http://www.ancestry.com. Accessed July 2007.

Thomas Vaughan, editor. *Space Style and Structure: Building in Northwest America.* Portland, Oregon: Oregon Historical Society, 1974.

Walling, Albert G. *History of Southern Oregon, comprising Jackson, Josephine, Douglas, Curry and Coos countries, comp. from the most authentic sources.* Portland, Oregon: A.G. Walling, 1884.

Winterbotham, Jerry. *Umpqua, The Lost County of Oregon.* Brownsville, OR.: Creative Images
Printing, 1994.

VERBAL BOUNDARY DESCRIPTION:

The nominated area is located in Township 24S, Range 4W, Section 18 of the Willamette Meridian in Douglas County, Oregon. It is the same as tax lot 200 (14.21 acres) plus tax lot 500 (4.40 acres), totaling 18.61 acres.

BOUNDARY JUSTIFICATION:

The boundary encompasses the entire tax parcel described in the Verbal Boundary Description and includes all important historic resources related to the property including the described house, agricultural outbuildings, heritage orchard, associated features, and several acres encompassing the view sheds from the buildings that convey the property's historic rural setting.

A BRIEF HISTORY TIMELINE

200 million years ago – Oregon was under the ocean. About that time North America broke away from Europe and has moved 1-2 inches to the west ever since.

70,000-11,000 years ago – Ice Age

14,000-10,000 years ago – Man arrived – Oakland area - Yoncalla Indians (Southernmost band of Kalapuya Indians)

1500's - From 1500's Spanish ships passed by mouth of the Umpqua River but did not stop.

1791 – American Brig, Jenny

1792 – English Captain Robert Gray

1826 – British botanist David Douglas visited the area

1830-1833 – Many Indians died from fever introduced by whites

1832 – Fort MacKay trading post established at junction of Kalapuya creek and Umpqua River

1836 – Hudson Bay Company built fort at Elkton

1843 – Settlers began arriving

1850 – Donation Land Claim Act

1850's - Town of Oakland established

1853 - Winslow Powers obtained 320 acres DLC

1854 – Joseph Deardorff obtained 327.66 acres DLC

1855-56 – Indian Uprising

1856 – Truce – Indians removed to Grand Ronde Reservation

1859 – Winslow Powers purchased Deardorff land, now having 647.66 acres

February 14, 1859 - Oregon became a State.

18when? – Historic house built on Deardorff Donation Land Claim (by whom?)

1869 – Transcontinental Railroad completed

1870 – Mildred Kanipe's maternal grandparents, Thomas and Emily Baimbridge, arrived from England with 5 children and moved to English Settlement East of Oakland.

May, 1872 – Railroad arrived at Oakland, Oregon, from the north. (Town moved by railroad.)

June 10, 1872 – Thomas Baimbridge rented Powers ranch

October, 1872 – Railroad completed to Roseburg (ended there for 15 years)

July 21, 1876 - Sarah Alice Baimbridge born (Mildred Kanipe's Mother)

1878 – Thomas Baimbridge purchased ranch

1887 – Railroad completed to California

September 30, 1907 - Mildred born in same house as her mother

December 28, 1907 – Mildred's mother died

1933 – Mildred purchased 167 acres (SW corner of park)

1940 – Mildred's father passed away – Mildred inherited 290.77 acres (East side of park)

1949 – Mildred purchased 633 acre Underwood ranch (connecting the two above parcels)

July 13, 1983 – Mildred passed away leaving her 1,090.77 acre ranch to Douglas County for a park.

1994 – Douglas County dedicated park

2005 – Friends of Mildred Kanipe Park was formed

September 4, 2007 – English Settlement School added to National Register

January 29, 2008 – Baimbridge-Kanipe Farmstead Historic District added to National Register

ABOUT THE AUTHOR

Lois Christiansen Eagleton was first exposed to writing history in the seventh grade when her teacher, frustrated with a bored student whose work was always done, sent her out to talk to old folks and record the history of her home town, Junction City, Oregon.

As an adult she immersed herself in writing her family histories. This was no small task, as the first one she did was about her maternal great-grandfather who had twenty-one children.

She writes for several local newspapers and has been featured in anthologies published by the AAW (An Association of Writers), of Roseburg, Oregon, of which she is a member. This is her first book.

Lois has four grown children and seven grandchildren. She lives with her husband and a menagerie of animals at the foot of Tyee Mountain in Umpqua, Oregon.

She is Executive Director/Chair of Friends of Mildred Kanipe Memorial Park Association, Inc.

SOURCES

Publications

A.G.M. Markers, Compiled by Jerry Winterbothom, *"Footsteps on the Umpqua"*, 2000, Dalton Press, Lebanon, OR

David D. Alt & Donald W. Hyndman, *"Roadside Geology of Oregon"*, 1978, Mountain Press Publishing Co., Missoula, Montana

Douglas County Historical Society, *"Historic Douglas County, Oregon"*, 1982, Taylor Publishing Company, Dallas, OR

Ellen Morris Bishop, *"In Search of ANCIENT OREGON, A Geological and Natural History"*, 2003, Timber Press, Portland, Oregon

Harold A. Minter, *"Umpqua Valley, Oregon and Its Pioneers"*, 1967, Binford & Mort, Publishers, Portland, Oregon

James W. Powers, *"Frontier Days, The Life of Winslow Powers and the Early Settlement of Eastern Oregon"*, 1940, Bear Creek Press, Wallowa, Oregon

Jerry Winterbothom, *"UMPQUA, The Lost County of Oregon"*, 1994, Creative Images Printing, Brownsville, Oregon

Larry Moulton, *"DOUGLAS COUNTY SCHOOLS, A History Outline"*, Self Published Roseburg, Oregon

Stephen Dow Beckham, "*Land of the Umpqua, A History of Douglas County, Oregon*", 1986, Douglas County Commissioners, Roseburg, Oregon

Stephen Dow Beckham, "*The Indians of Western Oregon, This Land Was Theirs*". 1977, Arago Books, Coos Bay, Oregon

Theresa Jordan, "*COWGIRLS, Women of the American West*", 1982, University of Nebraska Press, Lincoln & London

Other

Douglas County Courthouse and Ticor Title Company, Roseburg, Oregon, Land Records

Douglas County Museum of History and Natural History, Mildred Kanipe personal papers, photos, maps, and documents

Douglas County Park Department, records and taped interview with Ed Boehrs

Internet: wikipedia.org, Donation Land Claim Act

Interviews with Mildred Kanipe's sister's children, John Howard and Kathryn Weathers. Kathryn also provided many family photos and stories written by her mother and Mildred.

Interview with Maxine Baimbridge, relative of Mildred Kanipe who knew her well and cared for her before she died.

Interviews and casual conversations with a large number of people who knew something of history of the area and/or knew Mildred Kanipe.

INDEX

Shambrook, George, 132
sheep
    diseases and, 85
    raising, 179
    ranching, 179, 184
    shearing shed, 173, 188
    wool production and, 182
Sheep Shearing Shed, 173, 188
Shoestring Cemetery, 88
"Shorty" (grey horse), 85
SHPO. *See* State Historic Preservation
    Office (SHPO)
Soap Creek School, Adir Village,
    Oregon, 140, 141
Southern Oregon Normal School,
    Ashland, 83
Spalding, Miss Alta, 83
Spitzenburg apple, 153
State Advisory Committee on Historic
    Preservation, 115
State Historic Preservation Office
    (SHPO), 56, 115, 116
Stayman apple, 154
Stearns Hardware, 10
steerage, origin of term, 5
Stienhoff, Itha Green, 79
Steinhoff, Roy Green, 74
Stricker's Auction Yard, Sutherlin, 63

T
Talburt, Bill, 49
teachers
    education and testing, 133
    salaries, 134
teaching methods, 133
Thanksgiving, 86
Thomas, Dick, 11
Thomas Baimbridge Diary, The, 11
Thumper, Jed, 87
timeline, Douglas County, Oregon
    history, 197–198
Tower, Harriet, 184
tractors, steam-powered, 181
transcontinental railroad, 7, 11

transparent apple, 152–153
"triple stumpage" contract, 32
"Turkey Capital." *See* Oakland

U
Umpqua County, Oregon, 3, 8
Umpqua Valley Agricultural Society
    meeting, 181
Umpqua Valley Oregon and Its Pioneers
    (Minter), 9
Underwood, G. R., 29
Underwood House, 52–54
United States
    boundary between Canada and, 5
    economy in Eastern region, 5
    Homestead Act, 7
    schoolhouse architecture in, 137–
139
    schooling in (*See* American
schooling)
uranium mines, 85, 86
U.S. Census Bureau
    of 1860, 183
    of 1870, 1880, 1900 and 1910, 133
U.S. Forest Service, 94
U.S. government
    Donation Land Claim Act (1850),
5, 132
    Homestead Act (1862), 7

V
Van Slyke, Dan, 51
Vian, Bill, 46
Victor Point School, Oregon, 40
Virginia City, Montana, 86

W
wagon trains, 5
Walling, A. G., 166, 182
Wallowa County, Oregon, 184
Western Oregon
    birds spreading over, 54
    breeding sheep in, 179
    building material available in, 140

roads of, 1
weather of, 2
"white male citizens," 7
Whittaker, Elizabeth, 80
Wild Bill. *See* Cantrell, Bill James
Winslow Powers Donation Land
      Claim, 136
Witt, Bill, 88
Wonderful One Hoss Shay, 91
World War II, 84

Y
Yellowstone Park, 86
Yoncalla Indians, 3
Young, E. G., 75
Young, Edwin, 70
Young, James, 74
Young, Jim, 74

CONTACTS

Douglas County Park Department
P.O. Box 800
6536 Old Hwy 99, Winchester, OR 97495
TEL 541-957-7001 or 541-672-3311

If you wish to make a reservation to have a function at Mildred Kanipe Memorial Park, contact Douglas County Park Department. There is a nominal fee for functions that require a reservation. For casual picnics, hiking, or trail riding no reservation is required and there is no charge. Motor vehicles are not allowed in the park beyond the parking areas except for the purpose of park maintenance.

Mildred Kanipe Memorial Park
16513 Elkhead Rd, Oakland, OR 97462
TEL 541-459-9567

The Day Use area of the park is open daily year round from 7am to dusk. Trails are available in winter months for hiking only. The equestrian area and all trails are closed to horses from November 1 through March 15.

Friends of Mildred Kanipe Memorial Park Association, Inc.
P.O. Box 105, Umpqua, OR 97486

Membership is $10 per family per year. Donations are tax deductible and are used for park projects only. Members receive organization newsletters and information on work parties and other functions sponsored by the organization. They have the opportunity to help develop plans and future direction for the group and participate in a meaningful way in assisting the Douglas County Park Department with the huge responsibility of caring for this valuable resource.

A 501 (c) (3) tax exempt charitable organization: since November, 2005. Charitable Trust and Corporation Act registration: #35437. IRS Employment Identification: #20-2378046. Oregon Secretary of State Corporation Division Registration: #284132-92.